THEY CALL HER REGRET

Books by Channelle Desamours

Needy Little Things
They Call Her Regret

THEY CALL HER REGRET

Channelle Desamours

BLOOMSBURY
LONDON OXFORD NEW YORK NEW DELHI SYDNEY

BLOOMSBURY YA
Bloomsbury Publishing Plc
50 Bedford Square, London WC1B 3DP, UK
Bloomsbury Publishing Ireland Limited
29 Earlsfort Terrace, Dublin 2, D02 AY28, Ireland

BLOOMSBURY, BLOOMSBURY YA and the Diana logo
are trademarks of Bloomsbury Publishing Plc

First published in the United States of America in 2026 by Wednesday Books,
an imprint of St. Martin's Publishing Group
First published in Great Britain in 2026 by Bloomsbury Publishing Plc

Copyright © Channelle Desamours, 2026

Channelle Desamours has asserted her right under the Copyright,
Designs and Patents Act, 1988, to be identified as Author of this work

All emojis designed by OpenMoji – the open-source emoji and icon project.
License: CC BY-SA 4.0

All rights reserved. No part of this publication may be: i) reproduced or transmitted
in any form, electronic or mechanical, including photocopying, recording or by
means of any information storage or retrieval system without prior permission in
writing from the publishers; or ii) used or reproduced in any way for the training,
development or operation of artificial intelligence (AI) technologies, including
generative AI technologies. The rights holders expressly reserve this publication from
the text and data mining exception as per Article 4(3) of the Digital Single Market
Directive (EU) 2019/790

A catalogue record for this book is available from the British Library

ISBN: PB: 978-1-5266-7501-9; eBook: 978-1-5266-7500-2

2 4 6 8 10 9 7 5 3 1

Printed and bound in Great Britain by Clays Ltd, Elcograf S.p.A.

To find out more about our authors and books visit www.bloomsbury.com
and sign up for our newsletters
For product safety related questions contact productsafety@bloomsbury.com

For my dad, who made me fall in love with stories, and for my mom, who got me hooked on the spooky ones

CHAPTER 1

The third stall in the restroom of Ozzy's Pizza is my favorite spot in town. It's not anything I'd say out loud because it suggests something . . . well, nasty about the place I've called home my whole life—Fairville, Georgia, isn't great, but it's not public toilet bad. For me, this third stall, with its rusty hinges and eternally sticky tiles, holds sentimental value in the form of small, boxy letters written in permanent marker. CAMILLE + TONY FOREVER, surrounded by a sea of other declarations of love, obscene doodles, and phone numbers. Camille and Tony, my parents. The sixteen-year-old version of my mother wrote their names here, but turns out happily ever after wasn't in the cards. They divorced two years ago. I haven't seen or spoken to Mom since, but she feels so present here that sometimes I wonder if it's possible for a living person to haunt a place. I'm pretty confident that dead people can, but for those who are gone, not from life in the literal sense but gone from *my* life, there must be some sort of gray area, and I'm all up for exploring it—even if it means frequent visits to a bathroom in the back of an ancient pizza shop. My little sad-girl haven and inferno all wrapped up in one.

"Simone, hurry up. What are you doing in there?" my best friend, Kira, shouts, banging on the stall door.

I slip on my happy-girl mask because the sad-girl thing is a secret tightly held between me, these metal graffitied walls, and Cory Gooding—the boy who made me seek refuge here tonight in the first place.

"Simone!" Kira shouts again before her heavily mascaraed lashes and amber iris appear in the obnoxiously large gap between the side of the stall and the door.

I slide open the lock and push out, nearly knocking her over. "And to think you would have been mad at me if you caught a glimpse of something you didn't want to see."

"Oh, stop. That toilet has been out of order since freshman year."

"As if there aren't a dozen other private things someone might do in a bathroom." I turn on the tap and pump some soap into my hands. "Does Rich know what a deviant you are?" I ask even though if anyone's a deviant in their relationship, it's him.

She grins mischievously and retouches her lip gloss. "Of course. Why do you think he asked me out?"

"You two are horrible for each other. You know that, right?"

She blows me a kiss in the mirror, thinking I'm joking around, and that's my own fault. Rich Pearson is your stereotypical hot, athletic, horny teenage boy. He doesn't have any business being anybody's boyfriend. I should have told Kira the truth when she asked what I thought about her dating him. Instead, I drop passive-aggressive hints about his wandering eyes and watch them float right through her head. But I'm going to make it right soon. I have to before she gives up her spot at art school and follows him to South Carolina where he'll play D2 football—and her.

Kira frowns in the mirror, gently pressing her fingers against the frizzy cornrows along her hairline. "Is my hair flat in the back?" She spins around, her golden-brown coils sending the fragrance of coconut into the air.

It rained for a few minutes at the end of the football game tonight, and shoving her hair under the hood of Rich's jacket did a number on it. I fluff it out for her and twirl a few curls around my finger to redefine them. Without prompting, she turns and fiddles with my braids, swooping some back and securing them with a clip for a half-up, half-down look. We both examine our refreshed reflections in the mirror, then exit the restroom as the version of ourselves that the general populace of Pinegrove Academy knows.

Unbothered. Assured. Unrivaled.

I have many masks.

KIRA and I weave through huddles of our classmates, all buzzing with excited energy after our final-quarter comeback. The captain of the team, Jeremiah Hutchinson, sits on his throne in the center of our curved booth, huge smile plastered on his face, dark skin gleaming. He and Rich replay his game-changing first down for a group of juniors who would kill to claim our booth when we graduate. There's a certain neediness about them that makes my skin tingle with the same sort of embarrassment you feel when you discover no one told you you've been walking around with food stuck between your two front teeth. Sometimes I worry that the neediness I feel every day shows on me as starkly, clings to me as tightly, as dark spinach across white teeth. But I know it's an irrational fear. I am a vault, expertly camouflaged. It's something I've learned to take pride in, which is why the presence of Cory Gooding rattles me so much.

"Excuse me," Kira says, and Jeremiah's fan club parts for us. Knowing their idols' attention won't return to them, they drift back toward the arcade area. They each wear a white T-shirt with a royal-blue letter painted on it. H-U-T-C-H.

Kira slips into the booth and scoots toward Jere to make room for me. Piper, whose platinum-blond hair is pulled into a tight ponytail and adorned with a ridiculously large cheer bow, has claimed the spot next to Rich. She sits unnecessarily close to him, arm to arm, leg to leg, but Kira doesn't notice. She never notices. And all the guys love to tell Rich how lucky he is to have such a chill girlfriend—one of those stupid not-like-other-girls things. Chill girls don't get jealous. Chill girls can "take a joke." They don't need a text back, or quality time, or any words of affirmation. Chill girls lie to win the affection of mediocre boys. Kira is not a chill girl. She just throws trust out like confetti. I balance my friend's naive energy by giving Rich a critical look up and down. He pulls a confused face, but he knows exactly why I'm shooting daggers because he scoots a few inches away from Piper before throwing himself back into the conversation.

I could not be less interested in the latest pair of beefing rappers, so I turn my attention to the muted big-back TV mounted in the corner across from us. The news shows the smiling face of Natalie Dawson—a nineteen-year-old who attended the local community college and went missing three months ago. I made a terrible mistake around that time, but talk of Natalie's disappearance was enough to distract me from the gnawing regret.

I'm so caught up trying to read the tiny closed captions that I don't register Cory walking over to us until he is there asking what everyone would like to drink. We haven't had a proper conversation in more than two years, but the smell of him will always be familiar to me. Woody and clean, sharp enough to cut through the rancidness of overused frying oil and the bite of cheap tomato sauce that is ever present in this place. I feel his eyes on me, but I keep my own glued to the TV. These encounters between me and him happen every few weeks, and I hate the way they shake me up. Just a glimpse of Cory and my focus is shot for the rest of the day.

Rich bumps the table with his knee. "Simone, tell the dude what you want to drink."

"No rush," Cory says.

He's traded what used to be his signature fro for two-strand twists, and they look frustratingly good on him. "Sprite, please," I say, eyes back on the news.

Cory points at the screen with his server pad. "Crazy she hasn't turned up yet, huh?"

Everyone else looks over at the TV as if it has appeared out of nowhere.

Rich tousles his wavy brown hair. "Doubt they'll find her alive at this point."

"You would know," Jere snickers.

Kira shoves his shoulder. "That's not funny." She scowls at Rich. "And stop being so negative."

"Sad, but he's probably right," Cory says, angling his head toward Rich.

"What makes you say that?" Piper asks.

Cory presses the back of his pen a few times, the clicking sound filling the space in the air while he decides how to answer. "Mama Dee saw her ghost."

Everyone, except me, sits smiling slightly, waiting for Cory's face to break, for him to reveal that he's joking, but that won't happen.

Jere snorts. "Wait, you lyin'. Mama Dee, that hundred-year-old lady that does psychic readings for like a hundred dollars a minute?"

"Yes."

5

Cory doesn't joke. Not with people he doesn't know well, at least. He says what he means and means what he says, and he is very intentional about every word he chooses.

Rich laughs. "You really believe she sees dead people?"

"Why shouldn't I?"

Rich points from Cory to me. "You and this dude would get along, Simone. Y'all are both into that spooky stuff."

"Yeah. I think we'd get along great," Cory says, playing like we don't already know each other. "Maybe we can find out at your Halloween party this year?"

"And he's smooth with it!" Jere leans over and daps Cory up.

My annual Halloween party is the biggest event at Pinegrove every year outside of prom. Each student gets a personal invite and I go all out. It's not just an excuse to drink and party. I fully embrace the spirit of the season. YOU WILL HAVE FUN. YOU WILL FEEL FEAR was stamped on the envelope of every invitation last year, and I did not fail to deliver. Horror feels like home to me.

"C'mon, Simone," Rich nudges. "Don't leave him hanging."

"It's Pinegrove only."

Cory shrugs. "That's too bad." He pops his pen once again. "I'll be right back with your drinks."

Rich stares after him, squinting. "Didn't he actually go to Pinegrove at some point?"

Realization dawns on Jere's face and he does a double take right as Cory slips behind the counter. "He did! He was in my ninth-grade math class. Piper, you used to cheat off all his tests, 'member?"

"Do I remember cheating off someone in freshman math? Sure. Do I remember it being that guy? No."

"Not surprised. You cheated off—and on—a lot of people that year."

Piper opens her mouth to retort, but Jere keeps talking. "I wonder if he can hoop. Coulda used his height on the basketball team."

Cory cannot hoop. The thought of him trying to do anything remotely athletic almost makes me crack a smile. He and I have that in common. Long limbs everyone expects us to put to use in competitive feats. We've both gone our whole lives letting people down when those limbs don't match their expectations. *A waste* is what I overheard my eighth-grade volleyball coach call my height. *A bitch* is what she overheard me call her. That was my last day on the team. That was my last day on *any* sports team.

"Hey, man," Rich says as Cory returns with our drinks, "I think you can get an invite to the party on a technicality. Once an Eagle, always an Eagle."

"Yeah? What do you say—"

"See you on the thirty-first." I rush the words out, just wanting him to go away already.

"Bet. I'll be there." He passes out straws to everyone. "Do y'all know what you want to eat?"

"One large pepperoni and one extra cheese for the table, please," Rich says.

"Anything else?" Cory asks, eyes on me.

"Nope. That's it," Rich answers.

Cory waits to see if I have anything to add. When I say nothing, he taps his notebook and smiles. "I'll be out with your order soon."

"Thank you!" Kira supplies in the overly cheerful way she tends to do when she senses any tension or awkwardness.

Jere waits until Cory is out of earshot but still whispers when he speaks. "He was friends with that kid who got run over the summer before tenth grade, wasn't he?"

My gut clenches, and goose bumps erupt across my skin. This conversation is taking a turn in the exact direction I wanted to avoid. Toward the exact reason I don't speak to Cory anymore.

"Yeah, you're right," Rich says. "Hit-and-run. What was his name? He went to Eastside. Trenton James?"

Jones, I correct in my head. Trenton Jones. I grit my teeth as they debate about his name. *Trey? Tristan?* Piper throws in *Michael* out of nowhere and I have to take a sip of my drink to busy my facial muscles and keep from scowling. But when they turn the conversation back to the accident, I pray for them to continue the name game. Because I can't hide how I feel about that. Not for long. My eyes dart around the shop, searching for something else to focus on. The news segment on Natalie is over, and a cringey used-car commercial plays. I recite the jingle in my head three times, trying to drown out the conversation around me. After that, I switch to counting ceiling tiles. I get to twenty-one before switching to the number of hat-covered heads and then to the number of posters on the wall. I can't concentrate on anything for long. Snippets of their conversation continue to break through, making my armpits sweat, making my throat dry. I tear at my paper straw wrapper, and when that's obliterated, I go at a bunch of napkins.

"Did they ever find the person who hit him?" Rich's question cuts through all my attempts to tune the conversation out.

"Yes," I say, fiddling with the row of piercings on my left ear. "Some old guy who should have been off the roads a decade ago." I shrug, trying to seem less affected than I am. Trying to pretend that I am okay with the fact that I will never have closure. "The news said he had a stroke and died before they were able to bring formal charges."

"Dang, that's messed up. So is that why Cory left Pinegrove? Couldn't cope?" Jere asks.

Kira places a firm hand on my bouncing thigh. "Um, y'all? Can we maybe not talk about the beginning of sophomore year?" she snaps, eyebrows near her hairline, head leaning in my direction.

It takes a few seconds before it clicks for Rich and Jere. A few seconds before sincere apologies pour out of them. The beginning of sophomore year is when Mom left. They know how hard it was on me and were surprisingly supportive despite typically showing the emotional intelligence of a brick wall. What they don't know is that I made friends with both Cory and Trenton a few months before that. They don't know the mess losing Trenton only two months before my mother made of me. The way it imploded the deep friendship Cory and I had so quickly formed. The way it destroyed the blossoming flirtation between us. They don't know because I never told them. Because that part, the part where I spent the summer playing video games with two nerdy boys while my parents finalized their divorce—while the friends in front of me went to fancy summer camps or flew to foreign countries for vacation—doesn't fit the version of myself I spent all of ninth grade formulating. My mom taught me how to do that. How to protect myself with smoke and mirrors. Me and all my masks. It's no wonder I throw the best Halloween parties.

I spot Cory staring at me across the room, always with an expression of knowing, and I'm suddenly feeling eager to outdo myself.

CHAPTER 2

My friends drop me off at home. I have my license because Dad forced me to take lessons and get it, but all my interest in driving died with Trenton. As I walk down the driveway toward the side door, with the floodlight from the garage illuminating my path, I am uncomfortably aware of how my night transitioned from being haunted by the living to being haunted by the dead. All I can think about is what Trenton's final moments must have been like. I didn't witness the accident myself, but I went to the site. Saw the tire marks in the road. The bit of ruined sod in the yard of 29 Edgewood Lane. My mind fills in the gaps that I don't want to be filled. Trenton walking down that dark street. Blinding light. The squeal of brakes. I pick up my pace, ready to get inside and make these thoughts stop.

Dad pulls open the door before I can get my key in the lock.

"Sim Simma!" he shouts, stepping aside to let me in. "How was the game?"

Dad was an NFL offensive tackle before he retired and started a real estate business. Despite pleas from the community, he stays a comfortable distance away from the high school football scene.

I set my bag down on the kitchen island and slip out of my shoes. "Close one, but we pulled it off."

He nods, unsurprised. "Homecoming next week, right?"

I walk over and give him a kiss on the side of his bald head. "Yes. Game Friday. Dance Saturday."

"Oh, homecoming dance on your birthday? How you feel about that?"

I shrug and don't share that I'm secretly hoping the dance will have everyone too distracted to remember it's my birthday. I have intentionally failed to remind people that it's coming up. I'm not one for the spotlight. Dad has always said his NFL days taught him that admiration and scrutiny walk a thin line. Offering myself up for that coin toss? Yeah, no thanks.

Dad sniffs the air hard as I move to turn on the light underneath the microwave.

"I smell Ozzy's. You got some leftovers for your old man?"

"You're not an old man yet, but I want you to be one someday, so no. I will not participate in worsening your already high cholesterol and blood pressure."

"Slightly elevated," he corrects.

I ignore him and sift through the stack of mail he set aside for me. It's mostly ads from local colleges encouraging me to *Apply Now!*, but I already have all my applications in, and after working hard for my 4.6 GPA, I have no doubt I'll get into my top choices and start making moves toward a career in biotech. Academics always came easily to me. It was the social stuff that took work, but I've never been averse to working hard.

I glance out the kitchen window and it's oddly dark out. "Hey, Dad?" I look over to where he is getting cozy on the couch with our black cat, Serling. "I think the light bulb in the flood—" No sooner do the words leave my mouth than the light blinks back on, just as it has sporadically done for the past several months.

"You good, Simma?" Dad calls.

"Yeah, never mind," I say distractedly, peering out the window. I've mentioned the bulb to him a few times, and he always checks and finds nothing wrong. "I'm tired. Gonna head up to bed."

"All right. Get some rest!" he calls over the Netflix *tudum*.

Upstairs, I make a beeline for my bedroom window. It has the same view as the kitchen one, only a higher vantage point. I push aside my blackout curtains and swear I see the light above the garage turn off and on in quick succession, not in the way of a dying bulb, but like someone is fiddling with the switch. That light taunts me. Fluttering. Blinking. Turning on and off at random moments. Sometimes it feels like it tracks me. An eye. Following. Watching. Boring through my masks. Peering at what's inside. Judging. My heart rate picks up. People are supposed to be afraid of the dark, not lights. I tell myself it must be a bad breaker or something, but it doesn't eliminate the tremble that has formed in my fingers.

The warm light flashes once again, this time taking on a reddish hue, and for the third time tonight, my thoughts drift toward hauntings. Rich was right. I love spooky stuff. But I prefer the kind that I orchestrate. I like to be in control of the horror. To talk about it. Read about it. To piece together terrors and mysteries. I like to set the eerie scenes and tell the scary stories. I do not like whatever is going on in that garage, electrician-fixable or not.

I close my curtains, stride to my desk, and open my laptop, eager to distract myself with some other mystery. I type *Fairville.legends.com* into the address bar. I visit this site a few times a week, always certain to clear my browser history after. There's nothing bad or embarrassing here, and no one uses my computer other than me, but it's part of my ritual because the site is run by

Cory. Erasing him from my browser history is my tiny symbolic way of erasing thoughts of him from my head each day. He uses this blog to piece together terrors and tell stories the way I do in my head. Local and nearby missing persons, murders, cold cases, urban legends. All things dark and mysterious. All possibilities explored in the search for answers, both natural and paranormal. I want to reread his series on Natalie Dawson. She became Fairville's sweetheart when everyone learned that she deferred her admission to Brown to care for her sick grandmother. That information didn't come out until she'd already been missing for two weeks—it was the thing that suddenly made people care. But I learned of her disappearance on day one, thanks to Cory's blog. I move my cursor to the archives section, but a fresh post from this morning steals my attention.

BLOG ENTRY 076 / OCTOBER 8

CATEGORY: FAIRVILLE URBAN LEGENDS
EPISODE 3, PART 1

Welcome back, fright fiends! Today we'll be sampling a bit of local lore straight out of Champlain Park and Recreation Center. Now, I'm sure you're staring at your screen, jaw slack. What's the CPRC done to land a spot on my dark and mysterious little blog? Champlain? Where so many of the good people of Fairville, Georgia, spend summer days splashing in its Olympic saltwater pool or playing tennis on its state-of-the-art courts? Surely there's nothing sordid about the beloved summer landing spot, right? Well, yes and no. The rec center sits on a plot of land that spans 216 acres—and not all of them have been developed. Next time you explore Champlain's sprawling hiking trails, stop at mile marker 2.5. Still your body, quiet your mind, and you just might sense a mysterious charge in the air.

If you're feeling brazen, hop off trail, travel thirty or forty paces to the southeast, and you'll see the first signs. Maybe the mud-caked hand of a marionette or a tiny porcelain foot. Maybe an acrylic eye, locked mid-blink, or a stained pillowy torso.

Follow the phony body parts, and you'll find Doll's Head Lake.

While the abandoned toys have certainly captured the attention and intrigue of the occasional hiker (scroll through the photos on Champlain's Google reviews), the mystery doesn't end there. Two weeks ago I stopped in Tandy's Thrifted Treasures, as I often do. In the book section, I found a tattered copy of <u>Fairville: A History</u>. I've checked this book out from the library two dozen times, often for references made in this very blog, so I was geeked to find a copy of my own. But the real treat came when I got home and flipped through the dusty pages only to find them annotated by an especially thorough individual. The words below were written on the page behind a photo of the Champlain groundbreaking back in 1957.

> A dark specter lives on the banks of Yearwood Lake.
> Do not enter the wood without offering stake.
> Make a deal and you're in her debt.
> Those who've met her call her Regret.

Upon further research, I discovered that Yearwood Lake is indeed the formal name of the body of water tucked behind the CPRC. It seems to have taken on the Doll's Head moniker around 1960, and I can't help but wonder if the scattered doll parts are tied to the ghost called Regret and the offerings the author of the annotations mentioned. More research to do on my end, so stay tuned for my next installment. But in the meantime, if you're feeling bold enough to explore the mysteries of Doll's Head Lake on your own, tread carefully, and maybe stop by the toy store for a gift before you go—just in case.

Until next time, may your adventures be filled with both terror and wonder.

Keep it creepy, friends.
C.

I open another tab on my browser and search for those Google reviews. I click through the photos and it's exactly as I imagined while reading the blog. Old broken toys arranged along an overgrown path leading to a marshy lake with a rickety dock. Deliciously eerie. An excited rush courses through me. How had I never heard of this? Those woods would make the perfect backdrop for my annual party. I navigate to the CPRC website and look up the cost of reserving the banquet hall. It's three hundred dollars an hour on such short notice, but that's no concern. Dad will gladly swipe his card. I grab my notepad as idea after idea pops into my mind. We could decorate the room to look like an old haunted house. I could hire a ventriloquist with one of those wooden dummies to put on a show. The whole football team could hide in the woods, ready to jump out and scare everyone during a midnight hike out to Doll's Head Lake for a bonfire.

I've generated a Pinterest board and am halfway through drafting a text to Kira with my ideas before I remember: Cory is going to be at the party. I'd rather die than have him find out I've read his blog. That I was fascinated enough to base my best and final Halloween party around his discovery. He can't know that I think of him every day. That I hear his voice in my head as I read his words. And he *will* know. I could lie up and down, say I stumbled upon the spot during a walk or saw the Google photos while trying to reserve the party room. Everyone else would buy it, no problem, but he will know, and he can't. I cannot give him that.

My whole body deflates. I chew my bottom lip and return to scrolling through the blog post when another idea hits me. I grab my phone, delete everything I was about to send Kira, and type something new.

Me
what do you think about throwing a seniors-only party next week after the homecoming game? October 15th.

A typing bubble appears right away.

Kira
Simone Washington! Are you actually trying to plan something for your birthday this year!?

Me
My birthday is the 16th.

Kira
And what? You planned to wrap up all the festivities before the clock strikes midnight?

Me
No. I just want it to be about us. Not me. And an exclusive event will get the underclassmen even more hype for my party at the end of the month

Kira
Did you come up with something for that yet?

Me
No and it'll be hard to top what I'm thinking for this, but that's a problem for future me.

Kira
Babe I already told you my motto for senior year is ALL THE THINGS. Only thing you gotta do is let me call it your birthday party.

My aversion to birthday celebrations will have to be put aside, because with only one week to plan, I'm going to need Kira's help to pull this off.

Me
Fine.

Kira
xoxoxox!! Come by Layla's place in the morning so we can brainstorm!

CHAPTER 3

Saturday morning, Layla's two massive goldendoodles—Kira's fur nephew and niece—wiggle their way out the front door and bound over to me, jumping and whining.

"Monty! Shee Shee!" Layla hollers. "Get back in here, now!"

The dogs don't pay her one mind, instead choosing to gallivant around the yard, sniffing for any changes since their morning pee.

Inside, Kira lounges on the couch, the pink bonnet covering her pineapple curls giving her a conehead look. She already has the Pinterest board I shared with her mirrored onto the living room TV from her iPad. "So are you going to tell me what's up with all these creepy doll pins?"

"Can't say I'm not curious too." Layla finally gets the dogs inside and takes a seat at the kitchen island. She and her husband, John, were high school sweethearts. They got married last year, exactly one year after their college graduation. Kira looks up to her sister so much that I'm worried she wants to follow in her footsteps with Rich. That thought is more horrifying than any haunted dolls.

I tell them both the lie that Cory would never buy. That I was poking around on Google, looking for a good spot to hold my party when I stumbled upon some weird photos in the woods by the CPRC.

Kira hops to her feet, bouncing with excited energy that gets the dogs worked up again. "Wait, are you sure you want to do this for the seniors-only thing?" She grabs the end of a tug toy that Monty presents to her. "This would be perfect for the big Halloween party."

I clear my throat, quickly trying to come up with an excuse that has nothing to do with Cory Gooding. "Yeah, but the party room at the CPRC was already booked for that date."

Monty tugs on the toy and a long string of drool falls to the floor. Kira laughs and I'm glad he has half of her attention so she won't double-check my claims.

"Damn." She twists her mouth to the side, thinking. Her lack of commitment to tug-of-war sends the dog off to go bother Layla instead. "That's okay. Who says your eighteenth birthday party can't be the big one? It's our last year. We should celebrate you and treat ourselves. Go all out."

"When are y'all thinking of having the party?" Layla asks.

"This coming Friday night. Short notice, but Kira and I work well under pressure."

Layla grimaces. "Sorry, girl. That's going to be a booking issue for the banquet hall, too. A friend of mine is having her engagement party there."

"Oh." I really should have checked the open dates.

"But . . . ," Layla draws out, asking us to wait with her index finger in the air while she searches for something on her phone. "Right!" she shouts. "I thought something sounded familiar about those doll parts! That lake back there is called Yearwood Lake."

I work to keep my expression neutral, worried Layla already managed to find the blog post.

The two sisters stare at me, eyes wide.

"What?"

"Oh my gosh, Simone." Kira laughs. "Yearwood Lake!" She points at a hand-painted sign on the wall that reads THE YEARWOOD FAMILY.

"Wait. That lake was named after your husband's family?" I ask Layla. Cory would eat that info up for his blog. But based on how these two are looking at me, he probably already knows.

"They bought up all that land to build the rec center. Sold it about thirty years ago . . . except for one small piece. And that's the part you two are going to love. John's great-aunt Margaret still owns a cabin out there. Could be the perfect spot for a party."

"Are you serious? Do you think she'd let us use it?" I ask.

"I need to give her a call, but Margaret loves me. I'm sure I can get her to agree. How many people are we talking though? Because I doubt the entire senior class is going to fly."

Kira scratches her chin. "How do you feel about close friends only, Sim? Something extra exclusive could be nice since you want to be all shy about your birthday anyway. Oooh, and fewer people would definitely make it scarier." She tucks her chin and wiggles her fingers at me.

"No, that sounds great. Especially on such short notice. Think your aunt would go for maybe ten people?" I ask.

"We'll find out." Layla disappears up the stairs.

"Let's think about the guest list!" Kira takes a seat.

"Shouldn't we wait until we get the go-ahead?"

"Layla gets what she wants, which means if Layla wants something for you, you get it," she says matter-of-factly. "Actually, how about *I* work on the guest list and invitations while you work on all the creepy little details."

I grab my phone, and a flurry of social media notifications distract me from my task. Piper's shared a set of new pictures of herself at the local pumpkin patch. She posted it only thirty minutes ago, but she already has two hundred likes, including one by Rich. He even left a heart-eyed emoji as a comment. I scroll through her other pictures, and he is there on every single one, liking and commenting.

"Kira, are you aware that Rich likes all of Piper's posts on social media?"

She lies back on the couch, rolling her eyes as she goes. "Yes, Simone. I am aware."

"Okay, and are you aware he does it on Rachel's pics, too? And Bianca's?"

"What can I say? My guy's an equal opportunity liker," she says with a snort.

"Kira, I'm serious. I don't want him to make a fool of you."

"Simone, please stop trying to plant insecurities where there are none. I know Rich. He's a flirt. That's all."

I know for a fact that's not all, but I choose to drop it for now and tap back over to Pinterest. The first picture on my home page is of a garage at night with a bright floodlight that is disturbingly similar to mine. I frown at the screen and quickly close the app. When I reopen it, every single picture is a garage. In darkness. Floodlight beaming. "What the f—"

"Yo! I'm back!" John bursts through the front door, setting off the dogs once again. Shee Shee leaps over me to get to him, knocking my phone from my hand. When I pick it up again, the garages are gone, replaced by a perfectly ordinary Pinterest home page that reflects my recent searches for *scary dolls* and *Halloween party*.

John, clad in his usual puffer vest and flannel shirt, holds a cup carrier above his head, far out of reach of his hyperactive pets. "I got pumpkin spice and chai lattes! Who's the best husband and brother-in-law in town?"

Kira grumbles something unintelligible from deep within the couch cushions, and Layla comes galloping down the stairs, happily accepting the drinks in exchange for a kiss. "You're the best husband and brother-in-law in town."

"Thought so." He lifts his hat and runs a hand through his dark hair before pressing the hat back down on his head. "What are y'all up to?"

"Party planning!" Layla says.

Kira greedily clenches her fingers in the air until her sister places a latte in her hand. "Thank you!"

"Who's throwing a party? Not you, I hope." John eyes his wife nervously.

Layla laughs him off and hands me a chai. "You'll get a kick out of this, babe. You know that cabin your great-aunt owns out behind the CPRC?"

He squints. "Yeah. What about it?"

"Kira and Simone are going to host a little senior Halloween get-together there!"

Kira winks at me. "Told you it was a done deal."

"Done deal?" He frowns. "You can't have a party there. That place is decrepit."

Layla sips her drink and raises her eyebrows, not sure what he's not getting. "I said Halloween. That's kind of the point."

"Aunt Maggie's a Scrooge. She'd never let a bunch of teenagers loose on her cabin."

Layla twirls one of her curls around her finger. "Seems you've forgotten just how persuasive your wife can be."

He gapes. "Wait, what? You asked her?"

"All I had to do was agree to help her with some social media promo for her jewelry store, but I'm happy to." She shows off her ring-adorned fingers.

John places his iced coffee on the console. "Aunt Margaret said some kids she doesn't know can stay at her place alone?"

"Well, no. Not alone."

Kira starts to whine, but Layla cuts her off. "I agreed to chaperone. I'll be at the CPRC most of the night anyway for Zaria's engagement party. What do you say, babe? Want to dip deeper into this adulting thing and watch over the young 'uns after?"

"No. I do not."

"John, shut up. Come on."

"That house is a wreck, Lay. An accident waiting to happen."

"Margaret said it's fine. We'll put out a bug bomb, hire up a cleaning crew. Make sure no one has an asthma attack from the dust."

He sighs, already relenting. "A buddy of mine at work, his mom owns a housekeeping company. I'll reach out to her." He takes his coffee out back, mumbling to himself while Kira and I dive back into planning.

"Okay," Kira says after a while. "I think I have a good list of people to invite. Of course, it'll be me, you, Rich, and Jere. I know Piper isn't your fave, but the girl knows how to have a good time."

"Won't argue with that."

Kira side-eyes me, suspecting extra meaning behind my words. She and I both know it's there, but she chooses to leave it alone. "I've also got Noor, Cameron, and Shaina. That's eight. I was thinking Kingston and Diego to round it off, unless you had someone else in mind?"

"No. That sounds good to me." Rich already flirts with both Piper and Shaina shamelessly. Add some alcohol to the mix, and he's likely to make my job easy by slipping up and telling on himself.

CHAPTER 4

Kira and I spent every spare moment of the school week planning the party and shopping for supplies. She handled the invitations, and her decision to put a picture of a creepy doll head in place of an address for the location had people who weren't even invited buzzing. As soon as the bell rings on Friday afternoon, we pile into her car and head out to the cabin for the first time. Layla, with some extra time on her hands before she starts a new job, volunteered to go out there early and start setting up.

"Are you sure you don't want to go to the game?" Kira asks. "There can't be that much left to do. Layla's pretty efficient."

"I'm sure. Plus, it's my goal to spook *everyone* tonight. That includes you, so I'll be needing some alone time."

Kira squeals and flicks her hair over her shoulder, revealing a pretty gold chain I haven't seen before. There's a circular pendant with a *K* engraved on it. Probably one of Rich's I-messed-up-please-forgive-me gifts. "Yes, girl! I expect to be in full danger of peeing my pants and nothing less."

I look out my window. The turn has come up faster than expected. "Here!" I shout.

Kira slams on the brakes and peers into the trees. An almost imperceptible dirt road stretches off to the right. "This? You're sure?" she asks.

I double-check the GPS. "Yeah. This is it."

She makes a slow, hesitant turn onto the road. The trees are dense and the path is narrow. So narrow I'm not even sure another car could fit by on the other side. We drive for another ten seconds down the winding road until the cabin comes into view. The exterior is painted a moody black, and it sits on a tall, stilted foundation. It's cleaner, bigger, and more modern looking than I imagined from John's description.

"Oh, this is cute!" Kira hunches over the steering wheel for a better look.

Layla hears our arrival and comes sauntering out the front door and onto the deck, waving. She looks like a movie star in her flowy, long-sleeved maxi dress and fresh boho braids.

Kira and I each load up with as much stuff as we can carry and hurry to greet her. The gravel path is lined with fake tombstones, and the railings are draped with cotton spiderwebs. A couple of spooky dolls rest in the rocking chairs on the porch, and caution tape forms an X over the large window by the front door.

Upon closer inspection, the house is showing its age. Chipped paint. Moss growing on the stone bits. A green algae tinge to some of the floorboards of the deck. But that only adds to the appeal.

"This place is perfect, Lay. Thank you so much."

She winks at me. "Wait till you see the inside."

We follow her in. Light spills into the cabin from the left wall, which is almost entirely glass. In the kitchen, she's lit a yummy-smelling seasonal candle from Bath & Body Works. The home has clearly had some updates over the years, but the cabinetry looks original—old natural pine with beautiful antique-looking hardware.

"John made it sound like this place was condemned," I say.

"Well, John is a little bit spoiled and a lot bit melodramatic. What he sees as two stars is five to the average Joe. And even my rich-ass family is an average Joe to the Yearwoods." She tucks her hair behind her ear. "There's a bathroom and two bedrooms down the hall. The lofted area upstairs has one bed and a half bath. Figured you two would want to claim that space."

"Dumping my stuff now!" Kira sprints up the wooden stairs.

"You and John don't want to stay up there?" I ask Layla.

She waves me off and leans in close like she's telling a secret. "John might have acted like this party was some huge inconvenience or horrible idea when we first told him about it, but it's literally all he has been able to talk about. He's embraced the idea of hauling himself over here to play Mr. Chaperone after the engagement party, but there's going to be an open bar, and he has always been the life of the party. Doubt he'll be able to put one foot in front of the other by the end of the night. His family has a suite at the CPRC, and I'm ninety-nine percent sure that's where we'll be crashing. But we are right up the road if y'all need anything. I can get here in two minutes flat." She wiggles her cell phone in her hand. "Signal is strong. That automatically means nothing too scary can go down."

Layla checks her watch as Kira comes jogging back down the stairs. "Got about an hour and a half before I need to leave. I was going to make y'all some pasta salad and buffalo chicken dip. The rest of the decorations are on the coffee table. Y'all can handle those."

Kira starts up some music and we get to work, taking two or three breaks to sing, dance, and eat way too many of the party snacks. I'd be content if this were the main event. Just me, Kira, and Lay goofing around. But we can do that any weekend. Kira's been reminding me all week that I'll only turn eighteen once, and I think I'm finally buying in.

"All right," Layla says. "There are extra chips and sweets in the pantry. The real food is in the fridge and Crock-Pot. Think you can handle the final touches on your own, Sim?"

"Absolutely. Y'all go ahead."

"Great. Let me go grab John so we can get a move on."

"Oh, John's here?"

Layla lets out a pop of a laugh. "You thought he let me drive his precious truck? He's been pulling lawn furniture out of the shed and getting a new firepit set up. The old one was rusted out. And I think he said he was going to chop some wood? Since when he became a lumberjack, I do not know."

"I'll go tell him you're ready to go. I want to see outside."

I walk across the living room and slide open the glass side door. The porch wraps around from the front, but this portion is massive. There's a hot tub on one side and a large dining table with a pergola above it on the other. The porch overlooks a small clearing with the firepit and several Adirondack chairs. John is hauling hunks of wood to a large storage container. Behind him is forest, but the faint line of a hiking trail stretches out to the left. That must lead to the lake. I trot down the deck steps and cross the yard to where he is loading up the last of the firewood.

"Yo!" He waves, hands hidden under thick working gloves.

"Hey! Thanks for cutting the wood. A bonfire will be fun later on."

"Thought y'all might like that. I threw a couple of starters in the bin. Just make sure the fire is totally out before you all go back inside."

"Yeah, of course. The cabin is amazing, by the way. The cleaning people did a great job. Do you have a card? My dad has been talking about wanting to get our house deep cleaned for months now."

John pushes his safety glasses up on his head and strips out of his gloves. "Don't have their card on me, but you can look them up online. Delia's Home Cleaning."

I type it in my Notes app so I won't forget. "Thanks." I gesture at the woods behind him. "Have you been out there? To the lake?"

He looks over his shoulder. "Not recently. You shouldn't go, either. Seriously. It's not safe, so don't get any ideas about swimming."

"No, I wasn't thinking about doing anything like that. It's too chilly anyway."

"Yeah, well, stay out of the woods completely. I know you wanted to see those freaky dolls, but it'll be dark. Somebody'll turn an ankle. Saw a couple Chucky dolls in the Halloween section at Walmart. Grabbed those for you instead. Happy birthday."

I laugh. "I saw them on the front porch when we got here. They're perfect. Thank you," I say, fully intending to ignore his advice.

After I see them off, I go back inside, grab the last bag of props and decorations, and hurry down the porch steps, eager to scope out the trail to Doll's Head before daylight is fully gone. Being scared with friends is cool. Alone? Not so much.

I walk boldly into the trees—making plenty of noise so any lurking animals will clear out—and spot some toys right away. A plastic baby carriage with a moldy fabric doll inside with the words GO BACK written across her chest sits next to a tree stump. I hide an old waterproof Bluetooth speaker in the carriage, scheming for scary stories by the fire later. Farther down the trail I find a rusty model train set and a four-foot-tall Black Barbie in a tattered princess dress, elbow frozen at a ninety-degree angle as if waving hello. Her welcoming flight attendant pose is kind of unsettling, but I continue on down the path. It's not long before

I stumble upon something else. A clown head pokes out from a dense patch of weeds. I push them aside and let out a cheerful gasp when I reveal the rest of it. "Not a jack-in-the-box!" I pick it up and dust it off. I thought these only existed in movies.

Not too far away, the sound of a snapping twig makes my head shoot upright. I peer through the trees, trying to put eyes on the cabin, but it's getting dark even faster than I thought it would. I bite my lip and take one more glance in the direction of the lake, considering just a moment before putting the toy in my bag and retracing my steps. I'm not trying to get turned around out here by myself.

The interior of the cabin has been stripped of any personal Yearwood family items, which is mildly disappointing. I'd hoped John's aunt Margaret would be into taxidermy or collecting bizarre artwork, but it's nothing a few more decorations won't fix. I write BLOODY MARY three times on the first-floor bathroom mirror with red lipstick and arrange a plastic knife with a flashlight behind the shower curtain for *Psycho* vibes. In the living room, I set up the perfect booby trap to go off as soon as everyone comes in.

Upstairs Kira has already left her messy mark. Her bag is upturned on the floor, and stuff is scattered everywhere. I all but burst into a rage when I step on—and break—one of her claw clips. I begin gathering up all her junk and unceremoniously squashing it back into her duffel. A bottle of body spray goes rolling under the bed. I lie on my stomach and shove my arm beneath the bed skirt, feeling around for it. I come back with a different bottle. A small glass dropper with a label that reads LX. A laxative, I guess. Kira has always had tummy issues. I set it on the end table along with the body spray and a rogue bottle of contact solution.

In the bathroom, I swap my T-shirt for a cute V-neck sweater.

My makeup from this morning is holding up well, but I add some plum-colored blush that Kira insisted would look magical on my dark skin. I smirk at my reflection, decide she's right, and finish getting ready.

Struggling to hold back a yawn, I head to the kitchen. It's going to be a long night, and I can't be the first to sleep at my own party. Luckily, there's a case of Red Bull in the fridge. I crack one open and take a big swig, but choke when I see a flash of something outside. I cough and use my hand to drink some water from the sink while taking a look out the window. It was like a flashlight, only bigger. Maybe more like the single headlight of a motorcycle. But there is no road out there, and the trees are too dense for anything other than walking. I wonder if anyone else in the world has been haunted by light. A chill licks across my skin, just like the other night when I was looking out at my garage, just like every time I imagine the last thing Trenton probably ever saw. Light. Blinding light.

I slap my cheeks and shake out my hands before clicking on all the exterior lights and marching outside. "Hello?" I call.

Crickets have begun chirping, and there are a few other random animal noises, but I don't see anyone. I sigh, relieved, like a child after their parent confirms that there is, in fact, no monster under the bed. I turn to go back inside, but a scream catches in my throat as soon as I do.

Someone is standing at the other end of the porch. Their body is large and completely cast in shadow. I pat my pockets for my phone. "W-who's there?"

Heavy boots clunk across the wood panels as they take a few steps closer.

Finally, the porch light illuminates their face. A man. Fortyish. Brown skin. Stubbly beard. Strong.

"Who are you?" I ask, voice less steady than I want.

He crosses his arms and raises an eyebrow. "No, who are *you*? Cause you damn sure ain't Ms. Margaret."

I relax some at the mention of her name, but I need him to know I'm no pushover. "Well, forgive me, but you sure aren't Ms. Margaret, either."

He runs a hand over his stubble, and I can tell he is holding back a smile. "She did say something about some kids having a Halloween party here. Silly me for thinking a Halloween party would take place on Halloween."

"It's a birthday party, technically. How do you know Ms. Margaret?"

"All right, twenty-one questions." He stomps his boot a few times, some caked-on mud crumbling away. "I'm a groundskeeper. Name's Nate. This is my first visit to the property. She hired me on a few days ago and wanted me to get things in order for a party at the end of the month." He emphasizes the last few words.

"She must have had her wires crossed about the dates. I—I'll text her nephew."

"Don't bother," he says quickly. Too quickly. "Was probably on me. Doesn't seem like there's much to be done anyway."

I nod, but the only question circulating through my head is why a groundskeeper would come inspect a property for the first time at eight thirty at night. "Was that you out there a minute ago?" I throw my thumb over my shoulder. "With a big light?"

He scratches the side of his head and looks at me like I don't have a brain in mine. "You just seen me come from round the way, right?"

"Yeah, but I thought . . . I don't know, is someone with you?"

"Just me." He peers through the living room window, then looks back at me. "What time's the party start?"

"Guests will be here any minute now," I lie.

He studies me for a couple of seconds. "What'd you say your name was?"

"Simone," I offer for the first time. "And sorry, you're Mr. . . . ," I ask, hoping for a last name.

"Hightower." He pulls up his dirty khaki work pants, which sag slightly. "I guess I'll be on my way then."

I look out to the empty gravel drive. "Did you walk?"

He looks at me like I'm stupid again. "Parked at the CPRC. Didn't realize it was such a hike. But fresh air never hurt nobody." He nods goodbye and I scoot back as he skirts by me and down the ramp. He grabs a toolbox at the bottom and sets off into the woods toward the CPRC.

I watch until he is completely out of sight, then I dart back inside and call John.

"Hello?" he answers, laughter and music from the engagement party almost drowning him out.

"John, there was some man at the cabin just now. He scared the mess out of me."

"What? Hold on."

I wait as he makes his way somewhere quieter. "Sorry, what?"

"Do you know some guy named Nate Hightower? Someone your aunt hired as a groundskeeper?"

"Uh, no. But I can check with her. Did you say he was at the cabin just now?"

"Yeah. He said he walked all the way from the CPRC."

"That's weird. Look, keep the doors locked until everyone else gets there. I'll go out and see if I catch him when he comes off the trail. I'll call Margaret and keep an eye on the security cams, too. Are you okay? Do you need me to come down there?"

"I'm fine. I didn't realize there was surveillance. That makes me feel better."

"Good. Lay and I will come check on y'all when this is over."

We hang up, and I go back inside, resisting the temptation to close all the blinds and turn on all the interior lights. I watched the man walk away. John's keeping an eye out. It's safe here. That's what I love about book- and film-based horror, Halloween haunted houses, and telling scary stories. Being able to explore your fears in a controlled environment. To feel the rush of adrenaline while knowing in the back of your mind that everything will be okay. That's what I want to set up for my friends. So I make some final touches with the decorations, plunge the place into darkness, and lounge on the couch until I see lights again. Lights that I know the source of. Lights that don't scare me because Kira texted and told me they'd be coming.

I crack open the front door. Loud bass music thumps as Jere parks his Jeep, and his high beams cast bright streaks across the unfinished pine floors.

It's time.

CHAPTER 5

I squat down behind the kitchen island where I can see the front door without being spotted myself.

Laughter and the goofy noises of my friends trying to spook each other fill the air when Jere cuts the engine. Another vehicle pulls up, followed by the sounds of doors opening and closing and people chatting and grabbing their things. The boys replay events from the football game as they trudge across the gravel. Their steps grow louder and hollow when they make the transition to the wooden ramp that leads to the front porch.

"Oh, hell nah. That door is open," Diego says. "It's dark in there."

"'It's dark in there,'" Shaina mocks before the door swings open all the way, I assume by her hand. It makes a deliciously eerie groan before it thuds against the doorstop, eliciting a few giggles from the other girls. "Hello?" Shaina hesitantly calls, without entering.

"See, look. Wanted to act all brave," Diego says. "Go ahead. After you."

"Oh my God, move," Piper says, and I'm so glad it's her who will set off my booby trap.

She takes a step or two inside and flicks on the light.

A lamp next to the couch illuminates, shining a spotlight on the jack-in-the-box I found in the woods. Piper lets out a terrified squeal that sets everyone else off shouting and laughing, too.

"Look," Rich says, the smile on his face evident in his voice as everyone settles down. "The sign. *Crank me up*. Who's gonna do it?"

"I got it," Jeremiah says.

I come out of my hiding spot while they are all distracted. Their backs are to me as I tiptoe toward the light switch and Jere cranks the toy. I have to time this just right. At the end of the fifth rotation, I cut the lights. The dirty clown pops from the box with a programmed, earsplitting scream, which is quickly muffled by everyone else's shrieks. Jere drops the toy and punts it across the room, where it hits the wall and goes silent. I flip the lights back on, the lamp and the overhead this time. Everyone turns to me. It's quiet for a second or two, and then we all burst into laughter.

Cameron aggressively rakes a brush over his sandy-brown waves. "Rich, put on that playlist you had going in the car."

Rich connects to the house's sound system and cranks the music up loud. He mumbles along, only singing every fourth word or so with any confidence, which sets Jere off on a roasting session. The frights will continue after some fun. I pull a bowl of bloodred punch from the fridge and everyone fills their cups. I pretend not to notice the bottle of vodka getting passed around as Kira raises her cup high in the air. "To a senior year filled with the best memories yet. Let's leave a legacy that Pinegrove will never forget."

The boys start one of their obnoxious football chants. Kira waits patiently, cup still in the air, dripping condensation.

"And," she says, waiting for them to quiet. "And I want to wish our beautiful host, the most loyal friend, the thrower of the best parties, a very happy birthday. Love you, Sim!"

A chorus of "happy birthday"s follows, then each of them tries to get their licks. I let them do their thing, teasing and prodding me until I crack a smile.

"We got you a present!" Shaina announces before dipping out to the front porch, her sleek black bob moving behind her like silk.

She returns with a gift basket filled with cult classic horror movie posters, games, and figurines.

"Thank you, guys," I say, knowing full well Kira was 100 percent behind this. "I love it."

I find a corner of the kitchen to tuck it away so it won't get messed up. As soon as I place it down, the doorbell rings—a sharp buzz that startles me. Noor's the only other person who seems to have heard it. I shrug as I walk by her. "Guess that's Layla and John." I pull open the door and blink rapidly a few times, wondering why on earth Cory Gooding is standing in front of me. "What are you doing here? How'd you even—I didn't—"

"Oh, bet!" Rich shouts. "Pizza's here!"

Cory raises his eyebrows and the three extra-large pizza boxes in his hands.

"You did this on purpose," I say to Rich.

"Uh, yes. You are correct. I purposely ordered pizzas for your birthday party." He takes the boxes from Cory. "Hey, man, this had to be your last delivery for the night, right?"

Cory looks cautiously between me and Rich. "Yeah."

"Then hang with us for a minute."

I glare at Rich's profile, trying to figure out if this is an honest coincidence, some weird attempt to play Cupid, or a calculated effort to keep me distracted on a night when he is likely to do something stupid. A second or two more and I decide that Rich is not the type to think that far ahead. He just does whatever pops into his head at any given moment. "Cory's working, Rich. I'm sure he needs to go close up Ozzy's or something...."

"I don't, actually."

Cory may not be the best with social cues, in general, but I know he knows what I'm not saying. I know he knows I want out of this. And I know he is going to stand there until I say it plainly. So, to spite him, I open the door all the way. "Well, come on in then."

His eyes widen just slightly before he smirks and crosses the threshold. "I can't stay for too long. Grandma waits up for me."

At least this will be over quickly. And it's nothing personal. Next to Kira, Cory is my favorite person in the world. But sometimes our favorite things are bad for us. "I wasn't lying or trying to set you up at Ozzy's the other night, by the way. I'm still having a party at the end of the month, and you can still come."

The statement barely fazes him. "I didn't think you were trying to set me up, Simone." He takes a look around. "This place is nice. How'd you find it?"

Kira pops up out of nowhere, munching on a handful of pretzels. "My sister! Her husband's aunt owns it." She throws an arm over my shoulder. "Totally Sim's vibe, right?"

"Totally," he offers in the same tone she did, which makes her laugh.

"Ayo! It's Cory, right?" Jere shouts from across the room. "You play basketball?"

Cory locks eyes with me, and I roll my lips together to hold back a smile because I know we are both thinking the same thing.

"Nah, man," he starts as he heads in Jere's direction.

And just like that, he folds seamlessly in with the group.

Kira nudges me with her elbow. "He's cute!"

"I know," I grumble before grabbing a Coke from the fridge.

For the next hour, I am hyperaware of my body. I can't talk or laugh or dance without wondering what I look like from Cory's point of view. A dozen times, I convince myself he isn't paying me any mind, and a dozen different times our eyes meet across the room. I do my best to keep distance between us. It doesn't take long for him to pick up on it, and he seems content to give me space. That thoughtfulness warms me, but only for a moment. The next time I look over and see him and Kingston laughing, my brain coughs up a memory of him and Trenton doing the same. And when Piper tries to teach him and Cameron the latest viral dance moves, I can hear Trenton ragging on Cory's two left feet. And the same continues until he announces that he better get going.

I'm relieved as I watch him drive off, but the relief comes with a healthy dose of guilt for being glad to see him go. He doesn't deserve that. I pull my braids up like I'm going to make a ponytail, then let them fall across my shoulders with an exhale, beyond exhausted by my yo-yoing emotions. I slide open the side door, letting in a cool breeze. It's time for me to reclaim this night. "Anyone up for a bonfire?"

"Hell yeah," Rich says.

We all trek outside, and I quickly link to the Bluetooth speaker I hid in the woods earlier so no one will hear it confirm the connection. Diego marches straight to the bin with the firewood and starters. He has some decent flames going before the rest of us even make it to the pit.

"You pyro," Cameron teases.

He shrugs and smiles, apparently taking it as a compliment.

We cozy into the Adirondack chairs, Kira taking a place on Rich's lap. Diego and Kingston stand and roast marshmallows.

"So what we doing? Ghost stories?" Jere asks.

"You don't know any ghost stories," Rich says.

"Yeah, I do." He leans forward and rests his elbows on his

knees. "Okay, so you know that classroom in the science wing that they never use? The one where they put all the broken furniture and shit?"

Everyone offers up a nod or an eye roll or a rotation of the wrist, hurrying him along.

"Well, the classroom hasn't been used since 1998, and depending on who you ask, you'll get different answers as to why not. Custodian says it's a mold problem. Assistant principal says wiring issues. All lies. But I know the truth." He pauses for dramatic effect. "It's haunted."

We all sit there, straight-faced, waiting for more.

"Is that the end of the story?" Piper asks, a trapped giggle making her lips quiver.

Jere straightens and tugs on the hem of his jacket. "No. What happened was this kid, we'll call him . . . Richard."

"Bruh," Rich interjects.

Jere grins mischievously. "Richard got up to sharpen his pencil. On his way back to his seat, the class bully"—he scans the faces around the bonfire and smirks when his eyes meet Cameron's—"the class bully, Camden, stuck out his foot to trip him, and *BAM!*" Jere smacks his hands together. "He fell, and the pencil went straight into his eye. No one could prove that Richard had been tripped, so Camden didn't even get in trouble—and Richard wasn't havin' that. He wanted revenge, and he got it only a week after he returned to school. See, they were doing a lab that day, and he secretly sprayed a flammable substance on Camden's lab apron. When he went to light the Bunsen burner . . . poof. Up in flames. But there was a ripple effect that Richard didn't plan for. All the bottles on the table exploded. The whole room was engulfed. Everyone got out except the two of them. Now they say anyone who goes in that room today suspiciously trips over something. They get a stabbing pain in their right eye. Break out in a nasty sweat. Straight-up impossible to hold class in there."

Piper fakes a snore. "Oh my God, Jere. If you're going to tell a scary story about a real place we all know, it needs to be at least somewhat believable."

"And ideally scary," Kira adds.

"*Et tu*, Kira? You're supposed to be the nice one." Jere throws up his hands.

"Sorry," she says as everyone else joins in on clowning him.

"I can do better," I say, barely loud enough to cut through the noise.

"Oh, really?" Jere asks, leaning back in his chair. "All right. Let's hear it then."

Here's my moment to shine. To add my own creative spin to the story Cory has only started piecing together. To blend fact and fiction into something terrifying. Changing just enough details so that I can claim ignorance if anyone eventually stumbles upon Cory's blog.

"We all know about the two Pinegrove seniors that disappeared back in 1978."

"Amy Thompson and Dante Hill," Noor offers. "There's a memorial plaque for them in the greenhouse."

"Wait, there is?" Jere asks.

"He's never read anything other than the football playbook," Piper faux-whispers.

Jere bucks at her playfully.

"It's true," I say. "They chose to put the plaque in the greenhouse because Dante and Amy were inaugural members of the Pinegrove Nature Club. But what most people don't know is that they disappeared during a club outing."

Kingston and Diego provide some well-timed "oooh"s.

"All of the club members, including Dante and Amy's friend Lisa-Marie Hilliard, went for a hike out in these very woods. They'd done it a dozen times before, but they couldn't have known how differently things would go on that cool October day. The three friends drifted behind the rest of the club and decided to explore a different trail. Only Lisa-Marie would ever be seen again. Her recounting of the events that transpired was so bizarre that most people assumed the trauma had affected her memory, and they discredited her completely. But Lisa-Marie was eager to tell her story to anyone who would listen. One of those people was my father's older sister, which is how I learned what happened. Lisa-Marie said that about thirty minutes or so after splitting from the rest of the group, they heard what sounded like a young child crying and calling out, 'Mama! Mama!'

"Worried a toddler had gotten lost in the woods, they followed the sound, but it only seemed to get farther and farther away. Dante broke into a run, trying not to lose the voice, but he fell and twisted his ankle. When Amy went to see what tripped him up—"

"It was Camden!" Jere shouts. He snickers until there is a loud *thwap!*—the sound of someone smacking him upside the head. Shaina, I assume based on the clanking bangles.

I sigh and continue. "When Amy went to see what tripped him up, she found an almost pristine baby doll in a white dress. Thinking the doll might belong to the child they heard, Amy stuck it in her bag and took it with them. Dante's injury slowed them down, and they started to get turned around as the light faded. Unable to find their way back to the main trail, they began arguing among themselves. That's when they heard someone else moving in the trees. They could feel someone watching them, and when they started to walk again, she showed herself.

A ghostly woman in a long, flowing nightgown appeared and accused them of kidnapping her child. They denied it, and she became hysterical. Angry. They tried to run, but she would disappear and reappear right in front of them. Screaming with a mouth open wider than any human mouth should be capable of. Teeth sharper than human teeth should be. They pleaded with her, told her they thought they heard her baby calling for her and where. Suddenly, the woman froze in place and pointed a long skinny finger at Amy." I extend my arm and model the action. Kira cuddles up closer to Rich. "Lisa-Marie followed the woman's gaze and saw she was actually pointing at Amy's bag, where the white dress of the baby doll was peeking out. Lisa-Marie walked over to Amy and carefully removed the doll from the bag as if it were a real infant. 'Do you want this?' she asked the woman. 'Is this your baby?' The woman's eyes softened, and she held out her arms. Lisa-Marie said the moment the doll left her hands, she blacked out. When she woke, she was back on the trail near the entrance. She ran for help right away, but Dante and Amy were never found. Every year on the anniversary of their disappearance, Lisa-Marie comes down here and leaves a baby doll in the woods, hoping her friends will find it and have something to offer the ghost. Her story, like a game of telephone, has gotten distorted over the years. But some people who've heard a version of it will leave offerings of their own. Now the woods are riddled with children's toys."

I turn to Kingston, my sudden motion making everyone jump. "I dare you to go find one of Lisa-Marie's dolls." I point again, this time to the woods where the trail begins. "You shouldn't have to go far."

His posture goes a little rigid, but I know he won't turn down a dare.

He drops his stick, blackened marshmallow stuck to the end, into the flames. "Easy work," he says before jogging off into the woods.

We all wait, staring at the place where the trees consumed him. It's so quiet. We can hear every step he takes. Leaves rustling as he curses every sharp twig and spiderweb. "Dang, man!" he shouts with a laugh. "Lisa-Marie ain't never miss a year!"

Once he goes silent again, leaving us only with the sound of his shoes padding the ground, I press play on a YouTube video I found. The sound of a baby crying echoes through the trees. Everyone tears out of their seats, falling over each other, ripping back toward the house. I play along. Kingston manages to beat us all to the porch steps, his locs riddled with dry leaves. Everyone is laughing and panting now, knowing it's a joke as the baby cries transition into an ad for a nutritional supplement.

Kingston holds a doll up by the leg. "For the birthday girl!"

I take the horrifying thing in my arms. I'm not sure how I missed this one earlier. She's pretty big, with matted dark brown hair and a lilac dress. There is a pull string on her back. It's rotted and feels like it might snap when I tug on it, so I'm unsurprised when the doll makes no sound.

"What the hell is going on over there?" a male voice playfully shouts from a distance.

I look up to see John and Layla coming around the side of the cabin, bathed in the yellow light of the flood lamp near the security camera. I shake away thoughts of the garage at home, thoughts of Trenton.

Kira groans loudly.

"Relax," Layla says. "We'll be out of your hair in a minute. Just doing our chaperonely duties."

"Looks like y'all are having a great time," John says.

"We are," I say. "Thanks again for letting us use the place."

"I'll make sure Aunt Margaret gets the message. Speaking of, I did get in touch with her about that groundskeeper."

"Groundskeeper? What groundskeeper?" Kira asks.

"Oh, it's nothing." I turn to John and Layla. "Y'all want to play some cards?"

"Sure, I'm down," Layla says.

Rich jogs up to John and greets him with a quick round of shadowboxing. "Hey, man, you get us them tickets to the Hawks' season opener?"

"Yeah. I texted you like two days ago. You in or out?"

"Bro, why is that even a question? Of course I'm in."

Kira clears her throat. "It's a question because our anniversary is next week."

With all their on-again, off-again drama, I'm not sure how Kira is keeping count.

"I know." Rich winks at her, not missing a beat. "That's why I was trying to get *us* tickets. Courtside date night." He shoots an imaginary basket.

"What? No, man, wait a—" John starts, but Layla jabs him in the side.

"Happy early anniversary from us!" she shouts.

John grumbles. "I'm gonna go put that fire out."

Cameron and Jere go with him while the rest of us gather up some playing cards and board games and find a movie to put on in the background.

I bow out of the third round of UNO, and that's when John and Layla head back to the CPRC, sure to remind us all that they are only a phone call away. I say goodbye to them and go to the kitchen for a snack. Rich is there, forearms resting on the counter as he stares at his phone. I squeeze behind him to get to the fridge and see that he's texting someone. As soon as he is done, Shaina's phone dings. A coincidence, maybe—until I see the smile spread across her face. Until I see the way she sinks into the couch, thumbs going a hundred miles an hour. Rich picks up his phone as soon as she puts hers down.

"Seriously?" Another incoming text vibrates his phone. I glimpse that it's from John, and he seems to be rightly cussing him out about those basketball tickets.

Rich turns around like he's only just realized I'm standing here. "Oh, hey, Simone. You say something?"

I smile tightly, done trying to call him out privately. "No. Just looks like Jere ate all the buffalo chicken dip."

"Check the back of the fridge. I put some in a separate bowl for the rest of us when I saw him going to town on it earlier."

". . . Thanks." My brain short-circuits a little because this guy somehow manages to be awful and thoughtful at the same time.

I change my mind about a snack and rejoin everyone else in the living room, taking a seat right next to Shaina. *Scream* plays on the TV, but most eyes are locked in on the extremely tense UNO situation. Shaina's phone dings again. I wait until she unlocks it, then I tap her drink with my foot and watch the contents spill across the hardwood floors.

"Oops! Oh my gosh! I'm so sorry." No one else even hears me over the chaos of the game.

Tipsy, Shaina tosses her phone aside and starts clumsily scooping as much ice and liquid back into her cup as she can. I casually pick up her phone and open her messages.

"There's a mop in the pantry," I say, attention fully on her most recent thread with none other than Rich Pearson.

She's too drunk to point out that I am, in fact, the one who knocked the drink over and should, therefore, be the one most eager to get it cleaned up, but that's exactly what I need right now. For her to go away and give me a few more seconds to read. I scroll back a bit to some texts exchanged on Wednesday to make sure I have the full context.

Shaina
😃 heyy

Rich
hey Shay, what's up?

Shaina
Are you bringing a gift to Simone's party?

Rich
hit up Kira. She's setting up a group thing

I glance at my pretty gift basket and then at Kira, her mouth wide open in laughter. Shaina thumbs-upped Rich's text about the gift. The messages start up again a couple of hours ago after they started drinking.

Shaina
😉 You look good tonite

Rich
You always look good

Shaina
better than your gf?

Rich
meet up with me. Later tonight

Shaina
Way to dodge the question

Rich didn't immediately respond, and I can imagine Shaina watching him love and hug on Kira. Jealousy building.

Shaina
😳 Meet where? When?

Rich
out on the dock. After everyone goes to sleep.

Shaina
the dock? Like through those creepy ass woods?

Rich
Not like we can chill in the house . . . plus, I'll be with you. No worries

Shaina
Okay then. After everyone goes to sleep.

I frown at Shaina as she returns with a wad of paper towels and toss her phone back on the couch. I like Rich. I truly consider him a friend. But I like Kira more. And I'm angry at him for putting me in this awkward position. I haven't been as open with Kira about the kind of personal things that best friends should be open about, and it feels so wrong. But I'm not quite ready to work through that. What I *am* ready to do is expose whatever Rich and Shaina have planned. Kira never wants to hear about his BS from my mouth, but tonight she can see it for herself.

CHAPTER 6

People begin dozing off around two AM, earlier than I would have guessed, but it's been a long day. Shaina is curled up on the recliner, pretending to be asleep. Her eyes squint open every thirty seconds or so, probably checking to see if everyone else is still up. Rich is sprawled belly down on the rug. The tiny circle of drool next to his mouth proves he's *actually* out. Noor and Cam sit side by side, laughing quietly, their faces illuminated by some video on her phone. Piper, Diego, and Kingston all sit heavy-lidded around the coffee table, lazily throwing out playing cards. Jere, who's been conked out on the couch for an hour, lets out a loud snore that startles Kira. She rubs her eyes, peeks at her sleeping boyfriend, tosses a throw blanket from the couch over him, then whispers my name and points upstairs.

I follow her up to the loft, where we both change into sweats and T-shirts.

"Have you had a good time?" she asks, toothbrush wedged in the side of her mouth.

"The best." I fluff my pillow and slide into the right side of the bed.

"I'll make everyone waffles in the morning. Can you text John and Lay Lay? Tell them we're tucking in for the night?"

I do what she asks as she burritos herself into a quilt and lies down next to me. It's only a matter of seconds before she's out.

After I hear the others say their good nights and get settled in, I strain for any sound that might suggest Shaina and Rich are following through with their plan. But the only noise is an occasional grunt from Jere. I turn on my side and close my eyes, only intending to do so for a couple of minutes, but when I open them again and reach for my phone, I'm shocked to find it's 3:07. Damn. I probably missed them. I sit up to go check but freeze when some light sounds from downstairs reach my ears. Whispers. A boy and a girl. I pick out the sound of footsteps next. The squeaky floorboard by the TV creaks, then the back door slides slowly open. And then slowly closed. It has to be them. Going out to the dock. I fake sneeze to wake Kira. A light sleeper, she shoots straight up, startled.

"Sorry," I say.

She squints at me in the darkness. "What time is it?"

"Just after three."

She yawns. "I gotta pee."

While she's in the bathroom, I peer over the banister to confirm that Rich and Shaina are truly gone. They are. The blanket Kira so kindly covered him with is crumpled on the floor by the coffee table. The recliner is empty.

Kira returns and moves the sheets around, preparing to get comfortable. I debate back and forth about whether I really want to do this. Is it worth it? What if she sees for herself and stays with him? Could I even look at her the same? I'm not sure. But when the glint from the gold chain around her neck catches my eye once again, I can't help myself. "Kira, when did Rich give you that necklace?"

Her hand reflexively darts up to it. She tucks the pendant into her shirt, annoyed that I've seen it. That I've said something.

"So when did he give it to you? Or maybe I should ask *why* he gave it to you."

"He gave it to me because he's my boyfriend and people who love each other give each other gifts sometimes, Simone."

I sigh, sick of beating around the bush. "He is cheating on you, Kira. He is cheating on you right now."

"What?"

"He's not downstairs, and neither is Shaina. Go look for yourself."

She hesitates but eventually walks to the banister and looks down. When she turns around, her face is stony. "Where did they go? Do you know?"

I nod.

She sits at the foot of the bed and puts on her sneakers. I do too, and within two minutes, she is following me out the door and toward the woods. Kira doesn't speak, but angry energy radiates off her. She knows she can't trust him. She just wanted him to prove her wrong. And now she is pissed that he hasn't. I don't say anything. "I told you so" is not the move, and this isn't about making her feel bad. It's about making sure my best friend doesn't accept anything less than she deserves. And Kira deserves the world. I never got to be the friend I wanted and should have been to Trenton. And any chance of that with Cory is long gone, too. Kira is all I have left, and that means she will get my very best.

It's gotten even cooler outside, uncomfortably so, and the light from the full moon makes the trees cast eerie shadows across the lawn. We book it through the woods, agreeing without words that moving quickly and not looking at the abandoned toys will prevent them from coming to life and snatching our ankles.

Unfortunately, our determined pace doesn't eliminate the menacing noises that call from the shadows. A yelp that I can only guess belongs to a coyote makes us speed up to a jog. But the next sound to cut through the night halts us in our tracks. The familiar ding of an incoming text message.

"Was that your phone?"

"No," Kira says. "I didn't bring it. And that sounded like an Android."

Something moves in the trees ahead of us—a person, maybe, running in the direction of the lake.

We instinctively crouch down and cling to each other. When my fear begins to dissipate, I straighten. "Rich?" I shout. "Shaina? We know you're out here!" I grab Kira by the wrist and pull her along. "Come on. We're almost there."

We break from the trees and onto the bank of the lake. The dock is straight ahead, and someone is standing on it. One someone.

"Rich?" Kira questions. She anxiously scans the whole area, because whoever we heard in the woods couldn't have made it to the end of the dock that quickly. But there's no one beyond the three of us.

The person turns as we get closer, and yeah, it's Rich. I keep an eye out for signs of anyone else as we walk up the dock to meet him. It might just be my own anticipation of the coming confrontation, but the air has a heavy charge to it.

"What are y'all doing out here?" Rich asks when we reach him. He takes off his jacket and throws it over Kira's shoulders. "It's cold."

"Where's Shaina?" I ask.

He sucks his teeth. "Come on, Simone. This is getting old. Do you see anyone else out here? You think Shaina hopped into the lake or . . . ?"

"She wasn't in the house when we left, so where is she?"

He shrugs hard. "Hell if I know. In the bathroom? Not out here, obviously."

"We heard her. Just now in the woods. I know you had plans to meet her."

"Are you sure about that? Is that a fact?"

"Yeah. It is. You know it is." I hold out my hand. "Let me see your phone."

Kira's shoulders drop. "Simone, stop. Let it go. Please." She begins walking back to the shore.

"No, Kira. You were right there with me. We heard her phone!" I lose the smallest bit of confidence after saying it. I was holding Shaina's iPhone earlier and the two text tones don't match, but that doesn't change what I read, and I need Kira on board.

"I don't know what we heard, Simone! Let's go back. I know you meant well, but I don't want to be out here anymore. I don't want to talk about this."

I look at my friend, the resigned expression on her face, and all I feel is disappointment. "Buck up, Kira. He is a *liar*. You deserve so much more."

"You are such a fucking hypocrite," Rich says under his breath, only loud enough for me to hear.

I whip back around to face him. "Let me see your phone."

He takes his phone out of his back pocket and holds it out but yanks it away when I reach for it.

"Rich, don't do that," Kira snaps. "Will both of y'all just stop?"

I ignore her and reach for the phone again, incensed. He holds it high out of my reach and glares down at me. "Gotta be quicker than that," he teases.

I snatch for it again, this time accidentally scratching the back of his hand hard enough to break the skin.

He lets out a hiss of pain that sends Kira running back down the dock, yelling at us both to grow up. I take advantage of the distraction and finally grab his phone. He clenches my wrist and yanks hard, trying to get it back.

"Stop!" Kira shouts.

She tries to step in between us, but I push her away. I push her hard. Too hard. Time slows as I watch her eyes widen in alarm as she stumbles backward. There is no railing. Nothing to stop her.

Kira falls into the murky water with a surprisingly quiet splash.

CHAPTER 7

Rich and I stand there for a moment, staring at the place where Kira fell into the lake like the whole thing was a joke. Like she'll pop up, laughing, any second now.

"She—she can't swim," Rich stutters, breaking the silence. "She can't swim!" He dives in after her. I watch, my mind finally catching up to reality. When he resurfaces without her, I take a step back, then launch myself into the water, too. Every second is like an eternity, and I am keenly aware that too much time is passing as we search for her. I cling to one of the posts of the dock trying to catch my breath, when I see Rich swimming toward shore, hauling Kira with him, his letterman jacket like a weight on her slim frame. I kick away from the dock and swim faster than I ever have before. By the time I drag myself out of the water, he is already giving her CPR. CPR that I thank God we were just certified in through health class. Rich screams at her to wake up as he pumps aggressively on her chest. It's not long before he falls back on his heels, crying. Before panic prevents him from taking any further action.

"Move!" I shove him aside and resume compressions. "Call 911!"

"My phone is somewhere in the fucking lake!" He shoves his hands into his hair and stares at Kira, rocking back and forth. "You pushed her," he says softly, processing.

"It was an accident!"

"You pushed her," he says again, more hysterical. "Y-you killed her."

"Shut the hell up, Rich! She wasn't under that long. She isn't dead."

"Yes, she is," he cries. "Look at her! Look at her head."

I don't. I can't. I already caught a glimpse of the dark blood staining the sand beneath her, and I refuse to look again. I put all my focus on her chest, forcing every last molecule of oxygen from the last breath she took to be put to use. Doing all I can to widen the chances of her walking away from this. "Go back to the cabin, Rich. Go get help. Now!"

Rich stands and backs away slowly before breaking into a full sprint toward the trees.

I pump on my best friend's chest, begging her heart to take over for me, bawling all the while. The muscles in my arms ache. I pause for one second to wipe sweat and lake water from my eyes. As I pull my hand from my face, I see a flash of something. I think of the coyote we heard earlier, of the groundskeeper Nate Hightower, of the lights that have been haunting me. A fresh dose of fear courses through me, but I can't let it incapacitate me. I turn my attention back to Kira. The squelch of her cold, drenched clothes every time I press against her nauseates me. The way her body lolls lifelessly like a rag doll despite my best efforts.

"Come on!" I keep pumping until there is another flash. Closer this time. Too close. Startled, I fall backward, the heel of my hands pressing into the cool wet sand. A shiver courses down my spine as a distinctive fragrance filters through the air. Thick and sweet. Like honeysuckle and tobacco. My eyes dart back and forth, searching for a source. They land on a tiny cabin right at the edge of the tree line that I hadn't noticed before. The air around it is hazy—iridescent, almost. The windows glow as if someone has lit several candles inside, and a feminine silhouette passes behind the ratty sheer curtains. I jump to my feet, ready to shout for help, but the shack goes black. It is far more ominous in the dark, rousing something in the primitive part of my brain. Something defensive. Movement in my periphery pulls my gaze to the left. Something is there in the trees. The deep, floral fragrance slowly dissipates as I take in the humanlike form. "Who's there?" I call, stuck between fear and desperation. Somehow I know it's no one from the party. "Help!" I beg, assuming it can only be the woman I just saw in the window. "Please help me. My friend. My friend, she—"

"Is dead." Her voice echoes all around me. "Pity. Pity."

I scramble back, crab walking to put more distance between me and where she stands.

"Help me!" I shout again despite my terror, because this woman—whoever, whatever she is—is all I have. "Please!"

"Oh, darling girl." Her voice is delicate and crystal clear, as if we were face-to-face and not fifteen yards away from each other. "She is beyond saving, at least by . . . traditional means."

"Wha—" I start to ask, but she vanishes. "Hello?" I whip my head all around, searching for her.

"I am here." The voice comes from directly behind me now. Her breath is hot on my ear, and her tone is soft, coddling, like a mother speaking to a frightened child. I don't dare turn to look.

"How did you— What are you?"

Her body makes horrifying sounds as she rises to her feet. Sinew stretching. Bones cracking. Joints popping. She's bigger and taller now. I can feel her mass looming as she slowly walks around me until the skirt of her damp and tattered gray dress blocks my view. My lips tremble and I turn away from her.

She crouches down to my level. "Look at me, won't you, love?"

Her sour breath makes my eyes water. I blink rapidly to clear them of moisture, but I keep my face turned to the forest.

"I cannot help you if you do not *look*." The last word floats from her mouth, accompanied by a dozen soft whispers in different gentle, ghostly voices. *Look at me. Look at me. Look at me.*

My head turns and I know it's against my will, but whatever piece of me that might have been afraid is silenced by the sight in front of me. My brain reads it as a face, but I can't discern any specific features. Only staticky swirls of brown and gray and black. "A-are you a ghost?"

She tilts her head to the side, but the movement is jerky and unnatural. "Debatable, darling. What makes a ghost? I was born here in Fairville, crying and screaming—the way so many of us entered this world, and yet no one remembers their birth, do they? Can the same be said of death? I do not remember experiencing it, but does that mean it did not happen?" Her form pulsates in front of me. "It seems you've already spent a fair amount of time considering the spectrum between living"—she points a long, bony finger at me, then slowly shifts it toward Kira's body—"and dead. Some pass from one end to the other in a fraction of a second. Fast. Linear. Neat. Others play hopscotch. Languish somewhere in the middle. Sometimes indefinitely. I"—she stands upright again—"believe I belong to the latter."

I scramble back to Kira's side. "Please. Can you help her?" I plead. "Help me save her. She fell. She hit her head. She's not a swimmer."

"She fell?" For a moment, her facial features reveal themselves, like she's offered me a peek behind a mask.

I'm surprised by how young she looks—how close to my

own age. "Please. It was an accident. I—I pushed her, but I didn't mean to. Rich, he—"

"Shh." Her bare feet make a sucking sound as she lifts them from the wet sand and walks toward us, the imprints slowly filling with water behind her. Her dress is threadbare at the ends and patches of mold or algae grow on it. It hangs from her frame like a loose second skin. Her actual skin has the texture of crumpled, thin, wet paper. The color reminds me of the deck planks at the cabin. A once-rich brown, sun-bleached to a grayish hue. She reeks of dirty lake water, and her body glitches as if she were a hologram. She stops walking mere inches from Kira's body, then nudges her lightly with her foot, toenails long, curled, and yellowed. "Tsk, tsk. What a shame."

"Please," I beg.

Her body continues to glitch. There one second, gone the next, directly in front of me the second after that. I fall back onto my ass again, repulsed. Wanting help, but also distance. Every inch I scoot away, she draws closer and closer. Closer and closer until her face is only centimeters from mine. Her features come into focus again, but instead of looking into her cloudy pale gray eyes and seeing a girl my age, this time, I see a predator. She inhales deeply, and her eyelids flutter like I'm a plate of her favorite food. For a brief moment, I think she may kill me. Devour me on the spot. But she doesn't. She slides her wrist under her nose, inhaling and wiping away a mucusy substance.

She peers at me through hooded eyes. "I can bring back the girl, but death must be traded evenly—and you must do something for me in return."

"Traded evenly?"

She begins to pace. "A life for a life."

My teeth chatter violently. "Whose life?"

She halts, and her lips curve into a curious grin. "The question of the hour indeed. The answer is up to you." She spins in a few circles, the sodden tatters of her dress splaying out to the sides, spraying fresh lines of water across the sand. She stops short and holds up her index finger. "One rule."

"What's that?"

"The person you choose must be present on these grounds tonight."

I shake my head. This is ridiculous. This can't be real. I force myself to laugh. Like doing so will make my friends pop out from behind the bushes, screaming *Gotcha!* But that doesn't happen. "How can you— Who are you?"

The woman takes a few lazy steps across the sand, like she is bored with the conversation. "They call me Regret."

Cory's blog post spirals to the front of my mind. Everything that brought us here tonight seems like utter fiction, completely made up. I stutter, unsure what to say or do, unable to get any words out.

Regret growls, impatient. "What say you, girl? About my proposition? I haven't got all night and neither does your little friend."

A rush of frustration and anger hits me like a freight train. "Why would I make a deal with someone called Regret?"

"A fair question." She smirks at me and inhales deeply again, running both her hands from her forehead and back across her patchy, matted black hair. "They call me Regret because I feed on it." She crouches down and maneuvers to me on all fours, only standing up again once she is right in front of me. She is even taller now. Towering over me, blocking the light from the moon.

I am frozen in fear.

"They call me Regret because I consume it." Her chest rises

and falls dramatically with each breath. "I feast on it." Each inhale is shuddering, like she is barely in control of herself. Each new sentence a crescendo. "It is my blood. It is my beating heart. It is the air in my lungs." She pauses, eyes focused on the lake, as if recalling a distant memory. "Regret has kept me living far beyond my time. It is a comfort to me. It sustains me. But it does not belong to me." She considers me for a moment. Her voice is softer when she speaks again. "You have enough sitting just on your right shoulder to buy me much more time. And I. Want. Time."

This has to be some kind of nightmare.

"You'll want to make your choice quickly. Before she's been gone more than twenty minutes. Before the boy gets back to the cabin and calls the authorities."

"What happens then?"

"I cannot help you then. But"—her eyes sparkle—"I do have the gift of foresight. I can show you that fate, if you'd like?"

I nod and mumble a yes.

She rushes me, her physical form stuttering in the most terrifying way. She drags me to the edge of the water and submerges my face, her hand at the base of my skull, pressing hard so I can't come up. I kick and fight. Resist until an image starts to form around me. A courtroom. Rich on the stand. Tears streaming down his cheeks.

"And then what happened?" a voice from out of view asks.

"Simone pushed her. She pushed Kira into the water. She knew she couldn't swim. She knew what would happen."

"And can you explain for the jury what you believe to be the motive behind her actions that night?"

Rich swallows hard and drops his head in shame. "Me and Simone had this secret thing. It was forever ago and we'd both agreed it was nothing serious, but I think she was upset when I did want to start something real with Kira. Things were chill for a while but"—his voice cracks—*"summer before senior year, while I was in a relationship with Kira, me and Simone kissed. It was only one time. We just got caught up in a moment. I told Simone it was a mistake, but after that she went in on trying to convince Kira that I was a horrible boyfriend, like I was the only one who did something to betray her trust."* He stifles a sob. "I—I guess she was jealous, man, I don't know."

The image changes several times. A judge. A jury. A guilty verdict. A sentencing.

I'm abruptly yanked from the water, gasping for air. The only visuals swirling through my mind are ones of me and Rich. Me and Rich. After summer football conditioning. Under the bleachers. Standing closer than we ever had since he started dating Kira. Standing closer than two people with a history like ours ever should. Leaning into each other. Kissing each other. But it's not how it seems. I was— He—

"STOP!" I scream, pulling at my soaking-wet braids.

Regret sits on a rock that has appeared out of nowhere, picking at her fingernails. "Oh, I stopped several seconds ago. Whatever you are experiencing now is all you." She rises to her feet. "I must admit I am curious, though." She sniffs the air. "It smells awfully good. Will you tell me?"

"Tell you what?"

She dramatically throws one hand over her stomach and one over her forehead like she may faint. "I'm so hungry. Tell me your biggest regret, will you?" She disappears and reappears beside me, her mouth by my ear. "Tell me so I can taste it."

The images circulate through my mind again. Rich's lips on mine. His hands in my hair. Kira's smiling, unknowing face only half an hour later.

"Tell me!"

"You just showed it to me. You just showed me my biggest regret," I cry.

"No. I showed you your future, and you cannot regret something that has not yet happened."

"You know what I mean. You know what he'll say on the stand."

She rolls her eyes, impatient, annoyed. "That is what you want me to believe is your biggest regret? 'I kissed my best friend's disgusting boyfriend. How will I ever recover?'" She spits. "Mushy. Bland. You bore me." She rolls her neck in an exaggerated way as if to crack it, but there is no sound. "And you are a liar."

"I'm not! I'm not lying to you!"

"Oh, you are. You've just mastered lying to yourself as well. More reason to take my deal. Perhaps some time to reveal your own secrets will do you good."

"Show me the other version."

"What version?"

"You have the gift of foresight. Show me what happens if I take your deal."

"That would be nice, wouldn't it? But I am afraid I cannot see futures in which I am entwined."

"You said there is something I'd have to do for you if you make the trade. Why? Why isn't offering up someone else in Kira's place enough?"

"Oh, dear one, it is a force far greater than me that deals in souls. I am a middleman, but middlemen are owed their due, too. I've been stuck here for seventy years. Cursed. Accept my deal and the person you choose will perish forever while your friend here will be instantly revived." She raises an eyebrow. "But then starts the clock. Ticktock, ticktock. Figure out how to free me by eleven fifty-nine PM on Saturday, October thirtieth, and you will no longer be plagued by the true events of this evening. You will believe the same story as all the others. A tragic accident in which you played no part. I will ensure that all of your deepest regrets never threaten to creep into your consciousness again, even the ones you currently refuse to acknowledge."

"Why the thirtieth? And what if I can't figure out how? What then?"

She points up at the sky. "My magic flows with the lunar cycle. The window on this offer closes with the new moon. There can be no extension. And if you fail—" She sucks the end of each of her fingers and glances down at Kira again. "If you fail, she dies once more. This time, undoubtedly by your hand. A meal that will feed me for many, many years to come. Long enough to find someone else who may be able to set me free."

"But what—"

"Stop with your questions. There is no more time. You must make your decision now."

Taking this offer, choosing someone to *die*, will make me a killer. But the world will view me as one anyway if I decline. It all comes down to whose death I can live with being responsible for. Kira is not an option. I could choose anyone else here tonight. Shaina. Piper. Any of the others who I'm not as close to. But there is only one choice that saves her and *protects* me. I look at Rich's letterman jacket wrapped around Kira's body. I see him in it. Cocky smile. Always flirting. Always taking advantage. I see him holding that stupid phone above my head. *Gotta be quicker than that*. I hear him speak under his breath. *Hypocrite*.

"I choose him."

"You choose who?"

"Rich." He is going to lie. He is going to get on the stand and tell the world that I pushed Kira, that I *killed* her, out of jealousy over him. Whatever fondness I had for him as a friend evaporates, solidifying a choice I wish I didn't have to make. "I choose Rich Pearson. Trade his life for hers." I've already seen what happens if I do nothing. At least this choice gives me time. It gives me a chance to write a different ending.

"So it shall be."

CHAPTER 8

"Simone? Simone, are you okay?"

I blink rapidly a few times, clearing a stickiness from my eyes. Regret is gone. The dark gray sandy bank of the lake is gone. I'm in the middle of the woods.

"Simone, what the hell is wrong with you?"

I look over at the person talking to me. "Kira."

"Yes . . . that's my name." She laughs.

"Kira," I say again.

"What? You're freaking me out, girl. Did you accidentally pick up someone else's cup?" She mimes drinking.

I crash into her. Hug her with all my might. And I'm relieved to find she is strong and solid and breathing. It takes a moment before she returns the gesture.

She laughs against me, more nervously this time. "Love you too?"

I step back and scan her whole body for any sign of what just happened. She's completely dry. Her curls are neat and free of blood. Rich's letterman jacket is gone. She's here. Standing in front of me. Alive. "Are you okay? Do you remember?"

"Remember what? Is this another prank? Because I think I'm

good on the scary stories for tonight. You showed me the freaky giant Barbie doll. Can we get back already? You need to drink some water."

I look over my shoulder, my heart pounding like someone might be following us. "Where's— Have you seen Rich?"

She squints at me, confused. "He's back at the cabin with everyone else."

I want to ask if she is sure, but I shouldn't say anything that might seem strange or look incriminating later. Kira is alive, and I accepted a very specific, very dark deal to make that happen.

So it's the absolute shock of my life when we exit the woods and find Rich Pearson standing by the firepit.

"Baaaabe." He saunters over to us and throws an arm around Kira's shoulders, kissing her forehead.

I search his face and body for any sign that he remembers what just happened, too, but there is nothing. And I know what this boy looks like when he's hiding something. He's supposed to be dead, but he's here. Kira's here. Maybe I imagined it. Maybe none of it happened at all.

Rich's eyes meet mine for a fraction of a second, as they often do—the secrets in our minds briefly and silently acknowledging the presence of their other half. But this time I can hear him say it. *Hypocrite.* It enrages me, and I'm not too thick to understand that it's because it's true. But truth is complex. That's why I don't run my mouth about all the things that go on in my head. Some things can't properly be put into words. Like the deep feeling inside me that although both Rich and I betrayed Kira, he doesn't regret it like I do. He can't be trusted not to mess up again. I can. So there's no reason for her to know what I did. Telling her would take weight off my conscience while hurting her. Telling her would be for *me*. But exposing *him* was about shielding her from future harm. That was my intention. My actions weren't about jealousy. They were about protecting my friend. And somehow it got twisted into something ugly. I rub my temples as a throbbing pain kicks up in my head, along with the prickly anxiety of not being sure I can trust my own mind.

"Simone? What's wrong?" Kira's face is painted with worry.

"She's fine," Rich says. "You know she's a little dramatic." He leans too heavily on Kira, almost causing her to topple over. All I can see is her falling off that dock.

"Be careful!" The entire scene in front of me feels like it's balanced on a tightrope, and any second, I could be plunged back into . . . before.

"See what I mean?" His words are slightly slurred.

"Simone, relax. I'm okay." Kira laughs, pushing the massive hunk of flesh that is her boyfriend from her shoulder.

He downs the rest of whatever is in his Solo cup, then shouts at Cameron, who is climbing the steps to the deck. "Bring the whole punch bowl down, bro!"

Cameron raises his arms in a touchdown sign, then jogs the rest of the way up the stairs and into the house.

"Don't you think you've had enough?" I'm not trying to antagonize him. I just don't want a bunch of drunk football players tearing up the place. In fact, I'd like nothing more than to end the party right now. Stop while I'm on a peak of this wildly oscillating night. Go home and sleep for twelve hours because, clearly, obviously, my mind needs a reset.

"Oh," he says with a chuckle. "No, totally. I'm done for the night. I asked Cam to bring that down for you. Might loosen the stick up your—"

Kira presses her index finger to his lips. "Don't you dare. It's her birthday."

He gently pushes her arm away and tilts his head to the side. "I mean, that's technically tomorrow, right?"

I check the time. Eleven fifty-five. It was after three in the morning when we went into the woods. I open my text messages, searching for the one I sent to John and Layla telling them we were going to bed. It's not there. It's gone. Does that mean the texts between Rich and Shaina are gone too? Did they ever exist in the first place? I start walking back to the cabin, and Kira hurries to catch up with me. "Were Layla and John here earlier? Was Cory?" I ask when she reaches my side.

She plants her feet and grips my shoulder, turning me to face her. "Simone, John and Lay left right before we went to go look for the Barbie. You spoke to both of them yourself. Cory delivered the pizzas and stayed for like an hour. Did something happen? Are you all right?"

"I'm fine. Just a"—I gesture vaguely at my head—"migraine coming on or something. I think I need to lie down awhile."

"I'll come with you."

"No. Please. Go have fun." I force a smile. "Social battery on E. Twenty-minute recharge and I'll be back out."

"Okay," she says hesitantly, her golden eyes searching my face for signs of dishonesty, which she is absolutely terrible at spotting. "Text me if you need something."

All I can offer is a nod before turning on my heel and going inside.

My fears of us destroying the cabin were not unfounded. It's already a wreck. No signs of any serious damage, but plates, cups, trash, and games are scattered everywhere. I pick up a few pieces of garbage before I realize what I'm doing. My mother did it all the time. Clean to distract. Clean to avoid. Clean to disguise. No one would suspect the filthy state of your mind if the space around you is pristine. I drop the stuff in my hands and go to the bathroom. It takes me several seconds to look at my reflection and face everything I've been fighting back since we exited the woods. I burst into tears. Tears of relief. Concern. Disbelief . . . Confusion is what lingers after several minutes. What I experienced couldn't have been a dream. I might do more than most to earn a jump scare, but no way I'd take a nap in the woods in the middle of the night. It's also unlikely that what I experienced was real. I can wrap my head around ghosts, but people don't come back from the dead. And if you make a special deal with a ghost witch for an exception, no doubt the conditions of payment will be met. And they weren't. Kira *and* Rich are alive.

My memory and perception of time are so off that I wonder if I was talked into . . . taking something. Or even given something without my consent. I don't *feel* under the influence of anything. Not even alcohol. And what drug could cause a hallucination like that, I don't know. I splash water on my face and exit the bathroom, heading straight for the kitchen. Jeremiah might have thought it'd be fun to slip a little something extra into the communal food or drink. No one else seems to be experiencing anything like I did, but everyone's body reacts differently to that stuff. And I prefer the idea that this was some innocent attempt at increasing the fun rather than a targeted attack on me.

The punch bowl is gone, but cups with remnants of the sickly-sweet liquid litter the counter. I pick one up, sniff it, and gag, but only from the strong scent of sugar and liquor. An ugly batch of brownies sits in a disposable aluminum tin. I smell them too, but all I get is cocoa. Realizing I'd be unlikely to smell any drug slipped into a food item, I switch gears and eye the purses and duffel bags stashed in various nooks and corners. Rich's sits behind the recliner. I walk over and kneel in front of it. I grip the zipper and hold my breath, expecting it to smell like Fritos and sweat, but it doesn't. It smells good. It smells clean. And I bite my lip in shame because it also smells . . . familiar. More familiar than it should. I'm opening the zipper of the inside pocket when a strike of lightning and a crash of thunder end my alone time. Everyone comes running inside, laughing and damp with rain.

I grab a stack of towels and toss them to random people. I should be angry. It's possible that someone in this room drugged me. Regardless of their intentions, that's twisted. But maybe I just don't have the energy to scrounge up enough anger to override my sense of utter relief. Kira's across the room, excitedly trying to pick a scary movie with Noor. Her light brown cheeks are flushed, and her smile is gleaming, and it came at no cost. I may have hallucinated or imagined the whole thing, but I can't deny the grateful feeling deep in my chest.

It's only when they select *Scream* to watch that something else sprouts inside me. A tinge of doubt, a hint of fear that time won't move forward. That I'll be stuck in a loop of alternate endings for this night. But if I had some kind of premonition, at least I know what *not* to do. At least I know to leave well enough alone. To let Rich do what he does and let Kira figure things out for herself.

I wait until the room is dark to sneak away upstairs. I crawl into the bed, and my eyelids grow heavy. The banter among my friends, the slasher-movie music, and the thunderstorm outside lull me to sleep. I sink into my pillow, growing more comfortable with the idea that everything really might be okay.

But in the morning . . .

I wake to screams.

CHAPTER 9

I register the commotion downstairs before Kira. It's Piper. Outside. Screaming for help. Crying for it. Screeching. The sound triggers me. The room grows scorchingly hot, and my mouth goes as dry as sandpaper. My heart hammers, and my eyes flood with tears. Everything from last night hurtles back to me and turns my insides sour. I whip my head toward Kira, half expecting her to be cold and lifeless, but she's rubbing her eyes, confused. Trying to shake away sleep. Trying to process what's woken her.

"I told you your stories would give somebody nightmares. What time is it?" she asks groggily before gasping. "Oh my God! Happy birthday, bestie!"

She leaps from the bed, arms spread for a hug, but slows down when she catches my expression. I stare toward the window as new voices join Piper's.

"Rich! Rich, bro, wake up!" Jere shouts.

At the mention of his name, I turn back to Kira. Her face has blanched, and I watch her lips slightly part as she gathers that this is no bad dream, that this has nothing to do with scary stories.

Another frantic shout of Rich's name. A "Call 911!"

"Rich," Kira says, barely a whisper. She peers out the window, then quickly stumbles backward.

"Kira." I reach for her, but she dodges me and runs down the stairs.

I chase after her and we both join everyone else in the yard.

Rich's body is sprawled across the brown grass. Piper and Jere kneel beside him.

"He's dead," Kingston murmurs. "He's dead." He looks around at the rest of us for confirmation as Kira rushes to Rich's side.

"Be careful!" Noor shouts. "I think he got electrocuted." The long cord that belongs to the generator is still clutched in Rich's burned right hand. Long purple streaks extend across his skin, and a charred extension cord lies next to the side of his head. His dark hair is wet and plastered against his forehead. His eyes are open, and the usual deep chocolate brown of his irises has taken on a grayish and cloudy hue. A hue almost identical to Regret's.

Kira sways like she may faint, and Piper jumps to her feet to support her. Neither of them have shoes on.

I move my own toes, pressing them into the earth beneath my soles to steady myself as thoughts race through my mind too quickly to process.

John comes running down the hill from around the front of the house. Layla freezes a few yards behind him.

"What happened?" John demands. "What the hell happened? Move!"

He pushes Diego and Jere aside and checks Rich's neck for a pulse. "Did the power go out last night? In the storm?"

Everyone glances around, unsure.

"Shit." He throws his baseball cap on the ground and shoves his fingers into his hair, pacing. "Has someone already called 911?"

"I did," Cameron says.

Layla yanks her sobbing sister from Piper's arms and pulls her to her own chest. I look on in complete shock. Mouth hanging open like I don't know exactly what has happened here. But I do. Don't I? I take another hesitant glance at Rich's body. At the burns on his arm. Was this Regret, or was this truly an accident? A horrible coincidence that lined up with a horrible hallucination? I pray it's the latter because I don't want last night at the lake to be real. I don't want to think about what it means now if that was real.

Jeremiah collapses to his knees next to me, crying into his shirt. I look around at the others, suddenly concerned that my own reaction isn't normal. That I'm only seconds away from someone questioning me. From someone reading my mind and seeing all the horrible things circulating through it. I crouch down next to Jere and wrap my arms around him. He melts into me, sobbing. I rub his back and let my own tears fall, only my tears are not just for Rich Pearson. They're not even mostly for him. And I know in some way this reveals something dark about my character, because what did he do to deserve *this*? But then, that's the thing. It's not about what he did. It's about what he would have done. It's about who could have—would have—been lost in his place. I look at Kira, still held by her sister, and her pain physically hurts me. But it's nothing like seeing her the way I saw, dreamed, thought. . . . It's nothing like that. And it's nothing like the day I learned Trenton was gone. Or the day I realized my mom was never coming home. This is a tragedy, no doubt. But it is surmountable. We can all recover from this.

THE police arrive and secure the scene. My stomach twists as they remove the decorative caution tape from the front of the cabin and set up the real stuff around the area where Rich's body has been covered with a sheet. We are escorted inside to collect our essentials. I go upstairs and stuff my things into my bag. My top from yesterday gets caught up in the zipper when I try to close it, and I curse under my breath. I yank on it more aggressively than necessary, then freeze when I get the sense I'm being watched. I look over my shoulder, but no one is there. When I turn back around, I lock eyes with the doll Kingston pulled from the woods last night. It lies on its side on the nightstand, face forever frozen in a mask of a smile. Someone must have snuck it up here in the night to scare me and Kira. I'm surprised by a strong desire to take the doll home with me. I reach for it, but hesitate, feeling the muscles of my face contort into a frown. The doll is disgusting. I know that. I can see that. But I want it. I'm perfectly conscious that wanting the filthy thing is strange, but the feeling doesn't go away. It only intensifies. Someone calls for me to hurry up. I grab the doll by the arm and place it on top of my overflowing bag. Something to cling to, I guess. Something I can't hurt. Something from before everything got all twisty in my head.

We are all instructed to go back outside. On the way out of the cabin I grab my birthday basket from the kitchen and notice the time is wrong on the microwave. It spawns a warm feeling in my chest. A sign that the power *did* go out last night. I want to lean into the feeling. I want it to be proof that this had nothing to do with any dark deals. It wouldn't make sense for Regret to trade Rich's life for Kira's and make it look like foul play. I wouldn't be able to keep my end of the deal if I'm a murder suspect. She said herself that it would look like an accident to everyone else. But does that prevent it from *actually* being an accident? The answer is no. I need the answer to be no.

An officer questions John and Layla over by the firepit. We are directed to wait for our parents several yards away with a couple of other officers. Kira doesn't take her eyes off her sister for the entire time she is questioned. This is the only thing that has paused her tears in the last thirty minutes. She chews her bottom lip, face still wet and puffy as she watches. She's worried Layla will be in trouble. She and John were supposed to be the chaperones. They are the adults, and Rich died under their supposed watch. I want to comfort her. Tell her everything will be okay, but I don't know that. I can't know that.

It's impossible to hear anything being said from here, but John points at a security camera affixed to the cabin before taking out his phone and showing the cops something on it.

"Do you think the cameras caught what happened?" Noor asks.

Shaina huffs. "Do you know what generators are for?"

"Of course I do, but—"

"But nothing, then. The power was out, so the cameras were off."

"Not necessarily. Some are battery powered. Some use cellular for an internet connection."

"Nobody needs an IT lesson right now, Noor, but if you must go there, my parents have the exact same cameras. They don't work when the power is out."

"But the Yearwoods have money. Why would they get cameras that—"

"Can you please be quiet," Shaina snaps.

Cameron places a gentle hand on Noor's upper back and steps toward Shaina. "You need to chill."

"I need to chill?" Her voice trembles. "Rich is *dead*. He is dead, and we aren't going to get any answers from the stupid security cameras."

"What answers are you looking for, Shaina?" Jere turns his head so his ear is angled her way. "Huh? What exactly do you want to know? You saw his body the same as the rest of us. He had the damn cord in his hand."

"I want to know why he would give a crap about restoring the power at a cabin he's never been to before in the middle of the night when everyone was asleep. Does that make any sense to you?"

No one answers her.

"That's what I thought. Did anyone notice anything? Did he say anything to any of you? Did anyone hear him go outside?"

More silence.

"Kira?" she prods.

"Don't," I say.

"Don't what? She's his girlfriend. She should know him better than anyone. So why would he choose to do something like that? Hmm?"

I bite my tongue, wanting so desperately to ask how her and Rich's plans to meet up went. But I can't be sure those plans even existed after everything reset itself, and I won't risk being wrong in front of everyone. I won't do that to Kira.

"That's not fair," Piper says from where she sits on the ground, hugging her knees.

Shaina shrugs. "Y'all don't have to tell me, but you know the police are going to ask. That's why we are all still here. So you should probably start thinking about how you're going to answer."

"Well, what's your answer?" Kingston asks. "Since you want to interrogate people so bad."

Shaina opens her mouth, looking more ready to argue than contribute anything useful, but a car speeding up the drive silences her.

It's Kira's parents. Her mom is out of the passenger side before her dad can even get the car in park. Kira runs to them. They throw their arms around her shoulders and usher her into their BMW, where she disappears behind the tinted windows. They don't leave. The police really do need to speak with everyone before we can. But her being out of sight makes me feel so alone. It makes my anxiety ramp up, and I keep imagining some cruel magic trick where the car doors open again, and Kira is not there. That somehow the car is a portal. A portal that transports her under that sheet. That brings me back to that . . . horrible dream.

Piper's moms arrive next. She goes to them, tearfully trying to explain everything that's happened, but they silence her with a tight embrace.

Another police car pulls up a few minutes later, and Rich's parents emerge from it. The previously quiet crying and sniffling around me kicks up several notches. His parents' eyes are as wide as saucers. Mrs. Pearson looks like she was woken from bed. She wears pale pink pajama pants, a dressy cardigan, and what looks like Mr. Pearson's or Rich's sneakers. She stops walking several times on the way over to the body. Arms and legs twitching like she might sprint the other direction at any moment. A few officers attempt to block our view by standing between us and them, but I don't miss it when Mrs. Pearson collapses onto the white sheet, clutching her son and sobbing. John and Layla pass by, heading for her parents' car, sniping at each other through tears. I'm so busy tracking them, trying to get a read on what's to come, that I don't notice Dad's arrival until he is only feet away from me.

"I'm so sorry, Simma baby. I'm so sorry."

He reaches for me, and I let him pull me into his chest.

"Hush, baby," he says, even though I am not crying.

"I'm sorry to interrupt, Tony, but the sooner we talk with Simone, the sooner you can get her home," says Officer Long, one of Dad's oldest friends.

Dad squeezes my shoulder as he walks with me in the direction

Officer Long is motioning. We each take a seat on some foldout chairs nestled in a secluded corner of the porch.

Officer Long lets out a heavy sigh. "First and foremost, Simone, I am so very sorry for your loss."

My eyes dart toward the Davises' car, and I wish I could see Kira's face. Ensure that this terrible script hasn't been flipped to something horrific.

"Rich was a wonderful kid and a friend to so many." He swipes at the moisture that has collected in the corner of his left eye. "The whole town is gonna mourn his passing."

"Are we in trouble?" I know it's probably not the right thing to ask first, but I can't help it. I need to know. "Are John and Layla in trouble? Because it wasn't their fault. We—"

Officer Long holds up his hand and glances at Dad. "I'll be straight with you both. This looks like a freak accident. A terrible, terrible thing, but an accident nonetheless. Obviously, you kids were drinking, and you know better. Each of you is going to be putting in some community service for those mistakes. I'll see to that myself."

He eyes me sternly, but I don't tell him I didn't participate in the drinking. He may have my crimes wrong, but the scolding feels earned.

"As for the young Yearwoods"—he presses his lips together—"they should have known better than to leave y'all unsupervised all night."

"They didn't! They were right up the road at the CPRC. They checked on us. They have security cameras. They answered all my texts right away when I needed something. It's not like we're middle schoolers. It's my birthday. I'm eighteen. Five of us are already eighteen." The words tumble from my mouth, and they are all in an effort to spare Kira any additional stress and heartache.

"If the Pearsons choose to give them grace, then they may get off with community service, too, plus a stiff fine, and we all know that'll be no issue for them."

"And if they don't? Show grace, I mean . . ."

Officer Long glances at Dad again. "The Pearsons are good folk and longtime, close friends of the Davis family. If the autopsy report confirms what we already believe, then I'd set my bets that this is something that can be overcome."

I relax some, relieved that he arrived at the same conclusion I did. We can all get through this. "How long will it take? The autopsy report?" I regret asking right away. It's something someone concerned about his manner of death would ask. And I *am* concerned, but I certainly don't need Officer Long to know that.

"As I said, the Pearsons are well connected, and they've got deep pockets. What might take a few weeks for the average person will likely be cut down to a few days for him. I expect you all will have the closure you need before the week's end." He leans forward. "Now you listen to me good here, so nothing like this ever happens again. Don't you ever, *ever*, use an extension cord like this." He holds up his phone where several pictures of cords with prongs on both ends are displayed on Google Images. "They call these widow-maker cords and for good reason. Backfeed of that power is nothing to play around with. Wiring was bad on that generator, but it's dangerous even for one in great working order."

"Yes, sir."

He pauses for a few seconds to emphasize his point, then gets out a notepad.

"Do you know round about what time you saw Rich last?"

In my mind, I see Rich's soaking wet shirt clinging to his back as he runs for help. In that timeline, it was probably 3:30 in the morning. But in the version of events that led me to this moment, the *real* version: "I had a headache and went to bed before everyone else. It was around midnight, I think."

I talk with Officer Long for another couple of minutes, easily answering his generic questions. It's clear he's just going through the motions. That he has already made up his mind about what happened here. And that's for the best.

"Ready to go?" Dad asks, rubbing my shoulder once Officer Long dismisses us.

I nod.

He takes my things and carries them to the back seat of his SUV. I climb into the passenger seat without another word and without a second look at my friends still gathered in the side yard waiting to be questioned. I do text Kira, though. I tell her I'm sorry that this happened, and I ask her to please call me when she gets home. She probably won't. She just lost who she believed to be the love of her life, and despite my issues with him, I need her to know that I care. That I know how much she is hurting and that I'm here.

We reach the main road, and Dad stops the car, waiting for traffic to clear so he can make a left turn. Overgrown bushes make the visibility bad. Dad inches the car forward for a better line of sight, only to slam hard on the brakes as a pickup truck speeds by. My bag topples over in the back seat. We both startle at a sudden mechanical whirring.

Dad and I look back, and the doll I'd shoved in my bag is on its side, moving its head left to right and arms up and down.

"Hi! I'm Gabby Greta, and I love you!" comes a childlike robotic voice over the clicking internal gears. There's a bizarre emphasis on the word *love*.

"What the hell is that?" Dad asks.

"It's just a doll," I say.

Gabby Greta's head turns a few more times. *Click. Click. Click.*

"I'm Gabby Greta! Can you count to . . . fourteen? One, two, three—"

Dad gives the doll a few stern shakes, silencing it. The action is almost . . . comical—almost enough to dissipate all the fear the talking doll had caused.

Until another voice filters through the air.

One only I can hear.

Fourteen days.

CHAPTER 10

The voice replays in my head over and over. There are only two possible sources of it. Regret. Or myself. My own mind cracking under the weight of this massive trauma. The weight of *another* massive trauma.

"Dad, can you put some music on?" I can hear the sharpness in my tone. "Please," I add more gently. I cannot sit here in silence with my thoughts.

"You sure you don't want to talk? I can't even imagine—and on your birthday. I—"

"Right now I think I just need some noise, Dad. Music. Podcast. Something."

He looks at me out of the corner of his eye and hesitantly turns the volume knob from whatever near-silent status it was on when he drove up here. I press my temple against the window and watch the blur of the trees as we head for home. When we pull into the driveway, I grab my things and enter the house as quickly as possible.

"Simone," Dad calls before I can make it up the stairs.

I pause mid-stride and wait for him to continue.

"Talk to me. What can I do?"

I squint at him apologetically. "Let me sleep? I'm not ready to think or talk right now."

"Okay, but you need to come down and eat at some point."

I nod and continue walking up the stairs, Serling trotting at my heels. A lump forms in my throat when I see a small pile of birthday presents outside my bedroom door. Mom used to do that. Put all the gifts there so when I wake up and leave my room, it's the first thing I see. Dad didn't miss a beat keeping up with it the year Mom left. And the fact that he did it this year when I wasn't even home to wake up to it tugs at my heart. I want to call down to him and tell him thank you and hug him. But today isn't a day for celebrations. I drag the presents into my room, then I write *thank you* and draw a heart on a sticky note and press it to his bedroom door.

Serling tries to follow me into my room on my way back, but I close him out. He gives a pitiful whine and his shiny black paw darts under the door as I lean against it and look around my room. It feels foreign. My homecoming dress, emerald green and sparkly, rests on a hanger hooked over my open closet door. The strappy four-inch heels Kira convinced me to buy are still in their box on the floor. My AP bio textbook is still splayed open on my desk from the quiz I crammed for Friday morning. The person I was when I left this room just over twenty-four hours ago feels so far removed from the person I am in this moment. That person was not a happy girl, not by a long shot. But she could pretend. She could pick out outfits for dances, plan for parties, review for tests. All those things seem so ridiculous now. I cannot connect the person who cared about those things with the one I am now.

Last night I thought I had some kind of mystical encounter. Then I thought I'd been drugged. But now? Now, after hearing that voice, I feel uncomfortable in my own body. Unsure of my own brain. I do believe in ghosts and hauntings and witches and magic, but isn't the most logical explanation usually the right one? And in this case, there *is* a logical explanation. I've been through a lot. I'd been seeing things before the party even started. Add in some scary stories, sleep deprivation, and an ugly mess of secrets in the back of my mind. Is it any wonder I finally reached my breaking point?

I pull all my dirty clothes from my bag, dump them into the hamper, and place the Gabby Greta doll on a stack of plastic storage bins filled with arts and crafts in the corner of my room. I sit on the edge of the bed, studying her. She stares through me with that half-closed eye, a chunk of eyelashes missing from the center. My own eyes drift to the photo on my bulletin board behind her head. Me, Jere, Rich, and Kira sit on a blanket in the quad at school. Rich is the only one who is actually looking at the camera. I wait, expecting to feel something. I sit there for five minutes, ten minutes. Half an hour. I still feel relief for Kira, but I should be sad, too, right? Maybe not devastated, but someone I know, someone I spent so many hours with outside of school, someone I kissed, someone I touched, someone I shared one of my darkest secrets with, is dead. So shouldn't I feel guilt or grief or rage, even? Something besides this hollow nothingness?

I look down at my feet and let my thoughts openly drift to Cory. No resistance, for once. Because I wish he were here. The boy who can read me with a single glance. I want him to decode the things I can't see for myself. The things I don't understand. I want to talk through the entire situation with him because he is the only person in the world who would hear me out right now. And he wouldn't stop at hearing me out. Cory Gooding would believe me. I know that. He would help me. But there isn't anything I need help with because all of that with Regret . . . it didn't happen. It wasn't real. I lie down and repeat this to myself until I doze off.

Dad shakes me awake after what feels like only minutes later, so I'm shocked to find it's eleven PM. He gently pushes my braids away from my face as I sit up.

"I brought you a sandwich." He places a BLT and a glass of water on my end table. There's also a warm, freshly baked cookie on the plate. The kind he always bakes on my birthday because I don't like cake.

"We don't have to talk tonight if you're not ready," he says. "I'm sorry if I was pushy earlier. I'm just worried about you." His eyes scan my face, and I know what he's not saying. I know he is more worried about me than Piper's parents or Cameron's parents are about them, because while it's a tragedy to lose one friend in high school, two losses are unthinkable. Two should be unbearable.

"Kira's the one you should be worried about, Dad. She's the one I'm worried about. She loved Rich, and her sister could be in trouble." My breathing quickens as the reality of the situation smacks me in the face yet again.

He places his heavy, calloused hand on my shoulder. "Kira is going to be okay. She's got you. But, like you, she may or may not want to talk about everything right away, so give her time. As for Layla and John, like Officer Long said, I doubt the Pearsons will play the blame game. Neither will any of the other parents. The most horrible consequence has already been suffered. It's in everyone's best interest to forgive any perceived or real slights and move forward."

I make a face at that because he has used that same line to try to get me to reach out to Mom.

"I didn't mean it like that. I'm not dropping any hints about your mother. I wouldn't do that. Not on a day like today," Dad says. "What I meant was the Pearsons should forgive Layla and John for not chaperoning properly, or they'll find themselves stuck with some heartache that won't ever fade. At the end of the day, forgiveness is for you, not the other person. *But* if that makes you think about your relationship with your mother, then maybe it's something worth reflecting on." He pats my blanketed leg and stands. "Eat that sandwich," he says before leaving me alone again.

I look up at the ceiling, frustrated because he doesn't know what he's talking about. I want Mom to forgive *me*. I want the relief that'd come with that because I have been angry with myself for so long now. Angry because I made sure her career fell apart right before her family did. I made it so she had nothing worth staying here for. Of course it was yet another instance of me thinking I was doing something to help and it backfiring horribly. And of course I want to explain myself. But I won't push her to come back to somewhere she obviously doesn't want to be.

More than eager to break out of that chain of thought, I unlock my phone and find 118 texts waiting for me. Most of them are from various group chats. None are from Kira.

Me
Hey Kir. Checking on you. Love you.

I close out of my messages without expecting a response and open Instagram. My feed is cluttered with stories and pictures from homecoming. I'm surprised it wasn't canceled. Looks like only underclassmen ended up going and every single one of them has Rich's jersey number painted on their cheek or pinned to their clothes. The captain of the junior varsity football team posted a picture of the other players holding him up in the air in the middle of the dance floor. His fist is raised to the ceiling, and he's caught mid-shout as everyone else cheers. The caption reads **Rich bro, you were always the life of the party, and I can't**

think of a better way to celebrate your life than going hard tonight. Much love brother.

I roll my eyes at the irony. Life of the party? Rich literally *died* at a party.

I continue swiping and am surprised to find that even Jeremiah has already made a tribute post. I would think posting on social media less than a day after his best friend's death would be the last thing on his mind. If I'd lost Kira, there is no way, absolutely no way in hell, I'd be able to do anything. Simply keeping my heart beating, simply filling my lungs with oxygen, would be a feat, and after whatever happened last night, I know that for a fact. It was the same way with Trenton. But people grieve differently. I'm sure someone out there is wondering why I haven't posted. They might see it as a sign that I don't care enough. And I guess, in a way, they'd be right. So I choose to flip that idea on its head and do what most of my friends have done. I open my photos app and begin scrolling through my camera roll for a picture to share. One long swipe of my thumb and images blur down the screen. My stomach knots up when the photos stop. Hidden between dozens of pictures of the local stray cat and photos from a summer beach trip is an unfamiliar video. The still is the underside of the bleachers at our school's football stadium. My thumb trembles as I go to open it because this can only be one thing. I've only been there one time. And I sure as heck didn't record anything. So what the hell is this . . . ?

I take a steadying breath and play the video.

The camera moves erratically for a few seconds, but it's clear there are two people in the frame. Whoever is holding the phone is hiding behind some weeds and a metal support column. They zoom in, and immediately, I am so sick, so uncomfortable that the only thing I want in the world is to make what I'm seeing disappear. I cover the screen with my hands. Try to control the nausea that has overcome me. Someone was there that day. When Rich and I . . . Someone saw us. But how did this get on my phone? How did I not see it until now? AirDrop? Or could someone have slipped my phone from my bag without me noticing? With sweaty, shaky hands and without watching the rest, I delete the video, expecting my shame to go with it. It doesn't, so I go straight to my deleted album, ready to erase it permanently. But before I do, I swipe up to try to check all the details. The exact date and time it was recorded. The model of the phone that recorded it. It won't let me do it from the deleted album, so I recover the video and tap back to my camera roll. But when I scroll for it, I can't find it. It's gone. I know I hit recover and not delete. I think I did . . . or maybe—I throw my phone down and rub my hands over my face. I need to get some air.

I go downstairs and sneak past Dad snoring on the couch. A commercial for Mama Dee's Conjure Shop plays on the TV. The one-hundred-year-old woman dances in a white dress as she sings the jingle about her psychic readings that everyone in town can recite. *Come to Mama Dee's to get what you need. Come to Mama Dee's, set ya mind at ease!*

I slip out the front door. It feels good outside. A little chilly, but the crisp air forces some energy into me. I take a well-worn shortcut through the trees to the small playground behind my neighborhood. Someone is on the swings. I know it's Cory, even though he is cast in shadow. What I don't know for sure is if somewhere inside me, I knew he'd be here before I even left my house. If so, I've had a change of heart. Because all I want to do is turn around. I take one step backward.

"It's your birthday," he says.

My chest heaves, and even though I tell my feet to move, they don't. "Yeah."

"Stating the fact felt more appropriate than wishing you a

happy one. I heard what happened." He studies me and there is something about the way he looks at me. Something so undeservingly gentle. "Proceed or left turn?" he asks.

Proceed or left turn. Cory and I share some social anxieties, only I mask mine better. Or only I cared to bother with masks. Or maybe only I ever felt pressured to. It doesn't matter though. I could be me around him, and he could be him. And when he wasn't sure which way to take a conversation, when the cues were difficult to pick up on, he'd ask, *Proceed or left turn?*

"Left turn," I say, but I keep my feet planted firmly where they are.

He nudges the swing next to him. "Come sit with me."

I drift to him slowly. It's like I have no control over my legs because everything in my head says to go back home. Because this boy can read me so easily—or rather, he finds ways to get me to read myself. Out loud. And I do not wish to be read. I thought I did earlier, but now that I'm face-to-face with the possibility, I only want to run. But instead, I sit on the swing next to him. It's silent for a few minutes, aside from the quiet squeak of rusty metal.

"Do you remember when we went to that vintage horror exhibit at the museum?" he asks.

I watch our shadows sway in the dim light of the lamppost. "I remember."

"That was a good day, wasn't it?"

"Cory—"

"Wasn't it?"

"Cory, it's been so—"

He drags his heels in the mulch to stop his swing and sighs. "Simone, please. Just answer the question."

I let a few seconds pass before I decide that I don't have the energy to argue with him or the will to get up and leave. "Of course it was a good day. I found Serling in that Zaxby's parking lot after."

"That's not how I remember it."

"What?"

"You didn't find him. That mangy kitten snatched your chicken finger and ran. You caught him, and he wouldn't let go, so you took him and the chicken fingers home."

I snort out an actual laugh.

"You've had a lot of hard days," he says matter-of-factly. "And you probably have a lot of hard days to come. So I was thinking, for just a few minutes, while it's just me and you here with no obligations outside of this very moment, we could pretend that today was the exhibit day. We can pretend it's Serling's gotcha day."

Cory and I reminisce. Every time he sees the happy nostalgia in my expression slip, he dives deep and comes up with some memory I've kept long buried that sends us both into laughter and wry banter.

"It's late," he says after we catch our breath. "Let me walk you home."

I open my mouth to speak, but he cuts me off.

"It's late. It's not safe."

"My house is right around the corner."

"Yeah, and we were just talking about Natalie Dawson at Ozzy's the other day. She was staying with her grandmother the night she disappeared, and guess where Grandma Dawson lives?"

I don't meet his eyes because I know the answer, and it means I have no argument here. "Right around the corner."

"It's settled then. I'll walk you home." He slowly rocks his swing to a stop. "And one more thing. Just to clear the air. I hope you know I didn't intentionally crash your party. If I'd seen Rich's name on the order I wouldn't—"

"I don't want to talk about Rich."

"I know and I'm not. I'm trying to talk about me and you, and how you clam up so hard every time you see me and how it doesn't have to be that way. I'm not going to demand you open up or talk about uncomfortable things—I hate that stuff too," he says with a laugh. "I'm not even going to ask you to be friends again. But we can cross paths now and then without the earth rocking off its axis."

I take an exaggerated inhale and release it slowly because, no, we can't. Then I get off the swing and don't protest when he follows after me.

CHAPTER 11

I wake up Sunday from the kind of sleep that's so deep you feel disconnected from your own existence. It takes several seconds before I remember where I am, what day it is, and the terrors that occurred this weekend. Terrors that even thrill seekers like me want nothing to do with. I grab my phone from the nightstand, unsurprised to find it's nearly two PM. I check for messages from Kira. She hasn't written me anything, but she at least heart-reacted to the last text I sent checking in on her. I open Instagram, and my feed is flooded with even more tributes to Rich. I scroll, just trying to see posts from one of the dozen cat or dog accounts I follow. Something familiar catches my eye as I swipe through. Weeds. The underside of bleachers. Rich's size-thirteen cleats. My old Birkenstocks. I sit up so quickly my head gets light, and the room spins. When I'm able to focus on my phone again, the image is different. Weeds, yes. Bleachers, yes. But it's not me and Rich in the picture. It's a group of freshmen. I go to the account just to make sure, but I don't see any sign of what I thought I saw. What is this? Some Edgar Allan Poe "Tell-Tale Heart" mess? My own guilty conscience playing tricks on me? Or something more sinister? I put my phone on my nightstand

and take a deep breath. This is what happens when you suppress a memory for so long. When you've kept it under lock and key only for some outside force to crack it open. And I'm afraid now that the seal has been cracked, it won't stop leaking. I'm afraid even deeper buried ugly things will find their way out, too. So I lie back down and stop resisting. I confront it head-on.

July 29 of this year. About three months ago. The second anniversary of Trenton's death. I'd spent the first anniversary alone in my room and absolutely miserable, daydreaming about time travel. Wishing I could go back and change any one small detail about that day. Praying to see the butterfly effect in action. To see that day end with Trenton smiling and laughing instead of bloodied and broken. I was determined not to go through that torment again this year. So I slipped on a sundress and swiped on a bit of mascara to feel more alive. Then I grabbed my camera and headed to the school to get pictures of football summer conditioning for the yearbook. I stood on the track, leaning against the chain-link fence surrounding the field, snapping pictures. It was a win for the first hour. The heat and the gritty action on the field fully consumed me.

Eventually, Coach Brown blew the whistle to end practice. While the team huddled around the coolers, chugging Gatorade and pouring paper cups of water over their heads, I reviewed the photos. There was a good one of Rich and Jere smiling and waving when they first spotted me. I clicked through, examining each one as the boys slowly disappeared into the locker room or out to the student parking lot. My breath caught when I got to a picture of someone with Jones on the back of their conditioning T-shirt. On any other day, it would have been a perfectly ordinary, ridiculously common last name. It'd be something that blurred into the background. But that day. Seeing *that* Jones, the Jones who got to try out for varsity football. Who made the team along with his best friends. Who gets to fantasize about a senior-year deep playoff run. Seeing *that* Jones with big dreams and endless possibilities ahead while *my* Jones was six feet underground made me want to escape my own body. To hide from the world. I crossed the rubber track and kept walking until I saw the shade offered by the bleachers. The seclusion. I dipped under them to catch my breath. To let the horrible feelings pass. I closed my eyes. Counted to twenty.

When I opened them again, Rich Pearson was standing in front of me. I almost leaped out of my skin and promptly laid into him for scaring me. He apologized and laughed. And I remember my eyes being drawn to the crookedness of his grin. His white teeth. I remember his smile fading as he really took in my features. *Are you okay?* He asked me that. He asked me, and I was honest. I told him I wasn't okay at all. I figured he would assume it was about my mom, and that was fine. It still felt good to know that someone knew I was hurting. Someone other than Cory.

Rich took a step closer to me. Close enough that I could smell the fresh sweat, dirt, and grass on his skin. Close enough that I could feel the heat of his body on top of the already sweltering summer air. I enjoyed the way his presence, his closeness eclipsed everything else. I enjoyed the familiarity of it. He put his finger under my chin. Lifted up just slightly so I'd look at him. I remember thinking his eyes were pretty. So brown. So warm. Trenton's eyes were like that. And it was that thought, the thought of a friend, that brought me back to my senses. I opened my mouth to say her name. *Kira*. But Rich's lips silenced me. I knew it was wrong, but it was also less painful than the other things on my mind.

So I kissed him back.

It was only the sound of Jere shouting for him that broke us apart. Rich stepped away from me and looked in the direction of the parking lot. "Shit. Please don't say anything to Kira. We're already fighting. I gotta go." Then he ran off to meet Jere. And I was left there. Alone.

Rich wasn't lying. He and Kira *had* been fighting. They even briefly broke up a few days later. But *that* day, they'd been together. And I did what I did anyway. I'm sure that makes me irrevocably flawed. I wish goodness fit as comfortably in my body as it does in Kira's—I think that's why I find it so hard to confide in her. I wish virtue wasn't something I had to work at, but it seems all my attempts at doing the right thing morph into something to be ashamed of. Rich had every right to call me a hypocrite on that dock, but intentions are worth something, aren't they? He knew what he was doing, following me under those bleachers, and if he had a similar opportunity, I'm sure he'd do it again. But that's the thing. He *won't* have the opportunity. And if there was ever a possibility of me admitting to Kira what happened, it died with him.

I go downstairs and thank Dad for letting me sleep in. I eat lunch with him and say some things I think he expects and wants to hear: *I'll be okay. I just need some time to sort through things. I'm sad and worried about my friends. I miss Trenton and my mom. I feel bad for Rich's family. I know it's not my fault.* Only the last one feels like an outright lie, but I think it's enough to keep him off my case for a while.

I go back to my room and pull up my social studies essay that's due Monday, content to distract myself with homework. Mrs. Andino would probably give me an extension if I asked, considering everything going on, but I need to be consumed by something else for a couple of hours. So I research the electoral college and popular votes and outline and draft until my room is dark and the light from my laptop makes my eyes ache. I lean back in my chair, stretching until my joints pop and crack. I'm turning on my lamp and closing my laptop when a familiar whirring emanates from the corner of my room. My eyes dart to Greta, still sitting on the box I placed her on yesterday. Her head and arms move in the same repetitive way. Tiny mechanical clicks from the machinery inside her start up a couple of seconds before she speaks. "Hi! I'm Gabby Greta, and I love you!" I rise slowly from my seat and take a few steps toward her. "I'm Gabby Greta! Can you count to . . ." There's a heavy pause, and then, in a slower, warped voice, "Thirteen? One, two, three, four, five . . ."

She'd said fourteen yesterday. I don't need to look at a calendar. I'm now thirteen days away from the deadline Regret set. But there are no consequences for ignoring deadlines set by your imagination. I snatch the doll up as she continues to count. Flip her over, search for a switch or battery pack. Something to shut her up. I rip at her pull string, and it snaps off in my grasp. All other options exhausted, I try Dad's technique and bash her against the side of my desk. She goes silent.

"Simone!" Dad shouts. "What was that?"

I leave my bedroom carrying the doll by her leg. "Nothing."

Dad stands at the bottom of the stairs with Serling cradled in his arms. He brings the cat closer to his chest as I scoot by. "I know you didn't bring that spooky-ass thing in the house."

"Taking it to the trash now."

I dump Gabby Greta in the garbage can outside and go back up to my room. I hesitate at my door, half afraid I'll open it and she'll be right back where she was before. But she's not. Of course she's not. I can't say exactly where I draw the line between what's real and what isn't, what's possible and what's not, but today I am choosing not to believe in haunted dolls. Dolls with freaky mechanical glitches, sure. But even those can't take themselves out of the trash can and walk up steps. I laugh off the thought but go straight to my laptop to look up information on Gabby Greta dolls. I find a commercial from 1953 on YouTube and hit play.

One, two, three, four, she'll teach you how to count and more!
Five, six, seven, eight, she makes learning numbers great!
Hi! I'm Gabby Greta, and I love you!
I'm Gabby Greta! Can you count to . . . ten?
One, two, three . . .

The doll looks exactly like the one I threw away, only shiny and new and less squeaky. My stomach turns and I stare at my lap wondering if the advertised doll counted to numbers above ten, and as I'm convincing myself that it must have, that obviously it did, the YouTube video is interrupted by what I assume is an ad—until I look at the screen. It's the dock at Doll's Head Lake, but from an angle I haven't seen, like it was shot by someone wading in the water. I want to look away, but I can't take my eyes from the screen. I *literally* cannot move. My eyes well with tears and sting from the strain of trying to force them into a different position. I open my mouth to call for Dad, but no words escape. The sound of a heavy splash echoes through my laptop's speakers. The sound of a body hitting the water. It happens a dozen times before other noises mingle in. Voices. Familiar voices.

Hypocrite.
Let me see your phone.
Will both of y'all just stop?

The vantage point changes and now it's as if I'm at the end of the dock, looking out over the water. The surface ripples with bubbles as someone emerges from the depths. Pale gray eyes. Face glitching and staticky.

Regret.

I swear I feel a tiny blood vessel pop in my eye as I try in earnest to escape my desk chair. Her mouth opens slowly, revealing small, pointed teeth as she begins to speak.

Play ignorant if you wish, but we had a deal.
I assure you, girl.
This. Is. Real.

CHAPTER 12

My computer screen flashes to black before returning to normal. I push away from my desk, all the tension that was trapped in my body finally releasing. I pant, terrified, as the Gabby Greta commercial continues where it left off. If there are stages to accepting that you made a dark deal with a witch in the woods, then I sat in denial for a day and ripped through all the others in sixty seconds.

I roll back to my desk and x out of YouTube, hand trembling. This is real, which means I have to act. Now. I've already lost a day, but I can do this. I am on track to be first or second in our senior class. I am a problem solver. And while I am also a lot of negative things, one thing no one will ever catch me doing is quitting. Regret chose the right one.

I snatch an old, lightly used composition notebook from my bookshelf. The first thing I need to do is organize all the information I already have. Everything I learned that night. I close my eyes and rub my forehead. The memories are there. Clear as day, ready to be released from the cage they've been in since the moment I decided they weren't real. I don't want to revisit this. Of course I don't. But the clock is ticking and I need clues.

A few deep breaths and I set the memories loose. Fall deep

inside them. Regret's face is the first thing that rushes to the front of my mind. I have to swallow down a wave of fear and actually examine the features behind her terrifying expression. Her skin is gray. That stood out to me that night, but it's not *just* gray. It's dark with a brownish undertone. That and the texture of her hair, the coarse, curly strands—Regret is Black. I remember thinking she looked young, and that assessment holds. Every strand of her hair is as black as night. Muck and seaweed cling to her skin, giving the appearance of creases and wrinkles, but the exposed patches are smooth. Her teeth are coated in their own layer of grime, but they are all present. Early twenties would be my best guess, even though it doesn't feel right. Regret felt ancient. And in all the scary stories I know, the women who've been scorned enough to haunt a place are older. But that's silly, now that I think about it. As if age restricts trauma. Regret probably felt old because she said she'd been trapped there for seventy years. She might have been rounding, but it's still useful.

I take a second to list what I've recalled so far in bullet points down the page. "Okay," I mumble to myself. "Seventy years ago was 1956. That means I'm looking for a Black woman born in Fairville sometime in the mid to late 1930s."

I pull my laptop closer to me and navigate to Cory's website. I read the blog post again, combing for any small detail that might give me more information about Regret.

> A dark specter lives on the banks of Yearwood Lake.
> Do not enter the wood without offering stake.
> Make a deal and you're in her debt.
> Those who've met her call her Regret.

Make a deal and you're in her debt. My first thought is, *What have I done?* but I shake my head and force myself to revise it.

What other option did I have? It was either be in her debt or let Kira die. There was only one viable choice there. I add the part about "offering stake" to my notepad. Maybe resolving this could be as simple as bringing a gift, a new toy to the woods.

I go back to the Google reviews that Cory mentioned in the post and read every single one, hoping to find someone who had a strange experience at Doll's Head. I can't be the only person Regret has offered a deal to in seventy years. And I can't be the only one who accepted. But obviously anyone else who did failed. They failed, and they are probably out there suffering a consequence so terrible that they wouldn't be of any help to me. The Google reviews end up being no help either. I try Reddit next and then spend hours scouring half a dozen other forums. Come midnight, I slam my laptop closed, frustrated by encountering the same shallow information.

I debate whether to go to school tomorrow. No one is probably expecting me to, and I could use the day to do some research and make up for lost time. But Rich and Doll's Head will be the number one topic of conversation, and sometimes gems of truth are hidden in rumor mills. Someone at school might know more about the secrets in those woods and in this town than me.

HALFWAY through English, I realize school wasn't the best move after all. Teachers have been shutting down gossip and directing students to the small army of grief counselors posted up in the media center. More than one teacher tried to nudge me in that direction and more than once I wanted to take them up on it, but expressing what's going on with me right now would have everyone questioning my sanity. And for good reason. But I don't have time for that. I grab the hall pass and walk to the restroom.

Chatter carries over from the cafeteria as I slip into the bathroom stall. I stand there with my eyes closed, pretending I'm at Ozzy's Pizza. That I'm five again with a present mother and big dreams and zero trauma. A flood of girls leaving B lunch interrupt my peace and quiet.

"I just can't believe it," one of them says, voice breaking. "He was so sweet. We both had econ out in the trailers. One day, it was raining, and he saw me trying to cover my head with my book bag. He gave me his umbrella. Like literally gave it to me—I still have it. Then he ran ahead and held the door for me. He got soaking wet."

"Oh, I bet that was so hot. With his dark curls."

"Be serious, Lexi," she snaps before choking out a small laugh. "But yeah. Of course it was hot."

"You know Shaina Reyes thinks it wasn't an accident, right?" one of the girls says, voice lowered.

I perk up, lean closer to the stall door.

"Really?"

"Yeah. I overheard her talking to her cousin. He's in our grade."

"Was Shaina even at the party?"

"Mm-hmm. I heard her say she saw Rich and Kira go outside at like three o'clock in the morning. Said she heard them arguing, bad."

"About what?"

I see her shoulders rise and fall through the opening in the stall.

"You know Rich was a flirt. That's no secret. She was probably jealous."

"Do you think he cheated on her or something?"

"I mean, Rich is a good guy, but Kira seems sort of . . . clingy. A guy can only take so much, you know? It had to come to a head at some point."

"So does Shaina think Kira like . . . killed him or something?"

"I've been hearing that the police think it was an accident, but they don't always get it right, do they? Everyone is saying the official autopsy results won't be back until midweek."

"Why would the police be saying it was an accident if the results aren't even back?"

"You know Kira's brother-in-law is a Yearwood, right? I heard he and her sister were supposed to be chaperoning the whole thing. Papa Yearwood probably slid someone some cash. They have even more sway in this town than the Pearsons. I don't care what those results say. No one can convince me Kira wasn't involved."

This is not the type of gossip I came to school hoping to hear. I storm out of the stall, dead set on shutting it down. The door slams against the painted cinder block wall, and the girls gawk at me, mouths opening and closing like fish out of water.

"Say it again."

They continue to stand there, wordless.

I walk up to the girl who threw out the accusation and stop mere inches from her. I can feel her fear, and it only upsets me more. I've never fought anyone in my life, but she is afraid of me. "Since you know Kira so well, say it again. With your chest this time." I cup my hand around my ear. "No one can convince you that what?"

"I didn't mean—"

"That's what I thought. Stop talking about shit you don't know. Kira trusted Rich with everything in her. He was damn lucky to have her. And I don't know what you think you heard Shaina say, but I promise whatever ugliness you spread about Kira Davis will come back your way tenfold."

I leave the restroom fuming, wanting to shout Shaina's name up and down the halls until she shows her stank little face. Demand she explain what the hell is wrong with her. Make her tell me why she would dare verbalize something like that. Frankly, I can think of only one good reason. And knowing what I know about Shaina and Rich, it makes *her* look bad.

I wait for Shaina by her car after school. A few different emotions cross her features when she spots me, but she settles on the grieving friend.

"Hey, Simone."

I waste no time. "Why the hell are you telling people that Kira killed Rich?"

She stares at me, dumbfounded. "I . . . did not say that." Her voice lifts at the end like a question.

"Well, why are you suggesting it? Your loud and wrong mouth has people talking."

She sighs and pushes her bangs straight back from her forehead. Her eyes are watery when she looks back up at me. She raises her hands, palms up. "Simone, I'm sorry. I can tell you exactly what I said to exactly one person. I didn't mean for anyone to overhear it."

"Go ahead then."

"I heard Rich and Kira arguing outside early Saturday morning. It was still pitch-black out."

"She was next to me all night."

Shaina raises her shoulders up near her ears, at a loss. "She wasn't. I saw them with my own eyes. Heard them with my own ears."

"Okay, so what were they fighting about?"

"I'm not sure." She doesn't meet my eyes. "That wasn't super clear."

"Bullshit." I don't know if the exact text messages I saw exist in this corner of the universe, but Shaina and Rich definitely had some kind of exchange.

She scans the parking lot, searching for someone who can bail her out of this conversation, I assume.

"If you're going to drag Kira for filth, go ahead and drag yourself, too," I say.

Her eyes cut back to mine and she straightens her back. "As if I'm the only one who needs to be dragged."

I do not flinch. On the outside, my mask of choice is cold and secure. But on the inside, I am shaking with uncertainty and doubt. Could she know about me and Rich? Probably not. Her big mouth couldn't keep something like that a secret for so long. This is a bluff, a fair one, considering his history, but I won't fall for it. I will literally die before I ever speak my shame out loud. "No, you aren't the only one. Rich was a serial flirt."

"Exactly. And would anyone be surprised if Kira finally, *finally* got fed up with it?"

"No. No one would be surprised if she got 'fed up,' but you were implying something else entirely."

"Can you blame me? I couldn't make out the details of their argument, but what else could it have even been? Either way, what I do know for sure is that it was bad, and Kira came back inside without him."

"Why didn't you go check on him?"

"Because I knew he wouldn't want to see me. I'm not stupid, Simone. I was just someone Rich called when he wanted to drink or smoke. Can't claim to be an angel and act like I didn't try for it, but nothing ever happened between us. I swear."

My heart grows heavy, humiliated that I, Kira's best friend, can't swear the same.

"I didn't go check on Rich because I figured he was down there brainstorming his apology to Kira. Dreaming up all the ways he was going to be a better guy from that moment on." She rolls her eyes. "I went back to sleep, and when I woke up a few hours later, he wasn't anywhere in the house. I told Cam I thought I heard him outside in the middle of the night. Told him to go look for him out there. I thought he'd be by the firepit moping. But he was dead. And Kira was the last one to see him alive, so please don't come for me because that idea crossed my mind. Because I needed to get it off my chest. I should have done it somewhere private. I'm sorry for that. But none of it matters because it sounds like the police already drew their conclusions. So can we just get through this funeral and graduation and move the hell on with our lives?"

She storms by me and gets into the driver's seat of her car, where she proceeds to rest her head against the steering wheel and cry.

I need to see Kira. I'm up to three good reasons to go right now. The first and most important—I miss her and I'm worried about her. The second popped into my head a few times throughout the day. I need to nudge her again to see if there is anything at all she remembers from what happened out at the lake. She is the only other person who was there that I can speak to, and maybe there is some tiny, important detail trapped in her subconscious. And now, thanks to Shaina, I have reason number three. There are obviously some huge things Kira hasn't told me, and I need to know why. I need to know the whole truth. For the briefest second, I consider how I'd feel if Shaina were right. If something dark did go down between Kira and Rich out there. I consider it only for that fraction of a second because it would change nothing. I'd reach hypocrite level ten if it did. I know how it feels to be connected to something horrible. To have at least some piece of responsibility for it. All I want is to be able to support her fully. Unconditionally. I don't text to ask if I can come see her. She either won't answer, or she'll say no. I just start walking.

CHAPTER 13

Mrs. Davis is at the mailbox shuffling through bills and junk when I get to her house. She wears tailored pants cropped at the ankle and a carefully pressed dress shirt.

"Oh, Simone, baby, I didn't see you there," she says, Jamaican accent hanging on by a thread. "How are you? Come here." She pulls me into a hug, and my eyes instantly sting. She smells and feels like Mom, the generic version. Not *my* mom, but *a* mom. Soft and safe and sweet.

I pull away from her and hold up the bag in my hand. "I brought Kira's favorite."

She glances at the house. Kira probably asked for no visitors, but I guessed her mom might be having a hard time getting her to eat, that a takeout bag from Benny's Burgers might be my in.

"Come on inside."

I follow her to the front door, which she left cracked open.

"Are you okay?" I ask. "Layla?"

"We are all crushed, I mean absolutely devastated for the Pearsons. We loved that boy like family. But I'll tell you the way I told my girls, John and Layla being in the house wouldn't have stopped Rich from trying to turn on the generator when the power went out. He has one at his place. No way an independent young man like him would have gone and woken up John to do it. I only wish he would have waited. The outage only lasted thirty minutes or so." She motions for me to enter the house first. "Kira's in her bedroom, sweetie."

I go upstairs and quietly open Kira's door. Her room is a mess. Books, art supplies, makeup, and hair products litter the floor. The bag she brought to the cabin is sticking halfway out of her closet, unpacked. Her homecoming dress is shoved into the too-small trash can beside her desk.

"Kir?"

A lump under the blankets stirs.

"Kira, it's me."

She sits up and slides a black eye mask down her face. Her curls are in a messy bun on top of her head, and eyeliner, I guess from days ago, is smudged around her eyes.

"Mom wasn't supposed to let anyone in," she says, nostrils already flaring as the scent from the bag in my hand reaches her nose.

"I'm not anyone. I'm me."

She scoots over, silently welcoming me in. I sit next to her, and she greedily takes the bag, digging inside for a handful of fries. She chews silently for a minute. "Thank you."

"You're welcome."

"How was school?"

"Not great."

"Figured. Good thing I didn't go." She tosses me her phone, messages app open.

The first three texts are from unknown numbers. The message preview on the first says *bitch*. The second says *killer*. The third says *it's your fault*.

"I'm so sorry, Kira. I just laid into Shaina for spreading stuff around, but I didn't know it was already so bad."

"Yeah. Well, it is."

I pause, not sure what to say next. I have questions, so many. But I'm her friend first, so I turn to face her and wrap my arms around her. "I'm sorry. I'm sorry about all of it," I say, apologizing for so much more than she knows.

"You were right, Sim." She sniffles into my chest. "You were right. About Rich. About not being able to trust him."

I stiffen, overwhelmed by an emotion I can't place. Relief? Joy? Apprehension? I've been waiting to hear her say those words for so long, but after what Shaina said . . .

Kira pulls away from me and wipes her eyes. "That night, after we all went to bed, he sent me a text by accident. He unsent it right away, but I'd already seen."

"What'd it say?"

"'Still down?' with a tongue sticking out and rocket ship emoji. If he hadn't unsent it, if it hadn't been in the middle of the night in a cabin in the woods, I might have been able to convince myself it was something innocent. But my gut said it wasn't."

"What'd you do?"

"I confronted him. I knew it was gonna get heated, and I didn't want us to wake everyone up, so we went outside." She looks down at her phone. "Clearly that didn't help much."

So Shaina was telling the truth.

Her bottom lip trembles. "Sim, I said the most awful things to him. I was cruel. I was trying to hurt him. And I did. I could see it on his face."

"I'm sure he knew he had every word you said to him coming."

She nods. "He stood there and took it. But he didn't expect"—she pauses, fighting back tears—"he didn't expect me to break up with him. And that's what I did. I told him it was forever this time. He begged me. He apologized a hundred times. Made promises. I didn't want to hear any of it. I broke up with him,

Sim. I broke up with him and left him out there. He was so upset. So, so upset. I thought for a second that I should wake up Jere to go be with him, but I wanted him to hurt. I wanted him to hurt like he hurt me." She stares straight ahead, eyes unblinking and tormented.

I feel a curious mix of pride and shame at her trusting me with this information so easily. Without even needing to ask me to keep it to myself. "Did your argument get caught on the security cameras? Or was the power already out when y'all went out there?"

She doesn't answer, so I reframe. "Are you worried about the texts you've been getting?"

"No." She picks at her burger bun. "John gave the police full access to the security footage from the entire night before I could even tell him and Layla what happened. I lost it when I found out. I knew it'd look terrible, us arguing out there. I told John, Layla, and my parents everything. We knew it'd be a bad idea to try to manipulate any of the footage, but John pulled it up so we could at least watch it and see what it might look like to the police. The cameras don't pick up sound, but you could tell I wasn't happy with him. My saving grace was that I lost steam toward the end. I hugged him and kissed his cheek before I went back upstairs. He followed after me only a few seconds later. Then there was nothing for an hour. We fast-forwarded through. Just trees swaying in the wind and rain until the power cut. When it came back on . . . his body was there. I couldn't look. But John pointed out that you could see Rich's footprints in the mud. That there was just *one* set of footprints. So I was mostly honest when the police asked me about it."

"Mostly?"

"I told them we were arguing about college plans and how

much time he spends obsessing over football. I didn't tell them that I broke up with him. How upset he was. I don't think I could have if I'd wanted to. That morning . . . when the screaming started. I—Simone, he was so sad. At first, I thought he might have—"

"It was an accident, Kira." I look her in the eyes, and the half-truths buried in my words weigh heavy on my shoulders. But I am used to things left unsaid, unexplained, between us. "It was an accident." I fumble for a reasonable chain of events that might make her feel better. "He came back inside shortly after you. That was literally caught on camera. He probably tried to . . . I don't know, reheat some food in the microwave or something before the power went out. You know he liked to play Mr. Fix-It. He remembered he saw a generator outside, went to try to plug it in, and . . . and it was a freak accident." I can see it so perfectly in my head, and I wish I could still be living in the comfort of denial. Of thinking all this was a figment of my imagination or just a string of terrible luck.

"I want to believe that, I do. And at the end of the day, I know he wouldn't have hurt himself or anything, but there's . . . something else I can't get out of my head," she says, voice thick. "I was so angry with him when I went to sleep. But I had this dream. . . ." She fiddles with the patchwork quilt strewn over her comforter. "The three of us were out at that lake you told me about."

I perk up. Maybe she *does* remember something.

"You"—Kira pauses, carefully choosing her words—"there was a commotion, and I fell into the water." She doesn't look up at me.

"You fell?" I ask. "How?"

She plays with a stray curl near her ear. "I can't remember."

She is such a bad liar. My heart pangs because she thinks I'm so much better than I really am. She won't say it out loud. She won't say that I pushed her. In her mind, that detail alone likely confirms the whole thing as a dream. In her mind, I would *never* do anything to hurt her. And I wouldn't. Not intentionally—Rich brought out something feral in me. He brought out something dark. But he's gone now. Forever.

"What happened after you fell?" I need to know just how far her "dream" stretched.

"Rich saved me. He pulled me from the water, then ran off to get help."

"He left you alone?"

"No." She looks up at me now. "You were there. You stayed with me. It's fuzzy, but I remember you talking. I think you were praying. . . ." Her voice becomes a detached mumble as fragments from that night return. The smell. Honeysuckle and tobacco. The chilly water. The full moon. The bloodstained sand. Something primal surges through me. Something hungry, alive, and angry.

My stomach roils, and the room feels ten degrees warmer. Kira's voice shifts from a mumble to a grating buzz that makes my skin crawl. The buzz grows louder and louder until suddenly words begin to break through again, but it's not only Kira's voice this time. There's another. And it repeats the same thing over and over.

Twelve days.
Twelve days.
Twelve days.

I am overwhelmed by the urge to cover Kira's mouth with my hand. To force her to be quiet. "Kira, please stop talking."

She doesn't hear me. She never does once she's on a roll.

I watch her lips move, recounting all those horrible things that happened at the lake, the number of days until my deadline echoing on repeat in the background, and that feeling, untamed and aggressive, swells inside me, so dangerously close to bursting free. It frightens me, and I force myself to look away from her. My eyes land on her fluffy down-filled pillow. I can hear Regret in my head. I can feel her urgency. Her impatience. *If you fail, she dies once more. This time, undoubtedly by your hand.* And I can see it. I can visualize it perfectly. Me, grabbing the pillow. Me, forcing Kira to *shut up*.

CHAPTER 14

I stumble from Kira's bed, heart thundering.

"What is wrong with you, Simone?"

"Nothing. I have to go. I'll call you later."

"Simone, what the hell? You came here. You said you wanted to talk and now you're up and leaving?"

"I'm sorry. I'm not feeling well. Something I ate."

I leave her room before she can say another word and speed down the stairs and out of the house, gasping in gulps of fresh air. The rage that was bubbling in my stomach dissipates, but what's left is anxiety so fierce that I actually run home.

As soon as I make it inside the house, I rush to the kitchen, drop to my knees, and practically put my entire head in the trash can, dry heaving so much it's painful. The exertion of physically pushing my body harder than I have in years violently catching up with me. The fear of what lies ahead. Of what could lie ahead if I fail. Again, I heave over the trash can. When nothing but spittle comes up, I sit on the floor, resting my back against the cool metal of the dishwasher, face covered in a fine layer of sweat. How did I even get here? All I wanted to do was make Kira see. My intentions were pure. Help a friend. And somehow, everything got warped in the most disgusting way. How does helping Kira morph into her lying dead on that wet gray sand? How does her lying dead on that wet gray sand morph into Rich lying dead on that muddy brown grass? And the answers to those questions are the least of my concern if I can't hold up my end of the deal. I won't gamble with Kira's life by trying to figure this out alone. I need help. I need to talk to Cory. He's my best option and I need the best. But there are things I have to confront first. Things I have to face head-on so all my energy can go where it's needed right now.

I go to my room and pull a plastic storage bin from the top shelf of my closet. I wipe a layer of dust from the lid before opening it, knowing the contents will put a vise around my heart. Part of me knows I deserve the searing ache that tears through me every time I look inside. It's a box of keepsakes. A time capsule holding all the small physical connections I have to people I've lost. To my mom. To Trenton. I run my fingers across the cover of my water-stained copy of *Bridge to Terabithia*. Mom gave me this shortly after Trenton died. I read it from front to back in one night, then cried every day for a week. Over the book. Over Trenton. Over that day that changed everything.

We were supposed to see a movie. Me, Cory, and Trenton. I had to pass Cory's house on the way to the theater, so I stopped by so we could walk the rest of the way together. But first we raided his kitchen pantry for snacks to sneak inside in my oversized purse. It was in that pantry, Oreos and Doritos in hand, that Cory told me he'd been crushing on me all year. I told him I felt the same and I can't remember a happier moment. Not before then, and certainly not after. Because while we were laughing, Trenton was waiting for us. While we were flirting, Trenton was looking for us. And while we were kissing, Trenton was dying. A hit-and-run while he walked from the theater to Cory's house to see what was holding us up. That's what he'd said on his mother's voicemail. He told her he'd made it to the movies safely, checking in like a good son should. He told her he was waiting for us, called us by name. Cory and Simone. He joked about how we are always late. How he didn't want to miss the previews. How walking around the corner to Cory's house would probably be faster than waiting for us to show up on our own.

Trenton was found dead at the start of Cory's long, winding street. Yvette, Cory's older sister, is the one who told us. She busted into the house, hysterical. We hadn't realized just how late we were. Forty minutes, by then. Ten minutes after the movie had started. Yvette told us she'd walked by the scene of the accident on her way home from work. She said her friend, who lived nearby, came out of her house after hearing the screeching tires of a car speeding away. It was through the whispers of people standing in their yards that Yvette heard the name Trenton Jones. And then she saw his backpack. The one that had been propped against the sofa in her house countless times. The rest of that evening is a blur. I cannot pull any complete memories from my brain. Only fragments. Cory shaking his head in denial. Dad picking me up . . . or maybe it was Yvette dropping me off. I don't know. All I can grasp on to is riding in a car and random town landmarks between Cory's house and mine.

But those details don't matter. What matters is that Cory and I made a choice. We knew we were running late. We knew what time we promised Trenton we'd be there. We put ourselves first. And it was our choices that led our friend to come look for us. It was our choices that landed him on that road at that exact moment in time. So it was our choices that got him killed. And maybe this whole situation is tied to that. Because I know now. I am admitting it to myself now—that is what Regret meant. That night. Kissing Cory—that was the biggest regret of my life, not kissing Rich. And that's why looking at Cory, why even just sharing space with him, hurts me so much. I can see my own guilt reflected back in him. But I guess this is the season for facing demons.

I'M irritated all day at school on Tuesday. I only bothered to go to shut down rumors about Kira if needed, but I spend every class period researching witches, ghosts, lunar cycles, and curses. People grieve Rich loudly and dramatically. Underclassmen who never even spoke to him wear tribute shirts and form prayer circles. Girls he played like toys cling to each other in the hallway crying. All of it infuriates me. And it doesn't help that I feel eyes lingering on me. The girl who threw the cursed birthday party. Some people abruptly stop talking when I turn a corner or enter a room. They whisper and giggle when I walk away. I catch myself being surprised that I haven't received any nasty anonymous messages like Kira, but the universe rights that by lunchtime.

> Unknown
> Now that Rich is out of the picture I guess you and Kira can have your happily ever after

> Unknown
> was just a matter of time before one of your satanic ass parties ended with someone dead

> Unknown
> We're losing our shot at state because of your stupid party

I swipe through six more, just skimming the words before blocking the numbers and deleting the threads to ensure I don't make any petty replies. These texts don't incapacitate me the way they are undoubtedly continuing to do to Kira. The things that mattered to me last week are irrelevant now. They can talk shit all day. They can talk it for eternity if it'd mean me getting the answers I need. I feel that so intensely—until one more message comes through.

Unknown
they say three murders makes a serial killer.
Eleven days til you earn your stripes

My palms go sweaty and my heart rate spikes as I watch the message dissolve with a *pop*.

Unknown unsent a message.

I'm not dodging my role in the death of Trenton and Rich, but I haven't killed anyone. Not directly. Not intentionally. And I'm not going to. This is just another scare tactic. Another nudge from Regret. Thumb quivering, I tap the number and hit call.

It rings once. *Your call cannot be completed as dialed. Please check the number and dial again.* I slowly pull my phone from my ear and hang up, feeling strangely numb and knowing there is no use trying again.

CHAPTER 15

When school lets out, I head for Cory's without any hesitation. The last time I walked to his house, it led me to one of the biggest heartbreaks of my life. But I have to do it. I have to get his help, or the heartbreak to come will trump everything else.

There's a freshly printed missing person sign for Natalie Dawson stapled to a utility pole on the corner. It's so weird to me that she lived here in town, and was so close to my age, yet I never crossed paths with her. I think that's partly what pulled me into her case so intensely. She lived a whole life I knew nothing about. It reminds me how small and insignificant we all are—and not in a negative way. It's strangely comforting, actually.

Cory said old Mama Dee the psychic saw Natalie's ghost, and I wonder if it's true. I never had any trouble believing in the supernatural and certainly don't now, but mediums who charge people money to connect with other realms always gave me pause. Emphasis on *gave* because she is for sure going on my list of people to speak to.

I knock on Cory's door and knock again when there's no answer. When I'm finally considering turning around, I hear some rustling. The turning of a dead bolt. The door swings open, and Cory stands there in a wrinkled white T-shirt and gray sweatpants.

"Simone?"

"Hey." I rock back and forth on my heels.

"Hey," he replies, matching my tone. "What are you—"

"Is your grandma home?"

His left eyebrow raises just slightly. "You came to see my grandma?"

"You know I didn't. Please don't make this more difficult than it already is."

"Tuesday is karaoke night at the senior center. Grandma goes over early to help set up. And I'm not trying to be difficult. I'm just surprised you're here."

"Okay, well, can I come in? Can we talk?"

He opens the door wider and steps to the side. "Of course. We can talk whenever you want, Simone. And I meant I'm surprised you're *here*. At my house. Outside of the other night at the park, I don't think we've spoken more than a few words in over a year."

"Trying to hold a conversation while you're juggling hot pizzas at Ozzy's might have been tough, don't you think?"

"Sure, but aside from a few seconds at the door, I wasn't juggling pizzas at your party," he says, looking down at me.

I feel small beside him, something I don't often experience as a tall girl. "A party's not quite the vibe for a deep conversation."

"So you're trying to have a deep conversation?" he asks, failing to hide his surprise.

"No, Cory. I mean yes. I don't know. Can we go to your room, or . . . ?"

"Yeah," he says with a humored exhale. "We can go to my room and have a maybe not but possibly yes deep conversation."

I lead the way. I've taken this route through his one-story home at least a dozen times, and entering his room again doesn't feel like I imagined it would. I thought it'd be difficult. Painful. But the smell and dim lighting, the position of his posters and figurines—almost everything is exactly as I remember it, and I'm grateful to find that it's joyful memories that come rushing back first. Cory always leaves his curtains drawn but often opens the window, allowing in the scent of the pine trees from his backyard. It's tidy. Sterile, compared to Kira's room. Everything in its place. There's a photo of us on his bulletin board. I put it there myself one of the last times I was over here. I turn around and startle to find him just standing there, only a foot away from me.

"Jeez, Cory."

"Sorry. Was just—" He motions at the rolling chair at his desk, slips by me, and takes a seat. "So what did you want to talk about?"

"I don't know. Everything is a lot right now. I don't know where to start."

"Is there something I can do to help?"

I plop down on the foot of his bed. "Erase my memory. Make me forget."

"I would if I could."

Little does he know, he can. Or he can assist, at least. That was part of Regret's deal. Eliminating my memory of all the things I regret most. But I'm not telling him all that if I don't have to, and I don't think I do. "You can help distract me. I need to keep my brain occupied."

He scratches the back of his neck. "Yeah. Of course. D-did you have something in mind?"

He's nervous, and it makes me smile despite myself. "Loosen up. It's me." I know it's a wild thing to say considering how I've been behaving around him, but I'm surprisingly calm in this room. It's bizarre after years of associating him with stress and tension and anxiety. I'd convinced myself that he made me uncomfortable when he is, in fact, one of the safest, softest places in my world. But it's not any wonder I put up the walls I did. I've done nothing to earn safety and softness.

"I'm loose." Cory shakes out his arms. "And I'm glad you're here."

I clasp my hands together on my lap. "I should probably start with a confession. Your blog about the urban legends... I've been following it for a long time. Since you started it, to be honest. That's why I had the party out at Doll's Head."

"I thought so," he says casually, nothing boastful in his tone, no implied flattery, just a simple fact shared.

"I knew you would if you heard, but I didn't have you actually showing up on my bingo card."

He rolls back and forth in his chair. "So, did you see her?"

For a second, I'm not sure what he's talking about. It's going to take me a while to get used to how he speaks again. His frankness. How he turns conversations in unexpected directions. His mastery of left turns. You would expect him to ask about Rich, whether to offer a shoulder to cry on or just out of morbid curiosity. But no. This isn't just anyone. This is Cory, and Cory is asking me about Regret.

"Did you?" he pushes.

A small part of me wants to be completely honest and tell him everything. I know he'd take me seriously. Believe every word. Spend every waking moment helping me figure it out. But he'd do that even without knowing the details. And I don't think his choice to do it would have much to do with me specifically. Cory's the type to really lock in on a task if it's something he's into. I can get his help without opening myself up, without splaying everything inside out for him to see. I have a ghost witch inserting herself into my life and counting down the days until I murder my best friend. If I don't have to make myself even more vulnerable than I already am, I won't. "No. I chickened out. Didn't even make it out to the lake..."

"I'm sensing a *but*..."

I scramble for something to get him on board without triggering too many questions. "Someone dies at a haunted lake. It's normal to wonder if something... supernatural went down, right?"

He grabs a yellow stress ball from his desk and squeezes it absentmindedly. "I think that's normal, yeah. Not sure if everyone would agree, though."

"That's exactly why I came to you. Kira keeps an open mind about things, but she's grieving hard, and we... aren't connecting like we usually do." I don't add that my visit yesterday ended with me thinking about suffocating her. "And, despite my cold shoulder, it was nice to have you at my party for a little while. It was nice talking about the horror exhibit, too. I was thinking I could help you with your blog. I want to help you research more about Regret and Doll's Head Lake. And I know I must seem like the worst person ever showing up here now like you're some last-resort distraction from my problems."

"I'm not a last resort."

"I know. That's exactly what I'm saying."

"You don't need to say it, though. I know. Simone." He rolls closer to me, moves his index finger back and forth between us. "I've missed you a lot, and maybe I should've been more forward about hoping to reconnect recently, but the silence between us at the start wasn't one-sided."

My voice catches for a second. "No, yeah. I'm not suggesting you've just been waiting around for me to want to be friends again." I guess I knew he'd be open to it, but now I'm not so sure where that confidence came from.

Cory smiles at me, a dimple springing up in his left cheek.

"All I'm saying is I understand. And I'm more than happy to be your not-last-resort distraction."

I let out a shaky laugh. "In that case, can we get straight to it?"

He leaps from his chair and searches for something behind his desk for a few seconds before pulling out a scratched and dented whiteboard. He holds it up, grinning. "I've been waiting for my Sherlock Holmes moment. Just needed my Watson."

I shake my head. "Toss me a marker."

He does, then we both move to the floor to start planning. Across the top of the board, I write

GOAL 1: Gather enough info to update blog by Friday 10/22
GOAL 2: Solve the mystery of the witch called Regret by Friday 10/29

That will give me one day of wiggle room, but hopefully I won't need it.

Cory pushes his twists out of his face. "That's, uh, soon. . . ."

"Don't want to leave your loyal readers waiting!"

"I think you might be my only loyal reader."

"Maybe if you updated more regularly I wouldn't be." I tap the board with my marker. "Let's focus. I want to get a game plan together now so we can go all in tomorrow."

He chuckles. "Yes, ma'am."

Getting the next installment of his Doll's Head series posted by the end of the week might be lighting some fire under him, but keeping Kira alive and myself out of prison is undoubtedly the superior motivator. "Okay. Let's start with a list of people to talk to. Older folks who might have been alive around the same time as Regret."

"How do we know when she was alive?"

I fiddle with my braids, trying to play it cool. "Oh, uh, I already did a little research. Talk of a witch called Regret started up in the mid-fifties, and from what I could gather, she was fairly young. Early twenties, I'd guess."

"How—" he starts, but to my relief, he seems to rethink his question. "Yeah, so if that's true, most of her peers are probably dead by now. But if we can find some people who were in their really early teens around then, they might be able to recall some useful information." He starts scribbling names on the board.

"Do you volunteer at the senior center with your grandma or something?" I ask as his list of old-timey names grows.

"Yes, actually."

"Great. That'll come in handy. Add Mama Dee."

Cory snaps his fingers. "How didn't I think of her? Good idea." He adds her name, then starts a new list. "Let's pick some spots around town to go visit. I can organize everything into a schedule later tonight."

"That'd be perfect."

Done with his terrible handwriting, I nudge him away from the board and write as we brainstorm aloud. The library. Town hall. The memorabilia room at the CPRC.

I scoot back to admire our work so far.

"Nice," Cory says. "I think our starting hypothesis for what happened to Regret should be the most obvious thing."

"And what's that?"

"Classic vengeful, mourning mother did something . . . well, regrettable in an attempt to be reunited with her lost child, and her ghost is trapped here because of it. I think that's a fair assumption based on the toys and what was written in that book I thrifted, but it does feel generic. Almost too obvious. But that's what happens to stories over time. They get watered down to their bones and beefed back up with filler. We have to rediscover the uniqueness. The details. Weed out the falsehoods."

I think about the story I made up at the bonfire and how easily it came to me, wondering if it could be close to the truth. Could Regret have influenced me to tell that story somehow? "Agreed."

Cory is absolutely glowing. The stakes of the situation keep me from sharing in his excitement, but I slip on a mask from my collection anyway. An energized, zealous one. He'd usually be able to see right through it, but he's too consumed right now. And that's for the best. I need his fervor. Kira needs it.

CHAPTER 16

Wednesday afternoon I meet Cory at Ozzy's to begin our research in earnest.

"Hey!" Cory gives me the biggest smile when he spots me. Total 180 from the awkward avoidance-of-eye-contact game we've been playing for so long.

"Hi," I say, helpless to resist returning the grin.

"I still have twenty left in my shift. Are you hungry?"

"Yeah."

He gestures at the bar. "Have a seat."

I perch on a stool, and a few minutes later, he brings me sparkling water and two slices of veggie lovers. My other friends hate it, so we never get it when we buy a pie to share, but Cory remembered. Of course he did. "Thank you."

I eat my food so quickly there are still ten minutes left in Cory's shift when I'm done. I wander off to the restroom because I can't make a trip to Ozzy's without visiting stall number three. I slide the latch and touch the Sharpie words on the wall like I always do. There's a new sticker pressed right above my mom's name—a cartoon astronaut puking up a rainbow. I peel it off and throw it in the nonfunctional toilet so no one follows the lead of whoever stuck it there. It's bad enough the writing on the wall has begun to fade. I don't want it plastered over with stickers, too. *Thanks, baby.* It doesn't feel like my imagination. It's like Mom is right here with me, and that's what I wanted. That's why I came in here. "I'm sorry," I say aloud without specifying what for. She hated it when I did that, but I have too many things to be sorry for to name. I close my eyes, and I can see her. A living ghost. *Never assume an apology means you are forgiven.* She used to say that sometimes, and I can hear it so clearly now. I smile because somehow it feels good. Like punishment I deserve for getting into the messes I've gotten myself into. Thanks, Mom.

I exit the restroom, and someone leaves the men's room a second later. Their phone dings. An Android chime that sends a chill up my spine and transplants me back to the woods with Kira before we made it to the lake. I look over my shoulder, and it's him. Nate. The groundskeeper.

There's a moment of recognition before he nods. "Afternoon."

It could have been anyone out in the woods with us that night, and it may not be significant at all, but he feels like someone I should talk to. If it was him out there, or if he's been back since, it's possible he has seen Regret, too. But I miss the opportunity to speak to him. He's out the door before I can even gather my thoughts. It's okay, though. I make a mental note to get his contact information from John and I reenter the main dining room.

"Ready?" Cory asks, pulling his apron off. It's then I notice, with his arms stretched above his head, that he's . . . stronger . . . looking than he was the last time I really let myself take him in.

My cheeks heat when I realize I've taken a little too long to respond. I force my eyes away from his muscles and to his face, which is equally nice to look at. "Yep. I'm ready."

He disappears into the back and reappears a minute later.

Together we walk through the propped-open doors into the late-afternoon sunlight.

I check the schedule he emailed me last night. "First stop is . . . Mr. Otis?"

"Yep. He lives right up the street. I mow his grass for him in the summer. He's always out on his front porch this time of day, and he loves to talk."

We walk down the cracked sidewalk without saying much. Cory is clearly pumped to interview Mr. Otis and is probably tossing around questions to ask in his mind. I should be doing the same, and it's this realization that illuminates one flaw in my choice to rope Cory into my mess. I told him I did it because I needed a distraction. That was completely untrue, but Cory himself is a distraction. My attraction to him—which lingers despite everything—is a distraction. But pros and cons weighed, I'll accomplish more with him than without. So I break the silence. I eliminate the opportunity for my thoughts to go off track, and we trade some ideas back and forth about what to discuss with each person on the list until we come up on a narrow one-story house with a small front porch. Sure enough, there is an old man sitting there in a rocking chair with an iced tea in hand.

"Hi, Mr. Otis! It's me, Cory." He waves and then talks to me out of the side of his mouth. "His vision and hearing aren't too great anymore."

"Cory?" Mr. Otis stands up and squints at us. His entire body lights up once he confirms who has come to visit. "Well, I'll be. It's been a good minute, ain't it, son?"

"Yes, I'm sorry about that. Been busy with school and working at the pizza shop up the street."

"School? I thought you was a dropout."

Cory slaps the back of his neck. "Nope. Just homeschooled."

"Hm. Same difference if you ask me."

"Oh, don't let Grandma Bea hear you say that. She's the one doing my schooling."

Mr. Otis whistles. "My bad, son. I know better than to cross Ms. Beatrice Gooding. Who's that you got with you there?"

"This is my friend Simone."

He wags his cane in my direction. "Yes, yes. I know you. Tony Washington's little girl. How you doin', suga?"

"I'm good, thank you."

"Why don't y'all come on up here? 'Steada hollerin' from the sidewalk."

We join him on the porch, where he gives Cory a firm handshake and a slap on the back. He tips his newsboy hat to me. "What brings ya by?"

"Mr. Otis, do you remember that website I told you about? The one I run?"

"Sho' do." He sniffs and takes a swig of his tea. "You write articles about Fairville."

"Yes, exactly. Simone is helping me out with it, and we were hoping to interview you for the next entry."

He straightens up, clearly excited at the prospect of being interviewed. "Be happy to. Why don't y'all come on in for a bit? I'll get ya something to drink."

We follow Mr. Otis into his house. It's tidy. Not a thing out of place. There's a beautiful antique dresser in the hall that leads to the kitchen. Above it are shadow boxes filled with his military decorations and awards, along with old photographs.

He directs us to have a seat on the couch. "Tea, cola, or water?" he shouts on his way to the kitchen.

Cory shrugs, leaving it to me. "Tea, please," I answer, not missing Cory's slight grin at me remembering how much he loves it. How he never drinks it at home because he has no self-control with it.

Mr. Otis returns and passes us each a glass of sweet tea, rattling with fresh ice cubes. "So, what did y'all want to interview me about?"

"You've lived in Fairville all your life, right?" Cory asks.

"Born and raised. Spent some time in Korea when I was in the military, but Fairville is home."

"Do you remember when the CPRC was built? How old were you then?"

"Yeah, I remember." He leans back in his chair, thinking. "Oh boy, let's see . . . that had to be round what, 1957, 1958 they built that?"

"Yes, sir. 1957," I say.

"Then I would have been about fourteen years old. I remember the fuss everyone made. It was a big deal. Real exclusive, if you know what I mean." He taps the brown skin on the back of his hand. "But it wasn't just about color then. The CPRC was for rich folk only originally."

"Still is." Cory laughs.

My stomach tenses briefly at this gentle reminder of what Dad's NFL career has afforded me access to and what Cory's grandmother's teaching career did not. And I wonder if it's something harder for him to forget than it is for me.

"I didn't step foot inside the place until the mid-eighties after the grand reopening. That's when it became the Champlain Park and Recreation Center. Was the Champlain Country Club before that. 'A gathering place for the community.' That's what they advertised it as. But as you've pointed out, the change was in name only. Never did feel the community inside."

Cory opens his notebook and writes down the original name. "Mr. Otis, did you ever hear any stories about someone called Regret?"

He rubs his chin curiously. "I don't know nothing 'bout

nobody called Regret. But I did know of Ms. Evelyn Young. Wasn't no young man in town that didn't know of Ms. Evelyn."

Cory and I briefly make eye contact.

"Was that Regret's real name?"

"Again, I don't subscribe to all that nonsense. Folks was real cruel to that woman for no reason, and you two shouldn't go 'round calling her out of her name. Where'd you hear that anyway? Ain't heard mention of Regret in a decade at the least."

"I saw something someone had written inside a book about Fairville history."

"That's some history that needs to stay in the past."

"You don't have to tell us about that if you don't want to, Mr. Otis," Cory says.

I kick his ankle. He flinches and opens his eyes wide, silently asking me to trust him.

"But maybe you could just tell us about Ms. Evelyn? I bet she'd appreciate her story getting told outside of . . . whatever led to people calling her that."

"Look, I'll be straight with you. I didn't know her well myself. She had to be a good five years my senior, but I tell you what, I wanted to marry her just as much as the next fella. Fine as cherry wine, that one was. A little quiet and introverted, I heard. Got her a place on the outskirts of town and at one point was only really showing her face over at Fairville First Baptist on Sunday mornings. She vanished without a trace one day."

"Do you know what happened to her?" I ask, feeling eager and hopeful that I might get all the answers I need right now.

He lifts his cap, revealing wisps of cottony white hair. "There were rumors, and I won't indulge them. I do know she went and got her heart broke, though. That wasn't a secret to nobody."

"Do you know who broke her heart?"

He nods. "Her best friend, Violet Savoie. Them Savoies was probably the richest Black family in town at the time. Evelyn came from more humble means. Not a pair you'd expect to get on, but they did for a good long while."

"What happened?" I ask.

"Tale as old as time of course. Violet Savoie stole her man. They'd been friends far longer than she'd been dating that snake Willie Thompson, so it was her betrayal that hurt most."

I lower my gaze to my lap, disgustingly familiar with that particular brand of betrayal. But Regret knows what I did and seemed bored with it. If Violet really did steal her boyfriend, I'm going to go out on a limb and say sometime between now and seventy years ago, she got over it. "Mr. Otis, did you hear anything about a curse?"

He pushes his glasses up on his face. "Folks wanted to carry on about curses and witchcraft and all sorts of ridiculous shenanigans, but as I say, sweet Ms. Evelyn was a churchgoing woman! I believe the poor girl just skipped town and never looked back."

"What sort of witchcraft were people saying she was into?" I ask.

Mr. Otis shakes his head. "Honey, I ain't even know there were different kinds. You gon' have to ask somebody else if you want to hear more about that. I don't dabble in that mess. I'm too close to the finish line to go getting myself into funky shit now." He cackles. "And fine ol' Ms. Evelyn certainly don't deserve the gossip. I wonder if she's on the Facebook." He contemplates this for a moment. "She'd be pushin' ninety by now, though. Might be on to rest with her Maker, bless her." He slaps his knee and stands. "It was nice of y'all to come on by and chat for a spell, but I need to get ready for spades night with my boys."

Cory laughs. "Do you need a ride?"

"No, no, thank you. My nephew should be here any minute."

He walks us to the door. "Y'all take care. Don't you be no stranger, Cory!"

"I won't! Thank you, sir!"

Cory's walk has even more pep to it as we head back in the direction of the pizza shop. "That was really helpful."

"Was it?"

He stops short. "Are you kidding? We got a name out of the very first conversation. Three! Regret, the best friend, *and* the boyfriend. That's elite."

"But we need more than names. We need a story. We need to know what happened to her."

"We'll figure it out. Just be patient. The fun is in the research."

I puff out some air and push my braids out of my face. This is anything but fun, and I don't have time to be patient.

CHAPTER 17

At home, I walk up the steps to the side door, replaying the information we got from Mr. Otis. Cory is right, three names are worth something, but I'm afraid the story will spiral out in a dozen different directions that I won't have enough time to explore. I put my key in the lock, but before I can turn it, the faint sound of a girlish giggle freezes me in place. I move only my eyes, looking to my left and right for the source of the sound. After a few seconds of silence, I go to turn the key—

"Hi! I'm Gabby Greta, and I love you!"

I scream and jolt so hard my keys go flying into the yard. I peer around the corner of the house where our trash can lies on its side. Gabby Greta is there, moving in that staccato way, rusty gears grinding.

"I'm Gabby Greta! Can you count to . . . ten?"

"Yes!" I shout at her. "Yes, I can count to ten." I storm over to the trash can and right it. "Yes, I know how much time I have left! I don't need your creepy-ass reminders!" I shove the doll and a bulging white kitchen bag deep into the can, slam it shut, and roll it out to the curb for pickup tomorrow.

I'm so on edge as I walk back down the driveway that I scream again when I see Dad's head poking out the door.

"Simone! Baby, what's wrong with you?" He scans the yard. "Who were you talking to?"

"That stupid doll!"

The concern on Dad's face grows exponentially. "You were talking to . . . a doll?"

"She talked to me first." I drop to my hands and knees to search the grass for my keys.

"Simone, honey—"

"I'm fine, Dad," I say, lying through my teeth. "I threw that doll I brought back from the lake in the trash, and it started talking again. Scared me."

"Oh." He laughs, clearly still concerned. "Well, are you hungry? I made dinner."

I find my keys, shake the dirt off them, and stand. As Gabby Greta so kindly reminded me, I don't have time for things like worried fathers to slow me down. I need to take this opportunity to get him off my back. Hell, maybe he can even help me. "Yeah. Dinner sounds good."

We enter the house and I spy a big casserole dish with bubbling cheese on top. Lasagna won't be a good move for my stomach after the pizza I ate not too long ago, but I guess my digestive system is just going to have to take one for the team.

We both fix our plates. Dad walks to the couch, and I grab a soda from the fridge before sitting down next to him.

"Oh, I thought you'd take your plate upstairs. Should we sit at the table?" Dad's eyes absolutely sparkle, and it makes me feel bad for not spending more time with him. And for doing it with ulterior motives now.

I pop open my can and take a sip, playing it as cool as I can. "No, no. This is great."

After a couple of minutes of pretending to watch the car restoration show he has on TV, I clear my throat. "Hey, Dad, do you remember a family with the last name Young when you were growing up?"

He scratches his cheek and looks up at the ceiling. "Doesn't ring a bell. Why?"

"How about Savoie or Thompson?"

"There are five different Thompson families in town right now, so you'd have to be more specific there, but I do remember a Savoie. Older gentleman. Owned a tackle shop."

"Do you remember his first name?"

Dad frowns. "No. But he'll have passed on by now. Quick stroll through the cemetery might get you what you're looking for."

"Why didn't I think of that sooner?" Cory and I should have had that at the top of our locations list. I put my plate on the table and stand, patting around for my phone.

"Aht. Hold on. I know you don't think you're about to run off to the cemetery by yourself. It'll be dark soon."

"No, I wasn't going to do that," I lie. "I was just gonna go upstairs and tell Cory—" I bite my tongue as soon as his name escapes my mouth.

"Cory Gooding? Haven't heard that name in a while. Y'all let bygones be bygones?"

My instinct is to lie again, but people are bound to spot us around town together. "Yeah . . . I . . . he . . ."

"You don't have to explain it, Sim. And for what it's worth, I'm glad. I'm glad you're talking with someone who truly understands what you're going through."

I flinch. "I'm not going through anything, Dad." I mean, I am. I definitely am, but not what he thinks I'm going through. He thinks I've reconnected with Cory because of Rich, and I guess technically, in a twisted way, that is true. But I know Dad's view of it is so far from my reality. Dad can't see the difference between the loss of Trenton and the loss of Rich when the way I actually feel about those two things are on planes so far apart you could fit a solar system between them. But I can't let it show. How wrong he has this. I rub my forehead. "I'm sorry. It just took me a lot to reach out to Cory, and I don't really want to talk about it. He and I aren't talking about anything deep, either. I'm just helping him with this blog he runs. That's why I was asking about those families." I wave my hands around my head. "You know. Something to keep my mind occupied."

"Fair enough. Go on and put that plate in the dishwasher before you go upstairs."

I do as he says, then dart up to my room and go straight to Google, seeing what I can find through some generic searches. I don't text Cory about the cemetery. I wait a few hours until Dad's all hooked up to his CPAP machine in bed and slip quietly out the back door.

Sneaking out to a cemetery at night after a spooky encounter with a haunted doll has to be in some what-not-do-in-a-horror-movie handbook somewhere. But this isn't a horror movie; it's my life. And desperate times call for desperate measures. I stop in the garage to grab a heavy-duty flashlight, then hop on my bike and pedal out into the road. The streets around this side of town are well lit, and the lanes are wide, but I still feel a rush of adrenaline when I ride at night—the scary kind, not the excited kind. A car approaches from behind me, the headlights illuminating the area around me even more. It passes, giving me an extra-wide berth. But again, I can't help but think of Trenton and what his final moments must have been like. That street was, and still is, so dark and narrow. There are no sidewalks at all. In the summer, vegetation encroaches so close on the road that pedestrians have to choose between playing a balancing game on the curb or walking in the street. It's not a high-traffic area. Just a lonely residential road. But it doesn't need to be high traffic. It only takes one car at the wrong time. One old man not paying careful enough attention. I grip my handlebars tighter and pump my legs faster, releasing a bit of trapped rage. I'm sweating by the time I reach the cemetery.

I rest my bike against the stone archway entrance. A floodlight sits above the door to the visitor center and is bright enough to illuminate the first couple of rows of graves, but there is darkness beyond that. I wonder if there are cameras. The posted sign says visiting hours are dawn until dusk, but there's no gate or locks, so I stride through. A chill passes over me as the light breeze brushes against my sweat-dampened neck. I'm keenly aware that the last time I stepped foot in this place was for Trenton's funeral.

The deeper I travel inside, the more mature the trees. The larger shadows they cast. Spindly dark streaks across the cobblestone now merge into large swaths of blackness. The mystery of the emptiness is more terrifying than the nature-made Rorschach tests from moments ago. I take out my flashlight and turn it on. It flickers and I bang it hard against my palm until the stream of light steadies.

The pathway arcs upward, and at the top of the hill sits the Pearson family plot. The spot where Rich will be buried is already covered with flowers and cards, which seems wrong to me somehow. It seems like bad luck to decorate a grave site before a body has been placed there. But how much worse could Rich's luck get? If his death could even be attributed to bad luck in the first place. If anything, it's *my* bad luck that led to this. He and I had our issues, but I didn't wish him dead. I just wanted him exposed, which may or may not have had everything to do with guilt over my own sins. Maybe it really was the projection of my shame that sent Kira tumbling into that water. And it set a domino effect in motion where Rich ended up being the last piece.

I take a few steps toward his plot. The snap of a twig behind me makes me whip around, the beam from my flashlight throwing light chaotically, making it seem as if things are moving in the shadows. Dipping and diving behind bushes and headstones. I take a deep, steadying breath and go examine the things left on his plot. One handmade card catches my eye, and I pick it up for a closer look. That same sticker I saw in the bathroom at Ozzy's—the rainbow-vomiting astronaut—is stuck to the bottom of it. I inspect the sticker more carefully. There's a patch on the astronaut's arm of a rocket ship and what looks like the signature of the artist in the bottom corner, but it's too blurry to make out. I open the card. *We'll miss you like crazy dude* is the only thing written on it. I put it back and start my original mission.

It doesn't take long for me to find a Savoie. Three of the more extravagant headstones in the cemetery belong to them. I don't find Violet's, but I do notice a sharp drop-off in the family's fancy grave markers around the 1940s and I wonder if a change in taste or a change in funds was responsible. I take another loop around the grounds, searching for any Youngs, but after half an hour spent looking, I find nothing. The astronaut sticker in Rich's card felt significant, though. So on my way out I stop back by and snap a picture of it.

CHAPTER 18

I sleep through my alarm in the morning and tear out of bed when I realize what time it is. On the way to my dresser, I trip over the gift basket my friends gave me for my birthday. I go to push it aside when something catches my eye. It's the back of a small canvas painting and written on the wooden stretcher bars is *For my bestie on her 18th*. I smile, turn it to the front, and almost just as quickly drop it on the floor. It's a photorealistic painting of me and Kira. I remember that day perfectly. I remember the exact moment Rich snapped the picture she used as a reference. She'd just found out she'd received a scholarship for art school. I threw my arms around her neck for a hug and then we cheesed for the camera. The painting is near perfect—only in real life, I wasn't holding a knife to her throat. In real life, blood didn't drip down her shirt in the shape of the number nine.

I don't allow fear to take over. This is obviously my new normal, at least for the next nine days. I pick up the painting and place it on full display on my dresser. Serling hops up and sniffs it, nudging it with his forehead, probably picking up on Kira's scent. I throw on some clothes and when I glance at the painting one more time before leaving my room, it looks just as it's supposed to. A beautiful piece of my best friend's art. All gore and violence gone.

Dad, who conveniently overslept too, drives me to school. I stare out the window, playing back Regret's cruel reminders of how quickly time is passing. A seed of doubt sprouts in my stomach. *Make a deal and you're in her debt.* How do I know Regret will even hold up her end of the deal if I free her? She's clearly an angry ... entity. She might be bitter and petty too. Or maybe she's just desperate. Maybe she's hurt. I need to figure out which before it's time to confront her again, because that's the one moment when I'll actually hold some power.

I read a couple of texts from Cory as I walk into school an hour late. He's confirming our plans to meet later and exchange what we discovered during our independent research, which unfortunately on my end isn't much.

"HEY, Simone!" someone whisper-shouts at my back on my way to lunch.

I slow down, debating if I should even bother turning around.

"Sim! Over here!"

I spot Jeremiah poking his head out of the abandoned science classroom. He motions for me to come inside.

The look on his face concerns me. "What's going on, Jere?" I follow him into the room.

He closes the door and fidgets anxiously. "Have you heard?"

I absorb his nervous energy, and I hate it. "No. I have no idea what you're talking about. Can you get to it?"

"People are saying Rich's toxicology report came back."

"What people?" I ask, not even needing to clarify if it showed something unexpected because he wouldn't be sweating bullets right now if it didn't.

"I heard it from Cam first, but there's this junior, his mom works at the lab where they process all that stuff. Apparently, he overheard her talking or something. There was alcohol in his system, which we already knew. Some marijuana. But also GHB. I'm talking dangerously high levels. Suspiciously high."

"What's GHB?"

"Liquid X. That stuff can mess you up good."

Immediately I wonder if some of it somehow got into *my* system and if it could cause hallucinations, but I push the thought aside. While a party drug could explain what I experienced that night, I'm positive no one has been following me around and drugging me every day since. "Did you give it to him?"

"Hell no! That's why I wanted to talk to you. I know people are gonna be looking at me, but all I've ever brought to anybody's party is liquor." He tilts his head to the side. "Okay and maybe some edibles here or there, but I don't mess with that kind of stuff. I don't know anyone who does, which is why I wanted to ask you . . ."

"Ask me what, Jere?"

"That dude—the one who delivered the pizzas. Do you know anything about him?"

I hate myself for hesitating. For defaulting straight back to the world where I pretend Cory and I are pretty much strangers. "I know he didn't bring drugs to the party, if that's what you're asking."

"But how—"

"Any chance Rich brought it himself?" I interject because I cannot stand to listen to Jere make Cory out to be a suspect.

"Nah, that was my boy. He didn't do stuff like that, either."

"Everyone has secrets."

"Oh, I'm sure he had secrets." His eyes linger on mine a second too long before he continues. "I don't think hard drugs was one of them, but what the hell do I know? It doesn't matter anyway because Rich bringing it himself is not the story people are spreading. They're all like, 'Who does party drugs alone?' and talking like one of us killed him or something."

I think about that dropper bottle I found in Kira's bag. The one I assumed was a laxative. The one labeled LX. And I know. I feel it deep in my bones. That vial held the drugs that ended up in Rich's system. There were ample opportunities for anyone at the party to sneak up to the loft and take the vial. But I can't ignore the fact that it was in Kira's bag to start with. "Jere, the only people you need to be concerned about talking are the police. Have they said anything?"

"No, not yet."

"Okay, so don't make this into something until it's actually something. I have to go."

I leave the science room and walk straight out the back doors of the school. I need to talk to Kira. Right now. I'm nervous after last time, but my deadline isn't here yet. Kira should technically be safe until then. I don't think she would intentionally hurt Rich, but for all I know, Regret could have used Kira as some kind of . . . vessel to do her bidding. The more truth I can grasp about that night, the easier it should be to piece everything together.

I'm relieved to find only Kira's car in the Davises' driveway. I grab the spare key from its hiding spot and enter the home, hoping today isn't the day that Mrs. Davis decides to pay attention to her video doorbell notifications. I quietly climb the stairs and jump when I reach the top and find Kira standing in her doorway.

"What are you doing in here?" She looks awful, and she has on the same shirt she was wearing on Monday.

"I need to talk to you."

"I tried talking to you the other day, but you suddenly decided you weren't in the mood."

"I'm sorry. I told you. I wasn't feeling good. A little grace, maybe? Considering everything."

She sighs and steps aside. "Grace granted."

I enter her bedroom. "It stinks in here, Kira."

"If you get grace, I get a double serving." She opens the window as wide as it will go. A stiff breeze shifts the stale air. "Have you heard?" she asks, starting off exactly the way Jeremiah did. "What people have been saying about Rich's autopsy report?"

"Yes. And I knew if people were blowing you up before this, that it'd be worse now. Are you okay?"

"No, Simone! Of course I'm not okay."

"I know. I'm sorry. That was stupid. But there is something else I really do have to ask. . . ."

She crosses her arms. "And what's that?"

"His toxicology report. The drugs found in his system."

She simply raises an eyebrow, waiting.

"Kira, you were the last one with him. You said yourself you—"

"I *loved* him, Simone. What the hell are you trying to say right now?"

"I'm not saying you did anything, but . . ." I run my hands down the length of my braids, tugging lightly when I get to the ends. "Can you just . . . sit down for a second?"

She doesn't move an inch.

"Kira," I say, voice low. "I found a bottle of something in your stuff while you were at the football game."

Her eye twitches just slightly. "Why were you in my things?"

"Because you're a slob, and I was cleaning up. But that's beside the point."

She shrugs. "So what, you think I had some ecstasy? Where the hell would I get that? I haven't so much as touched an edible, Simone. You know that! The only pills I had in my bag were Tylenol and birth control."

I open my mouth to speak but pause. She said "pill." GHB, *liquid* X, is not a pill . . . and from what I googled on the way over, it's not even the same drug as ecstasy. I feel stupid and ashamed. "I'm sorry," I say.

"Nuh-uh. You don't get off that easy. Tell me what you think you saw."

I sigh. "No. I'm sorry. It—it was probably just . . . Gas-X or something."

She stares at me blankly for a few seconds, one hand firmly on her hip, the other pointing at her bag in the closet. "Gas-X?" The right side of her mouth quivers. "Gas— Simone, I—" She snorts violently, then slaps her hand over her mouth before bursting into hysterical laughter.

I watch her in shock for a few seconds, and then a few giggles escape my mouth, too. Before I know it, we are both rolling on her bed, gripping our stomachs, tears streaming down our faces, laughing so hard that no sound emanates from either of us. We make a few failed attempts to compose ourselves before finally settling. We look up at the glow-in-the-dark stars on her ceiling, breathing hard before Kira is overcome by a different variety of tears.

"Hey." I sit up and stroke some stray curls away from her forehead. "It's okay."

She draws her wrist under her nose as she sniffs. "I know you don't really think you saw Gas-X in my bag. But I'm telling you, I didn't put anything else in there. I—" She freezes for a second or two before launching herself off the bed and over to her closet. She upturns her bag, allowing the contents to scatter across the floor, much like they were at the cabin. She sifts through everything—way too much stuff for a single night away from home—and comes up with a medium-sized black toiletries bag. She holds it in the air like I'm supposed to know what it is. She wiggles the bag for emphasis. "It's Rich's!"

"What?"

"Last Wednesday night, my parents were out of town, so he snuck over here and stayed the night. He left this here and asked me to throw it in my bag so he'd have it at the cabin."

She hurries back to the bed and dumps the contents onto her messy quilt. A razor. Men's cologne. A comb. A couple of condoms. A toothbrush . . . No dropper bottle with LX on it, though. But of course there wouldn't be. It's all inside Rich's body.

I look at Kira, expression as gentle as I can make it, before taking her hand in my own. "Kir . . ."

She looks up at me, eyes so innocent. She hasn't connected the dots. She's not asking herself the important questions yet.

"Kir, do you think Rich had GHB in that bag?"

Her eyes darken. "Wha— No! Why would . . . ? He wouldn't. *He* was drugged."

"Something could have gotten mixed up. Maybe he was going to—"

"No." She shakes her head. "No, Simone. Rich was a lot of things, but I know you're not insinuating—"

"Stop, Kira. Just wait a second before this gets blown out of proportion. I'm not about to pretend like I know exactly what went down." I have absolutely no clue how all of this fits in with what happened by that lake. Every new thing I learn just complicates it further, and I only have a few days to unravel this mess. "I'm not insinuating anything. I asked about a bottle. You said it wasn't yours, and then you showed me Rich's bag. My question was the next most obvious thing."

"There's some other explanation if it was his, Simone. He wouldn't hurt anyone."

He would take advantage of someone, though. I know that firsthand. How far he'd let that go, I don't know, but he was no knight in shining armor.

Kira collapses onto her side, clutching the black pouch to her chest. It makes me nauseous to see her cry over him this way, to see just how deeply she was connected to him. My usual composed mask must slip. She must read it on my face because her eyes narrow, and she lets out a sarcastic laugh.

"You don't get it. You never will. You've never lost anyone you cared about the way I cared about Rich."

Heat rushes to my face. "Have you forgotten that I haven't seen my mom in two years?"

She sits up. "Your mom is not dead! You're just being stubborn. You could go to her if you really wanted. And I don't understand how that's not the first thing you did, how you wouldn't be eager to make that right after Rich."

"God, you sound like my dad." My brain assaults me with lightning-quick flashes of disjointed memories. Mom pulling up home late from work. Her mumbling, exhausted as she climbs the stairs to bed. An email, subject line: *Concern regarding Camille Washington*. "Why should I be the one to make it right? *She's* the mom. *She* left."

"My point is that you have options, Simone."

"Not with Trenton, I don't."

"With who?"

My teeth grind against each other. I hate that question. *With who?* That emphasis on the *who* that screams the insignificance of that person in their life. I hate the look on people's faces when they ask. I hate the look on Kira's face. I shift my jaw and bite my tongue.

"What is wrong with you, Simone?" she asks, the same stupid expression on her face.

"Trenton Jones." I do my best to keep my voice even. A light fragrance wafts through her open window. Familiar. Sweet. Leathery.

"Trenton? That kid who— Simone, you didn't even know him." Her eyebrows press together.

"Yes, I did. The summer my family was falling apart, he was here, and you weren't."

"You didn't say a thing about what was going on with your parents until summer was over. Was I supposed to read your mind? Ms. Simone, the self-proclaimed emotional vault? You act like you're this private little thing who can't stand any attention, but I'm starting to see through it. You can't even let me grieve my boyfriend without making it all about you."

She's pushing my worst buttons, and if it's her goal to get under my skin, it's working. "Rich wasn't your boyfriend. You dumped him." It feels like someone stuck their arm down my throat and ripped the words from some ugly place deep inside me. I can see the pain on Kira's face and know they are words I can never take back. In my head, I am sorry. I'm confused. But in my bones, in my skin, in my stomach, in my muscles—all I feel is rage. My fists clench at my sides. Kira is speaking. Shouting. But the only thing I hear is a high-pitched ringing. Again I want to press my hand over her mouth. Silence her. I take a quick step toward her, and something flashes in her eyes. Fear. I have never hurt Kira. Not in any way she's aware of. I take an anxious step backward, Regret's voice now the only sound I hear. *By your hand. By your hand. By your hand.* I turn and run out of the Davis house, not even bothering to pull the front door shut behind me.

CHAPTER 19

I run until I make it around the corner, heaving for air. Again, all the anger I felt toward Kira evaporates with the distance between us. The fury that clouded my mind and threatened to control my body only minutes ago is nowhere to be found. I rest against a tree, still breathing hard. I have to stay away from her. Regret may have *said* something bad would happen only if I don't make the deadline, but that's not how it *feels*. If I'm not near Kira, I can't get angry at her. If I'm not near her, I can't hurt her. It helps that she won't want to see me anyway. Not after what I said. And she said some cruel things too. Outside of the funeral, keeping away shouldn't be too difficult.

I walk home, hands on top of my head, stitch in my side. Serling greets me at the door, purring and rubbing against my calf. I grab a couple of treats for him and a bottle of water for myself before plopping onto the couch. The last text Cory sent me this morning was asking if I wanted him to pick me up from school at the end of the day.

Me
Actually, could you come get me from my house now-ish?

Cory
You left school? Why?

Me
Can you come? I'll explain then

Cory
on my way

Ten minutes later I climb into the passenger seat of Cory's truck. "Hey. Sorry for being so vague over text." What I have to share isn't the sort of thing I want in writing.

"It's okay. What's up?"

"Rumors have started going around about Rich's autopsy results."

"Wait, what? I thought his death was already ruled an accident."

"No. It was believed to be an accident. And for all I know, it still is. The police haven't said anything, but apparently, they found a lot of drugs in his system."

"What kind of drugs?"

I drum my fingers on my thighs. "GHB."

"GHB? As in the date—"

"Yep."

"Do people take that like . . . for fun . . . or is it just . . . ?"

"Yeah. I mean, I had to google it, but yeah. He could have taken it for fun. Only no one else who was there admits to taking anything with him. He wasn't the type to party alone."

"So, do you think someone gave it to him?"

A wicked witch in the woods. A jealous Shaina. A possessed version of myself. A possessed Kira. A heartbroken Kira, now stuck in denial. "I don't know. I went to bed before everyone else, but even after that, no one remembers him being high. He definitely wasn't passing anyone's Breathalyzer test, but he wasn't blackout level."

"And it seems unlikely that he'd randomly get up in the middle of the night and take a bunch of drugs by himself."

"Right. But apparently GHB leaves your system really quickly, so he had to have taken it not long before he died. Shaina heard him and Kira fighting after everyone went to sleep. And Kira admitted that herself. It was all caught on the security cameras. That was enough to make Shaina suspicious of her from the jump, but I'm sure this new info has her frothing at the mouth with accusations. I just came back from Kira's place. Tried to talk to her about it, but it turned into another argument."

"What do you think happened?"

I fiddle with the strings of my hoodie. I want to be completely honest with him. I want to replay every second of what happened at Kira's. At the lake. Let him dissect it for me. Give me his opinions. But it feels so wrong to let him in on my shame. It feels wrong to tell him things Kira shared with me in confidence. Things I cruelly threw back in her face. She might not ever forgive me, but I can't betray her that way. Not again. That's what separated me from Rich. I'd never, ever betray her again. "I don't know, Cory. Kira isn't acting herself, and I'm not acting myself, either. Everything is really confusing. Can we just . . . ?"

"Left turn?"

"Yeah." I nod. "I didn't find out much about Evelyn, Willie, or Violet. Well, except that maybe all that money Mr. Otis said the Savoies had ran out. Not sure that's useful info for us though. Did you find anything?"

He stops at a red light. "No, but we've got a visit to Tandy's Thrifted Treasures on our schedule today. She's the self-proclaimed town historian. Grandma says she's just a gossip, but that could be helpful, too. At the very least, she might be able to answer some questions that will get us going in the right direction."

"Okay. Let's go now."

Five minutes later, we enter the shop. It's uncomfortably warm and smells like mothballs and Pine-Sol, but Ms. Tandy greets us with a wide smile.

"Back again so soon?" she asks Cory.

"Oh, you know I can't stay away too long, Ms. Tandy."

She swats a dustrag in his direction. "Anything in particular y'all looking for?"

"No, actually, we were hoping to talk to you."

She throws her hands on her hips, curious. "Oh yeah? What about?"

Cory looks to me.

"Hi, Ms. Tandy, I'm Simone." I offer my hand, and she shakes it. "Cory and I have been doing some research for his urban legend blog."

"Oh, that sounds like a good time. How can I help?"

"We were wondering if you ever knew someone named Evelyn Young."

"Knew her, no. Knew *of* her, yes. That woman had a hard life. I assume since her name came up in relation to your urban legend blog, you've got questions about how she earned that infamous nickname of hers."

"Yes!" I take a deep breath, calm myself. "Yes, ma'am. Can you tell us what you know about it?"

She rests her elbows on the glass display case. "Evelyn Ruth Young was her given name. Beautiful woman she was. In fact, I might have some photos."

My eyes nearly bulge out of the sockets. "Wait, for real?"

"Yes, I've had a few photo albums end up in book donation boxes. I never had the heart to throw them out, but of course they don't sell. Let me pop back for a minute and see if I can find them," she says, already walking away.

"Nice!" Cory stage-whispers. "Exclusive photos for the next entry would be a first."

I can't even respond to him. I don't want to talk about the stupid blog when I might be seconds away from seeing Regret as she was when she was living. Possibly surrounded by other people who might help me connect some dots. A picture's worth a thousand words.

"I think she's coming back!" I say, stretching my neck at the first sign of movement from behind the curtain to the storeroom.

"Found them!" Ms. Tandy calls in a singsong voice. She reappears with a thick reddish-brown photo album and opens it to a page near the end. "Now, she's just caught in the background of this photo at the annual summer cookout we used to have. I was only a girl, but I stayed in everybody's business. Never was ashamed of it. That's how you keep folks alive long after they're gone. Here. Take a look."

I pull the album to me, unconcerned with whether Cory can see. My eyes don't focus at first, bouncing from person to person, looking for a familiar face. But the face wouldn't be familiar, not exactly. The person I saw in the woods would have been a warped version of whoever she used to be. So I consider Ms. Tandy's words—and Mr. Otis's comments—and scan the sepia-toned image for a young woman who might have attracted some admiring eyes around town. I tap on a woman toward the right side with my index finger. "Her?"

"Yep. Such a lovely air about her."

She wears a pale, collared short-sleeved dress that hits mid-calf with a matching hat that casts a slight shadow over her smirking face. Her dark hair is neatly curled, and her full lips are stained with dark lipstick. And when I look closely, I can see how that face was hidden behind what I saw at the lake that night. The one I saw was so frightening, but I guess I'm not the only one with a collection of masks.

"Look at that fella next to her," Ms. Tandy says. "Smitten as can be."

Ms. Tandy is right. There's a tall brown-skinned man with a paperboy hat and gleaming white teeth beaming at Regre—Evelyn. She was Evelyn then. I glance at Cory, certain he's thinking what I'm thinking.

"Is that Willie Thompson?" he asks.

"Oh, I'm not sure, darlin'. Wasn't a young man in town who didn't want to get into Ms. Evelyn's good graces. Could be anyone. But she was a bit of a free spirit. Not interested in being tied down."

Well, she's certainly tied down now. No wonder she's so angry.

"Do you mind if I record our conversation, Ms. Tandy?" Cory asks.

Her cheeks round with a grin. "Of course not, baby. Don't want to be misquoted on your blog!" She waits until Cory gets his phone set up and takes out his pen and notepad. "All set?"

We both nod.

"Everyone knew Evelyn was an independent outdoorsy type. Wouldn't be odd to catch her barefoot prancing through the fields. I'm sure she right about drove her mother up a wall with that. One of the most eligible young women in Fairville with a taste for freedom. Some whimsy. My auntie said when Evelyn finished high school she went and built herself a teeny little cabin by the lake and lived off the land best she could, but she'd come into town for supplies now and again."

"Yearwood Lake?" Cory asks.

"It wasn't Yearwood Lake yet. They didn't purchase the land until a few years later. Wasn't called Doll's Head, either. That didn't happen until Evelyn came to be known as Regret. It was just 'the lake' then. Just nature. Unclaimed."

"How'd Evelyn come to be known as Regret?" I ask.

"I'm getting there, I'm getting there. But I do need to start with a small disclaimer and say I'm glad this is an urban legend blog you're interviewing me for. I love Fairville history, but it's important to differentiate between facts and speculation. I'm sharing the story I heard whispered 'round town the most, knowing much of it can't be true, but it sure is interesting."

"Why can't it be true?"

"For one, people say Evelyn was into . . . let's call it . . . magic. Sounds nicer than"—she drops her voice to a whisper—"witchcraft. Sounds nicer, but still don't make it real," she adds, returning to normal volume. "Anyway. Way I heard 'em tell it was she fell hard for this fella taking over his daddy's convenience store. Like so many young folk of the time, they started themselves a love affair that ended with her expecting a little one."

"Do you know how old she was then?"

Ms. Tandy juts out her bottom lip, thinking. "Eighteen? Nineteen? The young man's parents did all they could to convince him she was no good and that the baby wasn't his. I doubt he believed that, but I guess he was too much of a coward to stand up to them. So Evelyn went back into them woods and had that baby on her own. 'Bout two years later, the young man's mother passed on, and she'd been the main one trying to keep them apart. So the lovebirds rekindled things. Apparently, one day, they had a date and were so caught up with each other they didn't see that the little one had snuck off outside. Poor thing was lost to the lake and she never forgave herself. Flew into a nasty rage and swore she'd curse anybody who came near her land again. Especially her old lover. Over time, kids started to dare each other to go out there, and the baby doll and toy offerings became a thing. The legend was the baby doll would protect you because she loved babies and leaving one with her when you visited was a kindness to a woman riddled with regret."

"Wow. Thank you for sharing all of that, Ms. Tandy," Cory says.

"No problem. You just make sure you come on by and let me know when my interview is published so I can see my name on the World Wide Web!"

"Of course." He points behind himself. "We're just going to take a look around the shop. See what new things you got in."

"Oh! Wait, I think I've got something you'd like. . . ."

Ms. Tandy and Cory walk to a corner of the shop with old books, and I drift toward the other side of the store, processing all this new information. I pass by an aisle filled with toys, and something catches my eye—something that makes the hairs on the back of my neck stand on end. I stop in my tracks, the object blurred, barely visible in my periphery. As I turn to confirm what I already know, a sound starts up.

Click. Click. Click.

"No," I breathe, facing Gabby Greta head-on as her scuffed limbs grind and whir.

I am overcome with panic because even after everything Ms. Tandy just told us, after everything we've learned, I'm not any closer to figuring out how to actually *free* Regret. Walking up to her and telling her the *Gossip Girl* version of her life story isn't going to cut it.

"Cory!" I call. I'm running out of time. I have to tell him everything. I need his urgency behind this with me.

"Simone?" He appears a few seconds after I hear his voice. "What's wrong?" He follows my gaze to the doll. "Oh, damn. That's . . . something out of a nightmare."

"Hi! I'm Gabby Greta, and I love you!"

"And it talks!" Cory laughs, quirking his head in fascination.

Ms. Tandy gasps and comes shuffling over to us. "It works! I tried for hours to fix that thing!"

"I—I want to buy it," I say.

Cory frowns. "You want to buy it? You seem terrified of it."

"I need it." I snatch it off the shelf.

"Hold on, sugar. Now that I know it works, I gotta do some research. Functional, that thing might be worth a pretty coin." She tugs it from my hands. "Not for sale just yet. Sorry darlings." She studies the doll. "Oh my goodness, how I wanted one of these when I was a girl."

The doll's speaker box crackles. "Can you count to . . . nine?"

Reminder after reminder. "Five days gone already," I say absently to Cory, knowing he won't understand.

"Oh, they must have made an advanced version," Ms. Tandy chuckles. "This one didn't get marketed in my neck of the woods. We got 123 ABC. Who knew Gabby Greta did algebra?"

Cory laughs. "Now, Ms. Tandy, since when is counting to nine algebra?"

"Cory, I've wasted too much time. I need to go. Please. Just . . . Ms. Tandy, how much do you want for the doll? I'll pay whatever you want."

A trace of irritation crosses her face. "Baby, I just told you I don't know yet. You can come on back in a few days, and we can talk then."

"But I—"

"Hey." Cory gently swipes a braid away from my face with his thumb and the feel of his skin against mine is bizarrely soothing. "Take a breath. Actually, go get some air. Wait for me outside."

"I need—"

"I got you. Go ahead."

I hurry out of the store, and Cory was right. The fresh air

feels good. A few minutes later he walks out with the doll tucked under his arm.

"How did you—"

"Just because you're resistant to my charm doesn't mean everyone else is."

"I'm not—"

He raises an eyebrow. "What's that?"

"Nothing. Thank you for the doll. Can you take me home?"

"Sure. After you tell me what got you so worked up in there."

"I will. When we get to my house."

CHAPTER 20

Cory and I sit on my back porch in silence. I didn't speak to him on the drive over, either, but he hasn't pushed. He stares out at the garage, a curious expression on his face. He's good at entertaining himself and would wait as long as I need to get this conversation started. If it were anyone else, I might take it as disinterest or avoidance. One of those things where people ask you what's wrong but don't actually want to know. Where they are happy to delay the conversation for their own comfort. It's hard to say if Cory's patience is something reserved for me or if it's just a general feature of his personality.

"I want to tell you everything. Need to, honestly. But I feel bad. It feels wrong to bog you down. To rope you into all of my drama, especially after keeping my distance for so long."

Cory pushes his twists away from his forehead and sinks deeper into his chair. "I hate when you do this." His tone is gentle.

"Do what?"

"Act like you're the only one who has ever done anything wrong. Like you're the only one with secrets. Like the nearly two years we went without having a proper conversation was all your doing. You put me on a pedestal, but you're smart, Simone. If you really thought about it, you'd understand why I enjoy your company so much. Or one of the reasons, at least."

He pauses, waiting for me to fill in, I guess, but I have no idea what he's talking about.

"Birds of a feather," he says. "Chip off the old block. Cut from the same cloth. Kindred spirit. Two sides of the same coin. You've always made me feel seen, which is both terrifying and . . . kind of the best thing ever."

If I wasn't positive that there were things I could tell him that'd make him eat his words, if I wasn't currently on the most horrifying deadline of my life, I'd lean over and kiss him.

"The doll," I say instead, a move that, for me, is equally as vulnerable. "A guy found it in the woods at my party and gave it to me. And I know this sounds weird when you look at the thing, but I felt . . . I guess you could say *pulled* to take it home with me. So I did. But it wasn't long before it started to creep me out."

He lifts Gabby Greta from the table in front of us and inspects it. "You seemed surprised to find it at Tandy's, so I'm guessing you didn't slip it in a donation box?"

"No. I threw it in the trash. Someone must have taken it out."

"You don't sound too convinced."

"Well, there is no other logical explanation."

"People put way too many constraints around what's logical and what's not. So, just for kicks, what's your nonlogical explanation?"

I take a long breath in and out, preparing to fully jump off the deep end here. "My nonlogical explanation would be that the doll is haunted and tracking me down to send me a message."

He looks at me, and his eyes make me feel so safe. "What message is it trying to send?"

I force myself not to break eye contact. "It's trying to tell me how many days I have left to figure this out."

"And what exactly is the *this* you're trying to figure out?" His face lights up a moment after he asks. "Unless . . ." He rubs his chin. "Okay. I think I'm putting some of this together now. Your party, then Rich, then you suddenly taking a strong interest in my blog post. Now this doll."

"Ask me again," I say.

He frowns, thrown by the question.

"Ask me what you asked when I showed up at your place on Tuesday. Ask me again, and I'll be honest this time."

"Simone, did you see the specter in the woods? Did you see Regret at your birthday party?"

"Yes."

He does not flinch. He sits there as if *yes* is the most ordinary answer. "Did something bad happen?"

"Yeah, something bad happened, Cory. Rich died."

"I know that. And you know I'm asking you if Regret had anything to do with it."

"No. I mean, sure, technically. I guess. But it was my decision." I feel the rush of emotions bubbling up inside and can do nothing to stop it. "I don't know everything that went down. I don't know how the drugs play in, or the generator, or if anyone else had a hand in it, but I know the blame starts with me. Because I had a choice. And the choice I made ended with him dead. And I knew it would before I made it." My eyes fill with tears. "Or maybe I'm just losing my mind."

"Tell me more, and I can help you decide."

"You'll tell me if you think I'm losing my mind?"

"I will. I promise. Tell me exactly what happened."

"I made a deal with Regret to save Kira." I take a shaky breath and recount almost the whole story for him. I tell him about Regret showing me a future where Rich accused me of intentionally pushing Kira. I even tell him Rich claimed it was done out of jealousy. The only part I leave out is the part I've already promised myself to take to my grave. The part about kissing Rich. The boy who briefly and weakly filled the space that once held Cory.

He nods slowly when I finish, face angled up toward the sky, fingers interlocked behind his head, processing. After half a minute or so, he sets his eyes back on mine. "Let me make sure I have it straight."

"Okay."

"You have to find out how to set Regret free by"—he mumbles as he does some quick counting on his fingers—"next Saturday or . . . you'll kill Kira?"

"That's what she said."

"It could be a bluff. You said the trade didn't happen right away. Why wouldn't it have if Rich hadn't made it back to the cabin yet? What if it really was an accident? Or what if someone else at the party had something to do with it? Maybe the toxicology rumors are true."

After the conversation I had with Kira, I'm sure those rumors are true. "But none of that means Regret didn't have a hand in it. I don't know what she's capable of. She could have taken control of someone."

"But who? Can we exclude you?"

"I'm not sure about anything, but I'd think so. It wouldn't make sense for Regret to involve me that way."

"Why do you say that?"

"Because the deal was to help me. To give me a chance to write a different fate. How could I do that if the police were investigating me for murder? How could I hold up my end of the deal to *her* through all of that? Regret wants me to succeed. That's in her best interest."

He concedes with a tilt of his head and a slight frown. "True. But if someone else killed him before Regret did, you might have a loophole in your deal with her. It'd be hard to prove one way or the other, but we can keep that in our back pocket. I think we can hold up your end of the agreement regardless. We're already more than halfway there."

"More than halfway?"

"Yeah. Look how much we learned from Ms. Tandy today."

"All she did was make it more complicated. Mr. Otis made it seem like something went down between Evelyn and her friend Violet. Ms. Tandy made it seem like it was about a man and a baby." As I say the words, something about them doesn't feel right. It sounds exactly like what Ms. Tandy said it was. Gossip. "If Regret had had a child who passed in some terrible, negligent accident, wouldn't people have talked to the police? Surely something like that would have made the papers."

"You're probably right, but that doesn't mean there's zero truth in it. Let's put it aside for a sec and focus on Mr. Otis's version of things."

"Okay."

Cory leans forward, resting his elbows on his knees. "Evelyn and Violet were best friends who had a falling-out. There were a lot of rumors circulating about Evelyn being into the occult, so it wouldn't be too much of a stretch to say Violet was too, right?"

"I guess not."

"Okay. So two witches get into a fight. What happens?"

"They curse each other."

He points at me. "This might be really straightforward. Think about all the Disney movies. How are most curses broken?"

"Love? Forgiveness?"

"Exactly! 'They call her Regret.' It's clear as day, isn't it? There's something she wishes she never did. We can try to figure out if it's linked to Violet, Willie, or a child—and that's worth considering, with all the dolls and stuff. And hell, maybe it's linked to all three. But we are homed in, Simone. Look what love did for the prince in *Beauty and the Beast*."

I raise my eyebrow. "Are you volunteering to move out to the shack on Doll's Head and fall in love with a ghost witch? Can you make that happen in nine days?"

"Once again, you underestimate my charm."

I shove his shoulder. "Cory this is serious. We can't use a bunch of stories in kid movies to solve this."

"But why not? Those stories are almost all based on tales that have been told for centuries, Simone. Is it so absurd to think the original started with some truth? Magic is real. You've seen it. So let go of what *should* be possible and trust what you've seen with your own eyes, experienced with your own body."

"Okay, but Violet and Willie are probably dead. And we haven't even confirmed whether or not Evelyn actually had a kid."

"Right, but bloodlines are relevant with this kind of stuff. Let's try to find some living relatives. Someone might be willing to offer Regret forgiveness on behalf of their families."

"Okay," I say, a hopeful spark of energy blossoming. "Let's do it."

CORY and I drive to the town clerk's office, wedged between the library and the post office.

"Welcome. How can I help you?" asks the woman at the front desk without looking up from her book.

"Hi," Cory says. "We were hoping to access some records. We're looking for living family members of some people who lived in Fairville a few decades ago."

The woman looks up at us over her glasses. "Sounds like you want to see vital records. Can't let you access those unless you have some relation yourself."

"Are there any records we're allowed to see?"

She points to a sign by the hallway that reads PUBLIC RECORDS. "Got some old newspapers back there, might find some marriage announcements and obituaries. Property records might paint a pretty picture for you, too. If not, I'd try the local churches. They may be a little more lax with their books." She winks at us.

"Thank you." I head in the direction she pointed. Cory follows closely behind me. "Oh," I say when I turn the corner into the large, carpeted, dimly lit room. "I was expecting something more . . . formal." There is a cheap folding table in the center of the space, three desks with computers on the left side, and a bookcase with some files in boxes on the other.

"It's never like the movies. But don't worry. I'll romanticize it for the blog."

"Cory, I mean this as gently as possible, but your blog is the last thing I'm worried about right now. You take Violet, and I'll take Evelyn, okay?"

"What about Willie?"

"His last name is so common. This place closes in two hours. We'll spend half of that time just filtering through other Thompsons. Let's focus on the girls for now."

"Sounds good."

I start with property records. Mr. Otis said Evelyn grew up in the church. He said she went to Fairville First Baptist, so it's likely her family lived around there. I pull up Google Maps on my phone and search the records for several streets around the church. I find a Harold Young who owned the home at 899 Shakers Avenue from 1933 to 1986. Could this be Evelyn's father? The property was vacant until 1992, when it was purchased by someone named Elmira Simpson, who still owns it today.

"El-who?" Cory asks.

His voice breaking the silence startles me. "I must have been thinking out loud. I think I found Evelyn's dad, though. Harold Young. They lived on Shakers Avenue."

"Is the house still owned by the Youngs?"

"No. Someone named Elmira Simpson. But I think it's worth making a trip out there. Could give us some clues."

"Agreed," Cory says, turning back to his computer.

For the next ninety minutes, the only sounds come from our fingers speeding across our keyboards, our pens scribbling across paper, and file boxes sliding on and off shelves.

"Oh my God!" I shout, still speed-reading through bleary eyes.

He leans over to my side of the table. "What is it?"

"I found something! An obituary. 'Cleveland Robert Simpson wishes to announce the death of his beloved aunt and former Fairville resident, Violet Simpson (née Savoie).'"

"Oh," Cory says, searching for the significance of it. "But we already expected Violet to have passed by now, right?"

"Simpson, Cory!"

"Okay, so she got married."

"No, not that. I just—" I hold up my hand and choose to keep reading instead. "'Mrs. Simpson is survived by her husband, Elliot Simpson, and her young daughter, Elmira Simpson.'"

His mouth drops open when he finally puts it together. "Elmira! On Shakers Ave."

"Yeah!"

"So you're saying Violet Savoie's daughter lives in Evelyn's old house, *right now*?"

I deflate a bit. "Well, maybe. She owns it. Could be renting it out or something." I check the time. "Damn. It's almost seven. This place is about to close, and it's kind of late to land on her doorstep."

"It's okay," Cory says. "We can go over there as soon as you get out of school tomorrow."

"I don't technically have school. The principal is holding a celebration of life for Rich in the morning. I'll be free by early afternoon."

"Great. We'll drive to Shakers after and put my fairy-tale bloodline idea to the test. See if we can get this Elmira person to write a letter offering Regret forgiveness."

"But what about Kira? She might be at the event. I don't know if it's safe for me to be around her."

"There will be loads of people there. If it doesn't feel right, dip out. I can hang around in the parking lot if you want."

"Would you?"

"Yeah, Simone. Of course."

THE whirring of Gabby Greta's gears wakes me up in the morning. I dart straight up in bed as she begins her sinister greeting in that childish robotic voice. "Hi! I'm Gabby Greta, and I love you! I'm Gabby Greta! Can you count to . . ."

"Eight," I breathe, heart pounding in the pause before she says the number herself. Instead of allowing her countdown to terrify me, I need to use it as a motivator. I crawl to the end of my bed and snatch my laptop from my desk, startling Serling in the process. He hops to the floor with a heavy thud and scurries under the bed. "Sorry!" I say, settling back onto my duvet cross-legged, back against the wall. Determined to maximize every minute before Rich's event at school, I open my computer and go straight to Google, searching again for someone who might have had a strange experience at Doll's Head Lake. I find a couple of posts from three years ago on a Georgia hiking forum discussing the CPRC trail and the toys, but there's nothing to suggest the posters even made it out to the lake. I click over to Cory's blog, which I now have bookmarked. The plan was for him to post his next entry today, and he has.

BLOG ENTRY 077 / OCTOBER 22

CATEGORY: FAIRVILLE URBAN LEGENDS
EPISODE 3, PART 2

Hi again, fright fiends. I'm here with a quick update on our mysterious ghost of Doll's Head Lake—the one they call Regret. I've recruited the help of a friend to assist me in my research for this series, and as it goes when working through any mystery, it seems things might get pretty messy before the answers reveal themselves. Here's what we know so far:

WHO IS REGRET?

My partner and I are confident that the true identity of Regret is Evelyn Ruth Young, born in Fairville during the mid-1930s.

WHY DOES REGRET HAUNT DOLL'S HEAD LAKE?

We don't have a clear answer to this yet—if we did, I'd be wrapping up this series! But we do suspect it has something to do with an incident between her and her best friend, Violet Savoie, back in the 1950s.

WHAT DO WE KNOW ABOUT VIOLET SAVOIE?

Sometime after Evelyn became known as Regret, Violet had a daughter named Elmira and passed away shortly thereafter. Lucky for us, not only is Ms. Elmira still alive today, but she lives right here in Fairville, Georgia—and my partner and I will be interviewing her. Tomorrow.

Stay tuned. Things are just heating up.

Keep it creepy, friends.
C.

I wish Cory and I could go straight to Ms. Elmira's right now, but it's time to get ready to go to school. The sooner I make it through this service, the sooner I can get back to searching for answers with Cory. The sooner I can make day eight useful. We were asked to wear Rich's favorite color, blue, today. It's easy enough since his favorite is the exact royal shade of our school colors. I slip on my Eagles sweatshirt and jeans and pull my braids into a ponytail. My phone dings.

Jere
About to pass your street. Need a ride?

Me
Yeah. I'm ready. Meet you outside.

Jere pulls up a minute or two later, and I climb inside his Jeep. "Thank you."

"It's nothing," he says as he backs out of the driveway.

"How are you doing?"

"Sim, the tox report stuff was true. The police already called Cameron and Piper in for another round of questioning."

"What? Seriously?"

"Yeah. I mean, they both said it was like a ten-minute thing, in and out, but . . ." He adjusts his hat. "Something just don't feel right. I'm not trying to put it on anybody that was there though. Some of us may have some quiet beef, but nobody would take anything that far."

I bet he'd be surprised by how far he'd take something if the life of someone he cared about was at stake. "What do you think happened?" I ask, staring out the passenger window.

"Didn't you say there was some guy creeping around before we all got there? A groundskeeper?"

I stiffen in my seat, remembering our brief encounter at Ozzy's. "Yeah."

"What if Rich drank some more after fighting with Kira, and something happened between him and that dude? A groundskeeper might know something about a generator, right?"

I think about the sound of his incoming text message and how we heard the same sound out there in the woods. John saw him leave the property, but that doesn't mean he didn't come back. No idea how he could have gotten his hands on the vial of drugs, but that's not for me to figure out. "You're right. I'm definitely going to bring him up to the police if and when they call me in." There's no telling if that man did something bad of his own volition or if he's just another potential puppet of Regret's, but my number one goal when it's my turn to be questioned is to take the police's attention away from me and Kira. Collateral damage be damned. I've already put everything on the line for her, and there's no use easing off the brakes now.

CHAPTER 21

I walk up to the school, grateful to have Jere by my side. I figure it will be easier to handle whispers and stares if he shares some of the heat of judgment with me. But I find the worry unfounded because no one gives us a second glance when we enter the gym. Music plays, one of Rich's favorite artists. Students stand around in groups, talking and eating snacks from a long buffet table. A stage has been set up at one end of the gym with balloons, flowers, and a microphone, and a slideshow of pictures is being projected onto the wall. The principal gets on the mic and encourages students to come up and share happy memories about Rich.

"I expected something more . . . somber," I say.

Jere doesn't answer, and I look over to find he has tears in his eyes.

"Oh, Jere." I grip his hand. "I'm sorry."

"Nah, I'm good. I'm good." He sniffs hard and wipes his face clear of all physical signs of sadness. "Rich wouldn't want people crying and moping around. That's what the funeral is for. That's why they call this a celebration of life, right?"

At that, Jere bounds into the crowd to join the rest of the

football team. I scan the room for Kira, but I don't find her, which means she probably isn't coming at all. That's for the best because I doubt she's ready for this vibe. Still, I need to talk to her before the police call either of us back in. I send her a text, knowing I won't get a response.

"Hey, Simone," comes a voice from behind me.

I turn around. "Oh hey, Cameron. How are you holding up?"

He shrugs. "Hanging in there, I guess."

"Jere told me you had to speak to the police again."

"Yeah. They had a couple of follow-up questions is all. Don't stress over it if you get asked to go in. I know people have been talking all out the side of their necks about what went down, but the police seem more concerned with what Rich was doing outside of our friend group."

"Really?" I never imagined Rich having much of a life outside of his Pinegrove friends. "Did you have anything to tell them?"

He shakes his head. "We weren't tight like that anymore. Not for the past year. I heard some stuff about him missing football practices, and I noticed he was sleeping through first block and skipping last block almost every day. I didn't read into it at the time—we all got senioritis. But maybe something else was up."

"Did you tell that to the police?" I ask, hoping he did.

"Yeah," he answers distractedly. He's spotted Noor by the drinks table. "Hey, I'm gonna . . ." He gestures vaguely in her direction.

"No, of course. Go ahead."

I spend the next forty-five minutes walking around, making sure to speak to my friends, making sure to be seen. I sign Rich's memorial book and clap for people sharing happy memories, but not without wondering how skewed they are by his death. When I feel like I have sufficiently played my role and done what's expected and normal, I sneak out the back door of the gym. If Kira can get away with not coming at all, I can be let off the hook for needing to excuse myself early.

I jog over to Cory's truck on the far side of the crowded parking lot.

"Hey," he says as I climb in the passenger side. "How was it?"

"The police have started calling in people who were at the party for questioning again."

"Really? Is it about the toxicology report?"

"Yep. Jere told me on the way over. They've spoken to Cameron and Piper already."

"Are they going to call you in?"

"I assume so, and I need to talk to Kira before it happens."

"She wasn't there today?"

"No. And she won't answer my texts. I'll have to talk to her at the funeral tomorrow. I don't want to try going back to her house." I buckle my seat belt. "Let's go before we get stuck in this parking lot."

Cory starts up the truck and drives us off campus, taking a left onto a small back road. The kind of road that stirs up ugly memories about Trenton. I look at Cory out of the corner of my eye, wondering if it does the same to him.

CORY parks by the curb in front of the third house on Shakers Avenue.

The home looks exactly like I hoped it would—old and full of secrets. The front door is open, with a closed glass storm door that gives us a peek at the interior. All I can see from here is a carpeted staircase. We get out of the truck and walk toward the house. There's a navy van in the driveway. I recognize the name on the window decal as Cory and I walk up the path to the front door.

"Delia's Home Cleaning."

"Huh?" Cory says absently.

I point at the van. "That's the cleaning company that John hired to get the cabin ready for my party." I casually wonder if he sent them back to deal with the aftermath.

Cory, rightfully uninterested in this information, shrugs and rings the doorbell.

An older woman in a dress shirt, slacks, and house shoes comes down the steps and speaks through the glass door. "I'm not buying anything!" she barks.

This clearly won't be as breezy as things were with Mr. Otis and Ms. Tandy. "Oh, we aren't selling anything, ma'am."

"Then why are you at my door?"

I work hard to shift my facial muscles into a smile. "My name is Simone and this is Cory." I pause so Cory can smile and wave. "We are seniors at Pinegrove Academy and we're writing a report on notable Fairville families," I say, hoping she has an ego I can appeal to. "Are you Ms. Elmira Simpson?"

"I am. And ain't nothin' notable about the Simpsons. Keep our heads down and work hard to make a living and that's just how we like it."

"And that's great! We wanted to be sure to highlight plenty of working-class families and all they have contributed to this community, but um"—Ms. Elmira looks over her shoulder as the cleaning guy walks a vacuum down the steps—"aren't you the daughter of Violet Savoie?"

She whips her head around. "Where on earth did you dig up that name?"

"Town hall," Cory offers.

Ms. Elmira crosses her arms. "Violet Savoie was my birth mother. I was an infant when she passed. My daddy's second wife adopted me and she's the only mama I knew, so I'm not likely to be able to help much with that little report of yours."

"Honestly any information you have could help. We—"

Ms. Elmira grips the edge of the wooden front door, looking ready to close it in our faces.

"Do you go to Fairville First Baptist, by any chance?" Cory rushes out.

Ms. Elmira shifts her eyes to Cory, her gaze landing softer on him. "I do."

"I think you may know my grandma then. Beatrice Gooding? She helps out with the choir."

"Of course I know Ms. Beatrice! And if you was a grandson worth any weight, I'd be familiar with you, too." She gives him a disapproving look, but I can tell Cory made the right move.

He hangs his head. "I know, I know, ma'am. Grandma has been getting on me about missing church so often lately."

Ms. Elmira unlocks and pushes open the storm door. "I'll be sure to tell her I spoke to you when I see her at rehearsal this afternoon. She'll be happy to hear you'll both be in attendance this Sunday."

"Yes, ma'am," we both say. And I'll have to make sure it isn't a lie. With all the dark stuff I've got myself wrapped up in right now, lying to an old woman about plans to attend church feels like an especially bad karma move.

"Come on in," she says, hurrying us along. "Like I said, I got rehearsal in a bit. Go on and have a seat in the living room."

Cory and I enter her home and sit stiffly at the end of a love seat. She sits across from us with a huff.

"Like I told ya a second ago, Violet Savoie birthed me, but she ain't raise me. I don't know much more about her family than any average Joe on the street. When I was real young, I heard some whispers here and there about Violet getting mixed up in some scandal, but they didn't follow me beyond grade school. You know how gossip goes. Folks prefer it hot and fresh, and somebody is always in the kitchen stirring up a new pot." She shakes her head.

"Do you remember hearing anything about a fight Violet had with her best friend? A woman named Evelyn Young? Maybe a fight over a guy?" I ask, hoping to high heaven that guy wasn't her father or something.

Ms. Elmira rolls her eyes. "People love centering men in stories that ain't got a lick to do with 'em. But you're right about them being friends. Unfortunately, they got themselves mixed up into some things they shouldn't have."

"Like what?" I ask.

"Evelyn lived in a shack of a home out by what's now Yearwood Lake. She would have been happy to live out her years there as a modern-day spinster, by the sound of it. Became pretty reclusive and rumors started going around about her and Violet dabbling in witchcraft. There were also rumors about Evelyn having a baby out of wedlock. Folks thought that was another reason why she kept to herself out there."

I find myself growing annoyed that it keeps coming back to this. "Do you think it was true? Do you think Evelyn had a baby?"

"Honey, I don't know and I don't care. I occasionally get a portion of that gossip stew forced on me, but won't catch me searching for the recipe." She bows her head and raises her hands in the air. "'Whoever goes about slandering reveals secrets, but he who is trustworthy in spirit keeps a thing covered!' Proverbs 11:13. Lord, I have already said too much. Y'all babies gon' have to go on now. This conversation not sitting right with my soul."

The cleaning guy walks by and toward the front door. "All done, Ms. Elmira. I'll see you next week!"

Ms. Elmira stands. "Oh wait, suga, let me give you a little something. Hold on." She scurries off to the back of the house, I assume to fetch her purse.

I let out a heavy sigh. Cory stands and offers a hand to help pull me up. I take it, and don't miss the smile that tugs at the corners of his mouth as soon as my skin meets his.

I sigh even louder and drop his hand once I'm securely on my feet. "Cory, that was useless."

He frowns. "Not entirely."

"I don't have—"

"Hey," the cleaning guy by the door starts, voice low. He glances down the hall, then takes a few quick steps over to us. "The attic. Tons of boxes and old stuff up there. Probably has all the info you're looking for and more."

I stutter a bit, grateful for this information, but unsure why he'd offer it. "Oh, uh, thanks . . . hopefully she'll let us take a look."

"She won't. But she's about to leave and I know where she keeps the spare key."

"Nah man, we aren't trying to do anything illegal," Cory says with a laugh, but my face remains straight.

The guy shrugs. "I graduated from Pinegrove four years ago. I remember those senior projects. I'm also broke as dirt and know who your"—he points at me—"daddy is. Elmira's gonna come back to tip me like seventy-five cents for four hours of work. Hook me up and I'll hook you up."

Ms. Elmira appears at the end of the hall, jangling her coin purse.

I whip my phone from my back pocket. "Give me your number. I'll send you something right now."

He pops his chewing gum. "A hundred dollars."

"Okay, fine."

"That was easy." He takes my phone and types in his number. "Should have asked for more."

I send him the money and he checks his phone to confirm.

"Sweet." Then he adds under his breath, "Backyard. Magnetic container under the flower box beneath the second window."

"Okay," Ms. Elmira says. "Here you go, darlin'." She hands him a dollar.

"Movin' on up! Thank you."

"No, thank you. I'll walk out with you all. Looks like my ride is here." She trades her house shoes for a pair of brown loafers underneath a tiny entry table.

A white sedan has pulled up behind the cleaning van. We all walk out of the house and Ms. Elmira locks up.

"Thank you for taking the time to speak with us." It feels awful to thank her knowing I intend to reenter her home without an invitation as soon as she leaves.

"Mm-hmm, you can show your thanks in the pews this Sunday!" She hustles down the drive and gets into the car.

Cory and I take our time and when we finally reach the truck, Ms. Elmira is long gone, and the Delia's cleaning van is backing out. The guy taps his horn before driving off.

"So we're seriously going to do this?" Cory asks.

"It doesn't have to be a *we* thing. And it's not like I want to, but what option do I have? For all we know, things that actually belonged to Regret are up there. All the answers I need could be up there, and what better opportunity are we going to have than now? Mission 'get a letter of forgiveness out of Ms. Elmira' is obviously a fail, but I can live with that if we dig up something even better in that attic."

"I'm not trying to dissuade you. Was just making sure. And don't give up on the forgiveness letter just yet. I have an idea."

"Tell me about it later. I don't want to waste too much time. Let's go."

Cory and I look up and down the street to make sure no one

is watching, then we casually walk around to the back of the house and locate the key.

I hesitate once I get it in the lock because this is escalating things to a point of no return. Cory places his hand on top of mine. "Murdering your best friend is worse." He turns my hand for me.

CHAPTER 22

I enter the house slowly, suddenly worried if it was right to trust that guy, but I might as well see it through at this point. It's weird once we're in. Almost like we aren't doing anything wrong at all. It's broad daylight out and we were here with permission only minutes ago. I know better than to try my luck, though. "Let's make this quick."

I follow Cory up the stairs, and we find the pull string to the attic in the hallway. He reaches it easily with his long arms and gives it a tug. I pull down the rickety wooden ladder and look up into the darkness.

"After you," Cory says.

I turn on the flashlight on my phone and hold it above my head as I ascend the steps. When I get to the top, I give the full room a quick scan for anything overly creepy or suspicious, but it's pretty generic as far as attics go. I climb all the way in, then search for a light switch. I find it and flick it on. A bare bulb in the center of the space illuminates weakly. Cory joins me and takes a look around.

"At least it's been cleaned recently. Won't leave any dusty fingerprints behind."

A prickly, hot sensation erupts across my skin. "Should we be worried about fingerprints? Of course we should! Why didn't we bring gloves?"

"Well, for one, we didn't know we'd be breaking and entering."

"Cory, I'm serious!"

He places his hands on my shoulders. "Calm down. She won't ever have any reason to suspect we were up here, so it won't ever matter. But let's get to it and leave."

I nod and we each stride over to separate stacks of boxes.

We both find potentially useful things in the first ones we open. Books, photo albums, journals.

"We can't take everything," I say. "Skim through. Set aside anything that has a direct connection to Violet or Evelyn."

Cory and I do some quick but thorough searching. Feeling defeated after coming up with nothing valuable, I open the last leather-bound notebook in my final box. Inside the front cover in pretty script are the words PROPERTY OF VIOLET SAVOIE. "Cory!" I shout. "I found something!"

"Me too! This box is full of like . . . I don't know, they look like spell books."

I flip through the pages of the notebook, and Evelyn's name pops out at me multiple times. "I can one-up you. I foun—"

The light bulb overhead flickers and goes out and it's like Cory disappears into thin air. I feel around for my phone. A strong breeze makes the house creak and I swear if Regret chooses right now to deliver one of her scary-ass countdown reminders, I will lose it.

"Cory?" I repeat myself when he doesn't immediately respond. "Cory, say something, damn!"

A beam of light blinds me for a second, and all I can imagine is the spirit of Violet Savoie rushing me, angry for tampering with her things. For attempting to undo her curse.

"Simone!" Cory shouts, moving the light of his phone out of my eyes.

"Cory, what the hell is wrong with you? Are you trying to give me a heart attack?"

"No. I couldn't—"

"Never mind. Let's get out of here. Right now. Just take that whole box."

"You don't think she'll notice?" he asks.

"No. I don't. I don't think she can get up here easily, but even if she did, that guy has been cleaning. It won't be any surprise to her that things have been moved around."

"Good point."

"WHERE are we going?" I ask as Cory drives toward the edge of town.

"It's nice out. I know a quiet spot where we can look through all this stuff."

He drives for a couple more minutes before turning down a dirt road and reversing the truck into an empty field.

"Uh . . ."

"I figure we'll be at this for a while and the sunsets here are great."

"The sunsets?" I laugh. "Cory, is this your secret date spot? Is this where you bring girls?"

"Nah, I come here to clear my head. Trenton showed me this place, actually. He'd come out here to fly his drone around."

His casual mention of Trenton dampens the mood and I feel bad about it. It shouldn't be that way. Trenton was bright and funny and warm. He was the opposite of how I feel right now.

"Do you ever feel guilty about what happened?" The words

just tumble out. It's time to address the elephant in the room. "The night Trenton died."

Cory looks like he's not quite sure what I'm asking, and it annoys me because it should be obvious.

"If we hadn't got caught up at your place, if we hadn't... kissed... do you think he'd still be here?"

He shrugs lightly. "I try to stay away from the what-ifs, but I mean, yeah. Sometimes."

"Sometimes what?" I push, desperately needing to know I haven't been alone in my feelings all this time.

"Sometimes I wonder if he'd still be here if we'd been on time." He does that thing where he matches my tone. Something I've learned he does when he doesn't have a confident read on the situation.

"So do you regret it?" I stare at the side of his face, wanting him to turn and make eye contact.

"Regret what?"

"Do you regret kissing me?"

He sits there rigidly staring out the windshield for a few moments before relaxing and finally turning to look at me, eyes as soft as ever. "No. I can't say that I do."

I wish I could say the same, but I don't understand how it's possible. "So sometimes you feel guilty that we were late, but you don't regret the reason why we were?"

He looks down, then rolls the end of one of my braids resting on the center console between his fingers. "You're not going to be able to make it make sense. Don't waste your time trying." He drops my hair and starts grabbing things from the back. "Bigger fish to fry right now anyway, right?"

"But—"

"Simone, you finding reasons to beat yourself up over it won't change anything. The whole thing was a freak accident. Okay?"

I think of Rich with that cable burned into his hand and wonder how many other accidents aren't so accidental. My thoughts bounce around erratically. It's happening too frequently now—snippets of uncomfortable things clawing their way up from the dark depths of my mind. Mom and Dad arguing. The shack at the lake, windows illuminated. A cracked windshield. A single headlight. Me and Rich.

"Simone?" Cory drops his head so his eyes are in line with mine.

"Huh?"

"Simone, are you all right?"

I inhale sharply and shake my head to free myself from the spiral. "Yeah, sorry. I'm fine. Left turn. Bigger fish."

Cory smiles and hops out of the truck. He spreads a blanket out in the bed, and we climb in with the box we stole from the attic. I dive straight into Violet's diary while Cory flips through the books on magic. For the first hour we go back and forth blurting out every new and seemingly important thing we find before agreeing that it's only slowing us down. We decide to work independently and share at sunset. Once the tiniest bit of pink erupts in the sky, I close the diary and start yapping.

"I should send that cleaning guy another hundred dollars because"—I gesture at the books in between us—"this right here is everything."

Cory picks up the diary and starts flipping through the pages. "Catch me up."

"Okay, so, it's clear that Evelyn and Violet were close, but I could sense some . . . resentment? For one, Evelyn was living the life she wanted while Violet's family was the traditional type. And they were definitely having some money problems like I thought. But also, it seemed like Violet was interested in some darker magic. She didn't call it that exactly, but she complained about wanting to try some things that sounded kind of shady and not being able to get Evelyn on board. And we have to keep in mind that all of this is just Violet's view of things, so it's bound to be biased, but the way she told it is that she and Evelyn had a third friend, and it wasn't some weird love triangle BS."

"Who was it?"

"Violet's first cousin, Dorothy Savoie. It wasn't super clear, but I think Dorothy was visiting for the summer or something and they all spent a lot of time hanging out at Evelyn's place by the lake."

"Was Evelyn's place the Yearwood cabin?"

"Oh, no. There's another cabin. More like a shack. It's right at the edge of the woods by the lake. Anyway, most of the entries were just boring rambling but"—I take the diary from Cory's hand and flip to the page dated June 23, 1956, so he can follow along—"the last few were major. So apparently, Dorothy and Evelyn get into an argument. It gets pretty heated. Physical. Violet runs for help in breaking them up, but she doesn't even make it off the beach before she hears a loud thud. She turns around, and Dorothy is there on the ground, bleeding from her head. Violet tries to help, but Dorothy takes her last breath right in front of her. She wrote that Evelyn said it was an accident. But from the way she described it, the only kind of accident that could cause something like that would be a ten-pound rock falling from a tree."

"What'd they do?" Cory asks, scanning the pages.

"Violet was heartbroken about her cousin, but she also didn't want Evelyn getting in trouble for something she claimed was an accident. She tried talking to her so they could get their story straight, but she said Evelyn started blaming *her*. She didn't want them both thrown under the bus over an accident so . . ." I take the book back again to search for the right word. "So she 'restricted' her to the lake."

"I saw something about restriction spells!" Cory grabs the composition book where he was taking notes. "Yeah. Right here." He moves his finger across the page as he reads. "Restriction spells are used to confine someone to a specific area—"

"Yeah, that much is obvious. How do you break it!?"

"Well, there are a few possibilities depending on the specific type of restriction spell that was cast. Some lift upon the caster's death."

"Okay, not that. Next."

"No, wait." He holds up a hand to slow me down. "There was an asterisk next to that one noting that the caster themselves can reverse it."

I open my mouth to interrupt but he cuts me off.

"Or"—he pauses for emphasis before continuing—"or a relative of the caster can act as a proxy."

"Ms. Elmira?"

"Yes! It's like we were already thinking! And from the other things I've read, I think a letter of forgiveness will be enough so long as she is the one to write and sign it. So long as she means it."

"How the hell are we going to get Ms. Elmira to write a letter forgiving Regret for killing Dorothy? You do remember we had to steal all this because she wouldn't talk? Rich's funeral is tomorrow at two thirty. I don't have time—"

"I do. Look, go home and throw some clothes in a bag. Leave it on your side porch or something. While you're at the funeral, I'll pick it up and check back in with Ms. Elmira. I'll do whatever I need to do to get the letter."

"But—"

"I promise I'll get it. I have an idea. She liked me better than you, anyway. Let me do it."

I run out of steam and just nod.

"After that, I'll get you from the cemetery, and we'll go straight out to Doll's Head with the letter. I'll buy a few new toys for offerings too, just in case. How's that sound?"

I smile, elated by how much came together today. "Sounds like this is almost over."

CHAPTER 23

Saturday afternoon, I sit in a pew toward the front of the church, anxiously twisting the hem of my knee-length skirt between my fingers. Two enormous photographs of Rich are at the front of the room, surrounded by fresh, fragrant flowers. It feels like his 2D eyes have been tracking me since I walked in. Boring into me, only to return to their correct position in the moments I'm brave enough to look directly at them. I've been brave enough just twice in the forty-five minutes I've been here. Rich's spirit has every reason to want to haunt me, so I've done my best to keep my head down. Dad sits next to me, one of his strong arms draped over my shoulders. I welcome his attempts to comfort me because the numbness I felt at the start of the week has evaporated. I'm frustrated and angry at Rich, even in death when people's wrongs are supposed to be magically erased. When we're expected to have grace. Give mercy. In the grand scheme of things, was he so horrible? Did he destroy anyone's life? Did he deserve to die? No. Not as far as I know. I can admit that. Hell, outside of him being completely wrong for Kira, I liked him. I considered him a friend. But the question I faced that night wasn't whether Rich deserved to die in general. It was whether he deserved it more than Kira. The obvious answer is yes. But the one I don't want to confront is whether someone else deserved it more than him—myself included. Because he wasn't the only choice that night. I love Kira, but I would not die for her. Who was I to decide that Rich should? A girl with the best intentions stuck between a rock and a hard place. Cornered by a predator. Forced to make life-altering decisions in the middle of a traumatic event. The dead are offered grace, but is it absurd to think that I should get some, too?

I look across the aisle, where Kira stares straight ahead, tears streaming down her cheeks. Layla and John sit next to her, expressions somber. Kira's a pretty crier. Her tears and red-rimmed eyes highlight her amber irises. She must have worn her expensive waterproof liner and mascara because the dark makeup hasn't bled at all. Her eyes flit in my direction like she can feel me studying her, and I quickly look away.

The pastor instructs us all to rise. We do and turn around as the back doors of the chapel open. Rich's casket is draped with his football jersey. His father and Jeremiah are the pallbearers at the front. My heart clenches when I see Rich's little brother, Max, in the back. His eyes are wet and puffy, and his fingertips barely reach the casket, an unnecessary addition to the six men ahead of him. But that's what makes it so touching. There's an uptick in sniffles and rustling tissue packets as people spot him, even a few wails. The little boy laying his big brother, his idol, to rest. I can't look at him knowing my role in all of this. I hang my head, the weight of cowardice heavy on my neck.

After the service, people gather outside in small family and friend groups, dabbing their eyes and offering long comforting hugs before setting off for the cemetery. Police officers are scattered here and there. I wonder if they are here to pay respects, or for crowd and traffic control, or to take note of any suspicious persons.

A combination of the three, probably. I need to find Kira and talk to her. We need to get our story straight. I spot her family, but she isn't with them. My eyes dart around, searching for her distinctive hair.

"Looking for me?"

I startle and spin on my heels at the sound of Kira's voice from right behind me.

"I need to talk to you. Privately." She turns and leads the way to the side of the church with an old rusted playground enclosed in a chain-link fence. A few young kids dressed in black chase each other while a woman in dark sunglasses keeps an eye on them from a bench. There's a cardboard box next to her with DONATION (7) written in black Sharpie on the side. The box is filled with old baby dolls, seven, I assume. Gabby Greta got her message through loud and clear this morning. I don't know if these extra reminders are the work of Regret, or just my subconscious assigning meaning to things that don't actually mean anything. But I'm not mad either way. I need this feeling of urgency. I need the extra dose of adrenaline to keep moving forward and prevent myself from falling to pieces before I resolve this.

Kira stops walking and faces me with a huff. I know she's heard about the second round of police questioning. That she wants to talk to me for the same reason I want to talk to her. I can tell by the look on her face that it's the *only* reason she's in front of me right now.

"Have they set a time for you to go in yet?" I ask, working to keep my eyes on her and off that creepy donation box.

"Dad thinks they'll pick it back up on Monday."

"And Rich's parents are okay with that? They're okay with them taking forever to figure it out?"

One of the kids on the playground falls and begins to cry. Kira watches him as he stretches his arms toward his caregiver. "They knew more about Rich than any of us did."

"What does that mean?"

"It means unlike everyone else, they weren't surprised by the toxicology report."

"So they think he took the drugs himself?"

"I guess. He got in trouble for sneaking out to a rave a few weeks ago, and he'd been having issues with his parents ever since."

"A . . . rave? What even is that? I thought it was a thing white kids in nineties movies did."

"Well, he was a white kid, and they still do it. All sorts of people do. But it's still a pretty underground thing here. At least, as far as I could tell from snooping around on social media. Rich never mentioned it to me, and that's not a surprise." She rolls her eyes. "I'm sure it was an easy place to meet girls that have no clue I exist. And a good place to get drugs, I guess. I feel like I barely knew him at all."

It seems Rich and I shared an affinity for masks.

"Let the police do whatever they are going to do on their own," Kira says. "Please don't say anything about that vial you found."

For once I find her expression difficult to read. I want to ask her why not. I want to ask if she's just nervous or if she has something to hide. But I know I can't do that without pissing her off, and lately, whenever she gets angry, I get angrier. So I just say okay. "I was thinking about bringing up that groundskeeper I saw before the party started. I forgot to mention him the first time I spoke to Officer Long. I'm not trying to accuse him of anything, but he *was* on the property that night."

Kira nods. "He was on the security camera footage, so I'm sure the police have been speaking with him."

The cameras. I forgot. Cory and I will have to steer clear of them when we go there today. "Do you think the grounds—"

"I don't want to talk about it, Simone."

A muscle under my eye twitches involuntarily. I bite back the confrontational words that so desperately want to come up and exchange them with something else. "I'm sorry about the other day. I know that doesn't mean much, but I am. There are just a lot of things I'm trying to figure out right now."

A strange expression passes across her face. "Yeah. Me too, Simone." She looks over my shoulder, and I follow her gaze. John and Layla are looking at us. Waiting for her. "I have to go." Without another word, she moves past me and joins them.

I find Dad, and he drives us to the cemetery for the burial service. There are far fewer people in attendance than were at the funeral, and the interment goes by rather quickly. I spot a few guys that I've never seen before. One wears a pin of that same astronaut sticker I saw in the bathroom at Ozzy's and in that card for Rich. I want to ask him about it, but they leave early and there's no way for me to chase them down without being disruptive.

One of Rich's cousins sings "How Great Thou Art" to close things off, which apparently was Rich's favorite hymn. I wouldn't have guessed he even knew what a hymn was. Her voice is beautiful, and a massive lump forms in my throat. At the same time, my collar dampens, and I can hear my grandmother's voice. *Sweating like a sinner in church.* I take a step back, ready to speed walk my way straight out of here. Ready to free myself from this discomfort. But I see Cory in the distance and having him there, knowing the truth of it all, or most of it at least, grounds me.

"READY to go?" Dad asks when the service concludes.

"Do you mind if I just meet you at home later? I want to take a walk. The fresh air is nice."

"Of course. That's fine, sweetheart. Be safe."

I walk slowly, giving Dad time to get in his car and for the rest of the crowd to thin before I approach Cory.

"Hey," I say, breathless after climbing the steep hill to get to him.

He leans against a tree not far from Trenton's grave, which has a Black Panther Funko Pop on the headstone. Brand-new. Still in the box.

"You're beautiful. Have I ever told you that before?"

"Uh, no. I don't think you have."

He holds out his hand to help me maneuver the tricky mound of roots between us. "I haven't said it, but you know I think it, right?"

I hold back a smile as we walk toward the parking lot. "I mean, I guess there have been signs. But isn't this an odd time to verbalize it? I did just leave a funeral. Like two minutes ago. We're still in the cemetery, actually. I don't know if you noticed."

"If there's any time to give someone a compliment, I think a difficult day is best."

"Today is difficult for Rich's parents. For Kira and her family."

"And you love Kira. So regardless of your complicated feelings toward Rich, a difficult day for her is a difficult day for you."

I am surprised by the tears that finally spring to my eyes when he finishes speaking.

"There it is." He slowly pulls me into a hug. The side of my face presses into his upper chest as more and more tears come. I let myself cry freely for a few minutes before sniffling and pulling away.

"Ugh. Thank you. I think I really needed that."

"I know you did. And while you were at the funeral, I was able to get something else you really need too."

My eyes go wide. "Did you get the letter, seriously?"

"Told you I would."

"But how?"

"I asked Ms. Elmira to tell me what the Bible has to say about forgiveness. That got her in the right headspace. Then I might have told her that her birth mother visited me in a dream and revealed all that stuff we read in her diary. Was cake from there."

"Cory!" I say in shock.

"It wasn't even a lie. Not exactly. I *did* dream about all this last night. Anyway, come on. Your change of clothes is in the truck."

I follow him around the corner to where he's parked, the setting sun painting the sky pink and orange. He stands outside with his back to the windows so I can have some privacy. When I reach for my duffel in the back seat, I see that he went to the store and picked up a few toys. There are some Walmart bags with baby dolls and stuffed animals inside. I grab my bag, shimmy out of my tights, and pull on some sweats. I slip off my skirt, pull a hoodie over my black shirt, and shove my feet into my dirty sneakers. "Okay!" I shout when I'm done.

Cory gets in the car.

"Is that what you're wearing?" I ask, eyeing his nice boots, clean black jeans, and navy button-up.

He shrugs. "I have a washing machine." He puts his hands on the steering wheel. "Ready to end this?"

"More than."

CHAPTER 24

My mouth goes papery dry as Cory drives up the path to the Yearwood cabin. He parks his truck in a spot where the gravel is laid evenly. After the party and all the police activity, the section closest to the house is muddy and patchy.

"Should we go now?" Cory asks.

"Yeah. It'll be dark soon. Better if we can make at least one trip through the woods while there's still daylight." I shove the dolls he purchased into my backpack and toss it over my shoulder, casually wondering what the groundskeeper's work schedule is like. "Don't walk too close to the house. There are security cameras."

We give the house a wide berth on our way to the side yard, and I do my best not to look at the spot where Rich died. We pass the firepit and are almost to the head of the trail that leads to the dock when I trip and fall onto my hands and knees.

"Damn. Are you okay?" Cory helps me to my feet.

We both eye the ground in search of what tripped me up.

"A whole-ass piece of firewood," Cory says, picking it up. "Who'd leave this here?"

I wipe my hands clean on my pants. "John probably did by

accident. He was cutting it himself before the party. The storage box is over there." I lead the way and open it up. Something catches my eye in the corner. Something black and rubbery. I nudge it with my finger, and it shifts to the side. A glass vial. *The vial?* The debate about whether to leave it and tell the police or grab it happens at record speed before I wrap my fingers around it and slip it into the pocket of my sweats just before Cory arrives with the log.

"Can I have that letter?" I ask after he puts the log away. "I should be the one to give it to her."

"Of course." He pulls an envelope from his back pocket and hands it to me.

I put it in my bag, mind still swimming with what finding that vial there might mean. What choosing to take it might mean. I do my best to shake the thoughts from my head. That's not my priority right now.

"Let's go." I start down the doll-laden path.

The forest is eerily dark, even though the sun hasn't fully set. My stomach twists and turns with every step. I'm afraid to reach the end of the woods. Afraid that I'll be plunged right back into one of the worst moments of my life. But I am also eager to end this. It'd be poetic to resolve everything on the day of Rich's funeral. To formally and permanently close this awful chapter with a week to spare. To begin rebuilding my friendship with Kira without those disgusting thoughts of harming her hanging over me.

When we reach the bank of the lake, the sun is right on the horizon. It looked so different in the darkness. Even that shack, which loomed so hauntingly, seems gentle and unassuming under the light of the golden hour. It's warmer today, too.

"Is this where it happened?"

"Yes."

"Should we go to the shack?"

I scan the dull wooden home. A little gnome sits out front, only tiny flecks of red paint remaining on its hat. There's something charming about it. It's like the place wants to lure you in. Like with every step the smell of cinnamon rolls and chocolate chip cookies would get stronger. Those scenes never ended well in the fairy tales, but I pray Cory's ideas for how this all relates to one are correct. "We should wait until dark. Let her come to us."

"You sure?"

"No, but I'm not ready."

"How about we at least put the dolls by the door?"

I nod. "Yeah. Okay."

We slowly approach the shack. There is no odor of baked goods. No creepy movements. Nothing. I put the stuffed animals and baby dolls next to the gnome, half praying for a burst of light and the little orb of Evelyn Young's spirit floating off into the afterlife. That doesn't happen, of course. Nothing happens.

"Want to go for a better view of the sunset while we wait?" Cory gestures toward the dock.

Maybe watching the sunset here with Cory can be one step toward erasing the other horrible memories. I'll need that if our plan doesn't work. We walk to the end and sit down. The water is low. Our feet dangle a couple of feet above it. We watch the sun slip away in silence. After a while, I lean back on my hands, absorbing the last dregs of heat lingering in the late fall air. My left little finger grazes something cool. I look back and see a tiny glint of gold between the wooden planks and pry it out with my nails. A circular pendant necklace with a *K* engraved on it.

"What'd you find?" Cory asks.

I inspect it closely. "This is Kira's. She was wearing it that night." And I wonder if it's a coincidence that I found this and that vial today. I slip it into my other pocket. "Rich gave it to her. She'll be happy to have it back."

"Such a thoughtful friend you are," comes a voice from behind us.

Cory and I whip around, but no one is there.

"It's her." I scramble to my feet and hurry back down the dock, the sky now a dusky purple. "Hello? Regret? Are you here?"

"I am always here," she says without showing herself. "You've brought a guest."

"Yes. He's been helping me. We—we think we figured out how to free you."

"Call me intrigued."

A shadowy form emerges from behind the shack. Cory takes a step back.

"Don't be afraid." Like slipping off a cloak, the dark form turns into a woman. I am bombarded by that familiar, heady scent. Summery and rich. It's so strong that I expect Cory to react, but he seems completely unaware. I recognize the woman before us as Regret, but she looks different from the first night I met her. She's cleaner. More pleasant. Less scary. She looks more like Evelyn Young. Despite her appearance, the way she moves, all twitchy and staticky, makes me uneasy.

Regret approaches until she is only inches from Cory's face. For a second, I think she is leaning in to kiss him, but she turns her head to the side and takes a long sniff of his neck. Her stomach rumbles loudly, and a bit of drool clings to the corners of her mouth as she pulls away. "Perhaps I will get a two-for-one meal if you should fail." She vanishes, then reappears a more comfortable distance away. A large stone materializes. She perches on it and spreads her arms wide. "Well then." She drops her chin ominously, her words coming out in a haunting double speak. "Release me."

"We learned that your name was Evelyn." I pause, stupidly waiting for her to confirm or something. "Sorry, um. We believe your friend Violet Savoie was the one who trapped you here after an . . . accident between you and . . . an accident between you and Violet's cousin Dorothy. We read that curses like this can sometimes be broken through forgiveness. Violet passed away a while ago now, but we found her daughter. She wrote a letter." With trembling hands, I pull the folded note from my bag and shake it open.

Regret tilts her head to the side, gray eyes cold, but curious. "Read."

I clear my throat. "'I, Elmira Simpson, on behalf of my birth mother, Violet Savoie, and the entire Savoie lineage, do hereby offer forgiveness to Evelyn 'Regret' Young for the events that took place on the banks of now-named Yearwood Lake in 1956. It is my hope that this offering of forgiveness will allow Ms. Young's spirit to finally rest in peace. With mercy and gentleness, Elmira Simpson.'"

Regret sits as still as the stone she rests on when I finish. Her eyes slowly darken until even the whites are completely black. The blackness spreads until it takes up each socket and then the entire upper half of her face. Could this be it? Is it working? Her skin grays, then her form rapidly doubles in size. She stands, towering over us. I know we got it wrong a half second before she snatches the letter from my hands. She crumples it in her fist and shoves it down the black hole that is now her mouth. Her voice is deep and painfully loud when she speaks.

"You think I desire the forgiveness of Violet Savoie? Violet Savoie is a MURDERER!" Her voice rumbles like thunder. "She is a liar and a greedy cheat, and I will never show sorrow for any ounce of pain that became her. I have nothing to be forgiven for. Stupid girl. I HAVE NO REGRETS!" This time, the crash of her voice magically opens the sky. Fat raindrops fall, even though there were no signs of a coming storm. "Save your fairy-tale solutions for children. I do not seek, nor do I want forgiveness from *anyone*. Tell me . . ." Her usual features return to her face, but her body takes on a serpentine quality as she approaches me. "Tell me. To what event in 1956 does this Elmira Simpson refer?"

Fear prevents any words from exiting my mouth. Regret grips me by the bottom of my jaw and squeezes. "SPEAK!"

Involuntarily, words in a voice that does not belong to me flow from my mouth—pulled like an anchor from the bottom of my stomach. The feeling nauseates me, but each time I think I may vomit, only more words come. "June 23, 1956. Dear Diary, I do believe today was the worst day of my life. It started out—"

"No!" Regret releases a feral roar and grips the hood of my sweatshirt, dragging me to the water like she did one week ago. Cory tries to run to my aid, but some unseen force blocks him. I struggle to free myself from Regret's grasp, not wanting to see that same scene she showed me before. She plunges my head under, and once again, the world around me morphs and shifts. It reshapes itself into a room I have never been in before. One I have never seen before. A woman with perfectly coifed dark hair sits at a wooden desk, writing. A pressed violet hangs in a frame on the wall. A delicate, feminine voice with a notable polite Southern accent—one my own vocal cords refused to replicate—begins to speak.

"June 23, 1956. Dear Diary, I do believe today was the worst day of my life. It started out fine as any other lately. I took a trip out to the lake to visit Evelyn. Cousin Dorothy has been back in town since her man left her, so she came along, too. I'm not sure what sparked it, but Evelyn and Dorothy got into a terrible, terrible

argument. I tried my best to break it up, but when it became clear I'd fail, I chose to run for help. Until the day I die, I'll wonder if that was the wrong choice because only moments after I turned round, Dorothy cried out. The scene when I looked back is one I will never forget. Poor, sweet cousin Dorothy lay on the ground, bleeding violently from her head. And my dear friend Evelyn stood over her, a rock gripped in her right hand. There wasn't a thing I could do to save Dorothy, and turning Evelyn into the authorities would surely have been a death sentence. I didn't have the heart to do it. Instead, I chose to use my magic to restrict her to that land."

Regret lifts my head from the water by my hair, drags me ashore, then shoves me to the ground. "LIES! FILTHY. DISGUSTING. LIES!"

"I'm sorry!" I cough. "Maybe we have it backward. M-maybe it's you who needs to offer forgiveness."

A violent bolt of lightning cuts through the sky. Regret pounces on me and pins me down. Her breath, cold against my skin, smells of lake water and rotting fish—all traces of the warm floral scent extinguished.

"You nasty little girl, am I a fool to have offered you this deal? Are you a waste of my time?"

I can see Cory freaking out in my periphery, still unable to reach me.

"No!" I plead with Regret. "I'm not a waste of time."

"Did you not hear me when I said Violet Savoie was a murderer?"

"I—I did. I'm sorry. I—"

"Why would I *ever* offer forgiveness to a murderer?"

"To free yourself!" I cry. "To free yourself from this anger. This curse." I search for the quote Dad often uses. "Forgiveness is not for the other person. It's for you."

Regret stares at me, eyes milky and unblinking, before

pushing me into the sand and standing. Suddenly she reverts to her Evelyn-like form. "There is only one way to test your theory. Bring me Violet Savoie and make her confess her deepest regret. Make her confess the *truth*. I do not have forgiveness in my heart today, but this is the only way to see if it will arise."

"But Violet Savoie is dead. We can't bring people back from the dead."

"Then I should wish you good fortune as you have just over one week to either figure out how or come up with another solution. And if you do not, you'll send your friend back where she was fated to be. And after that, You. Are. Mine. Do not return until dusk, Saturday next."

The world goes black, and when the light of the half-moon returns, Cory and I are in the middle of the woods, just like Kira and I were that night. "Do you remember what just happened?" I ask frantically, scared I'm in this alone.

"Yes. Yes, I remember. Let's get out of here, then we can talk." He grabs my hand, and we move fast, expertly avoiding roots and stones. I have to pause to catch my breath once we exit the trees.

"Come on. In the truck." Cory waits until we reach the main road to speak again. "One of them is lying."

"Violet," I say. "Violet lied in her diary."

"How can you be sure?"

"Because Regret doesn't want to be trapped there. And look how angry she was."

"Why would Violet lie in her diary?"

"To cover her back if Regret ever figured out how to break the curse. Or in case her cousin Dorothy's body ever washed up."

"So what now?"

"We obviously can't bring Violet back from the dead to apologize." I hear my mother's voice in my head. *Never assume an apology means you're forgiven.* "And I'm not sure that's the path we want to follow anyway. Regret might be uninterested in forgiveness, but I have a feeling she wouldn't mind some vengeance."

"We don't have to offer up Ms. Elmira, do we?"

"No, Cory! At least . . . not literally. I was thinking something . . . symbolic."

CHAPTER 25

I'm pulling my braids into a bun at my vanity Sunday morning when Gabby Greta begins to whir. It startles me less this time. Like a cuckoo clock I've grown used to.

"Hi, I'm Gabby Greta, and I love you! I'm Gabby Greta! Can you count to . . . six? One, two, three . . ."

I pull on a sweatshirt and hurry out of the house to meet Cory at the park. It's overcast and cool. Dry brown leaves litter the sidewalk. It makes me nostalgic and sad. I'm supposed to be in high gear planning for my last ever high school Halloween party right now. I'm supposed to be laughing with Kira, not stuck in some strange place between wanting to save her and wanting to kill her. This used to be my favorite time of year, and when I free Regret—which I will, because the alternative is not an option—I can only hope that her promise to eliminate all the awful memories of that night works.

Cory waits for me at the picnic table with baked goods and warm drinks.

He passes me a fat banana nut muffin. "Fuel."

"Thank you." I pinch a chunk off the top and stuff it into my mouth. It is disturbingly good.

Cory smirks and nudges one of the drinks closer to me. I take a sip to wash down the muffin, then pull the cup back in surprise. "What is this? It's delicious."

"Maple oat milk latte. Thought you might like it." He lifts the other drink. "But I did grab a chai, too, just in case."

"No, this is perfect. Thank you." And once again I find myself surprised by how well he knows me. How good he is at predicting things that will bring me joy.

I eat another piece of muffin and speak with my hand covering my mouth as I chew, anxious to get started. "Okay. Dorothy Savoie, Violet's cousin. Regret says Violet killed her, but Violet wrote in her diary that Regret killed her."

Cory twists his mouth to the side. "That's not exactly what Regret said."

"She said Violet was a murderer."

"Right. But she never said who she murdered."

"It's pretty obvious, though, isn't it? Who else could she be talking about?"

He shrugs. "I don't know, but I'll try to get some useful info out of someone at church today."

"Oh, I forgot! I said I'd go, too. Plus, that lady at town hall said churches might have old records. If I search while the service is going, I won't have to worry as much about getting busted."

THE early service is already in session when we pull into the packed parking lot of Fairville First Baptist.

I look down at my clothes. "I should have worn something else. I'm going to stick out like a sore thumb if someone sees me."

Cory holds up his index finger and reaches into the back seat. He returns with the skirt I wore to the funeral yesterday in hand. "You left it in here."

I grab it from him, excited by my luck, and slide it over my burgundy leggings. I pull at the stretchy fabric. "Think I can get away with leaving these on?"

"Yeah. It looks fine."

"Give me this." I tug on the sleeve of his black rain jacket before tearing out of my light gray sweatshirt and tossing it in the back. I can't help but snort when Cory falters at the sight of the tiny black tank I wore to bed.

He bites his knuckles and looks out of his window. "Can you blame me?"

I roll my eyes. "Give me the jacket."

Cory unzips his jacket and it's my turn to stare as he wiggles his way out of it. He wears a short-sleeved butter-yellow polo that makes his perfectly moisturized brown skin glow and grips his bicep . . . pleasantly. He catches me looking and smirks, but is gentlemanly enough not to say a word.

I slip on his jacket and let down my braids. My sneakers throw things off, but this is one thousand times better. "Okay. I think I'm good."

We both hop out of the car and start walking toward the church.

"Text me if you run into any problems, otherwise meet me at the truck after."

"I will. And thank you, Cory. Truly. You don't have to be doing any of this."

"I was interested in learning more about Regret before you knew Doll's Head existed. I'd be doing this anyway."

"Oh, right," I say with an awkward laugh.

"I'd be a creep if I said I was happy about the circumstances that led us to doing this together, but it's been nice spending time with you again."

He opens the front door for me and I go inside. The lobby

smells like coffee and fresh paint. Singing floats from the sanctuary and Cory heads off in that direction. There's a large fellowship hall to my left. A sign on the wall shows that the bathrooms, pastor's office, and rooms 1A through 1D are to my right. Two of the numbered rooms are full of children attending Sunday school. A little girl waves at me as I walk by, and I wave back. A woman exits the restroom when I get to the end of the hall and holds the door open for me. It's then that I realize there'd be nowhere else beyond this point anyone would expect me to be going. I enter the restroom just for show, count to ten, and then peek back into the hall. No one is there so I hurry to my right toward the pastor's office. The door is wooden with a frosted window with REV. EUGENE L. INGLEWOOD lettered on it. I try the knob, and, to no surprise, it doesn't turn.

At the end of the hall is the door to the basement. There is a closed folding chair wedged in the jam. I set the chair aside, push open the door, and call down, "Hello? Is anyone down there?" When no one answers, I descend the steps. It's cool and moldy smelling. Ancient furniture and boxes are everywhere, but in the back left corner, there is a large shelf, chair, and table with a lamp on it that seem well cared for. There's even a mug of tea sitting on a coaster. I figure whoever was working here went up for the services.

I scan the shelves, pleased to find them nicely organized. Records are sorted into boxes by year. I pull the box labeled 1956 and a plume of dust comes with it. I set it on the table and carefully remove the lid. Inside there are just a couple of logbooks and one file folder. I open the logbook on top. A table of contents is written on the first page:

Tab A: Births
Tab B: Deaths

Tab C: Marriages
Tab D: Divorces
Tab E: Adoptions

I scan through Tab A, looking for any familiar names. There had been rumors that Evelyn had a child, but if they were true, it either didn't happen in 1956, or Fairville First Baptist didn't keep a record of it. I move on to Tab B, this time specifically searching for Dorothy. My heart skips a beat when I see the name Savoie, but it's someone named Fabien. I skip over Tab C and D and contemplate E for a moment, wondering if a baby placed up for adoption would be listed in A first. I turn to the page, and I'm surprised to find eight entries. Data is organized into columns: date, adoption coordinator, birth mother, birth father, child DOB, and sex of the child. I frown, frustrated that the adoptive parents aren't listed, but I guess completely closed adoptions were more common back then. The adoption coordinator column has the same three names, with Deidra Hightower showing up most frequently. Deidra Hightower is Mama Dee, who's already on my list of people to speak to. Just last month the town threw a party celebrating her one hundredth birthday. She was surprisingly spry and lucid and ate three slices of cake, saying she wouldn't mind one bit if that was the thing to finally take her out of the game.

I run my finger down the birth mother column and nearly leap out of my skin when I see Evelyn Young written there on line seven. Birth father: unknown; child DOB: April 30, 1954; sex of child: M.

My eyebrows inch together. This boy was two years old at the time of his adoption. Is it possible she hid her pregnancy and child for so long? I trace my finger back to the adoption coordinator line and smile when I see Deidra Hightower.

CHAPTER 26

I explore a few more boxes and ledgers to make sure there is nothing else of value before sneaking back up the basement stairs. I make it to the lobby just as the early service is letting out. My stomach drops to my feet when I spot Trenton's parents talking with another couple. I make a beeline for the exit.

"Simone?" Trenton's mom calls when I'm only steps away from the doors.

If I didn't freeze at the sound of my name, I might have been able to pretend I didn't hear her. I take a deep breath and turn around. "Oh, hi, Mrs. Jones. How are you?"

"I'm well, thank you." Her once salt-and-pepper Afro has gone completely gray. "It's so good to see you. Did you come with Cory?"

"Yes, ma'am, I did."

Her eyes light up, crinkling at the corners. "I love to hear that. We are happy to have you. Why didn't I see you stand when Pastor welcomed the visitors?"

"I—I must have been in the restroom." What's the penalty for lying in church? Whatever it is can't be worse than what I've already done.

"Oh, I see." She pats my upper back. "I know my Trenton baby is up in heaven grinning ear to ear at me finding you here."

I grow queasy at the mention of his name. I can't imagine anything I could do that would make Trenton Jones smile down on me. All I can offer her is a nod. "I better go. I think Cory is waiting for me."

"Okay. See you next week."

I step outside and unzip Cory's jacket, desperate to let some of the heat trapped against my skin out. I walk to where his truck is parked, weaseling my way through clusters of people chatting about the service and brunch plans.

"Hey, I wasn't—" Cory starts as soon as I open the door, but pauses when he sees my face. "What's wrong? What happened?"

I get inside. "It's nothing. I'm fine. I just—I didn't know Trenton's parents went to this church."

Cory presses his hand to his forehead. "Damn, I'm sorry. I knew that. I could have warned you."

"No, it's okay. It's just . . ."

"What?"

"Mrs. Jones was so kind."

"She was always that way."

I shrug. "I never interacted with her much. And I don't deserve her kindness."

"Don't say that, Simone."

"I don't, Cory. All we had to do was be on time. That's it. And he'd still be here."

"That's . . . not true."

"It is!"

"We just talked about this the other day, Simone. It was a freak accident."

I can tell there is something he isn't saying. "What is it?"

He shakes his head. "Nothing."

"I thought you were an open book with me," I say, knowing it's the exact kind of statement to force him to open up.

He rests his hands at the bottom of the steering wheel. "I think it's not as simple as you're making it."

"How much simpler can it get? The only reason he was on that street was because he was looking for us."

"I'm just not so sure everything is always cause and effect. Sometimes things just happen."

"So what are you trying to say? That it was 'his time' or something? Because if so, you can shut all the way up with that. If you believe that, then why are you even bothering to help me? If *our time* is fated, if it's already written in the stars, then what's the point?"

"I don't mean—"

"Let's just drop it. It is what it is. Nothing we can do about the past, but I sure as hell won't just be accepting that I'm destined to kill Kira."

"I swear you're determined to misunderstand me." He starts up the truck and pulls out of the church parking lot.

"Okay, so tell me what other interpretation I was supposed to take from that."

"What I meant was, you have no way of knowing what would have happened if we got there on time. If it'd been me or you or anyone else on that street when that car came barreling down." He flicks on his turn signal. "The only person to blame is the driver, who wasn't paying attention."

I exhale and look out my window, completely over the conversation and mad that I can't go home and sit in my feelings. I can't do that, and it feels so incredibly unfair. I didn't mean to push Kira. I'm remorseful about the bad things I've done. Why does the cost of correcting my mistakes have to be so high?

We stop at a red light, and I feel Cory stare at me for a few seconds before speaking. "I'm sorry. Can we just . . . left turn?"

I don't look at him, but I nod.

"Did you find out anything useful at the church?"

"Yeah." My nerves settle some as the events from the basement come rushing back, temporarily pushing away thoughts of Trenton and his family. "Something huge, actually."

"Okay, let's hear it."

"I found a record saying Evelyn put a young son up for adoption."

"Are you serious?"

"As a heart attack."

"So some of the rumors were true then."

"I guess so."

"Well, we've already figured out that offering Regret toys does nothing. Was there anything else in the records that might help?"

"They had a few key people organizing the adoptions, and the one that did Evelyn's is a name you'll know."

"Who?"

"Deidra Hightower. Mama Dee."

"Hundred-year-old Mama Dee who owns that conjure shop in old downtown?"

"That's the one."

"Seriously? We were planning to talk to her anyway!"

"I know. Exactly."

"Call and see if they're open. We can go right now."

I search for the shop on Google and am surprised to find they have Sunday hours. Unfortunately, it says appointments are required to speak with Mama Dee. I tap the phone number to call. The line rings for a while before someone finally picks up. "Mama Dee's Conjure Shop."

"Hi, good morning. I was wondering if Mama Dee has any appointments open for today?"

"She is out of town today and tomorrow. But let me check the rest of the week." There is some clicking and typing in the background. I wait, wondering what business a one-hundred-year-old woman would have out of town. "Okaaay, let's see. She is booked up on Tuesday and Wednesday.... The first available is this Thursday at four PM."

"Is there any way you could squeeze us in on Tuesday or like, put us on a waitlist for cancellations?"

"No, ma'am. Mama Dee is strict on energies and the will of the universe. She's also quite elderly, and we look at cancellations as ordained opportunities for her to rest."

I sigh. "I understand. Is it okay if I bring someone with me?"

"Yes, we do allow one guest to be present. Would you like me to pencil you in for the Thursday appointment?"

"Yes. Yes, please."

"Wonderful. I'll need your phone number and email so I can send over a questionnaire before your meeting. You'll also have the opportunity to select which tier of her services will best suit your needs and budget."

I give her my information and hang up.

Cory looks at me nervously out of the corner of his eye. "When is it?"

"Thursday at four."

"Oh, that's not bad. I thought you were going to say Saturday."

"It's not bad to you! Cory, we are going to be pushing it to the wire. I can't put all my eggs in this basket. I need to explore other solutions in the meantime."

"Do you have any ideas?"

"No? I don't know. Maybe I need to back away from her life story altogether. I want to go through every one of those books on magic with a fine-tooth comb. You said there were a few different options for breaking restriction curses, right?"

"Yeah. There are."

Cory drives us to the library where we spend three hours flipping through books and scouring the internet for anything that might help us. I'm frustrated and overwhelmed by the end. I slap my book shut. "No way I'm going to be able to arrange for a priest to follow me out there with three gallons of holy water and fifty pounds of sage."

"Probably not. But I saw a few things that seemed like they could have some promise. Let's grab some lunch at Ozzy's, and we can talk about it."

We go to the pizza shop, and Cory places an order for us with one of his coworkers while I grab a booth in the back. He slides onto the bench across from me a minute or two later, Sprites in hand. Both our sets of long legs bump against each other under the table. We laugh a little as we struggle to find a comfortable arrangement.

"There we go." Cory relaxes into his seat, each of his knees on either side of one of mine.

"Sorry," I say.

He leans back and peers under the table before looking back up at me. "Simone Washington, you have absolutely nothing to be sorry about."

I smirk. "That's decidedly untrue, but okay. What's this super-promising discovery you made?"

"Pretty sure I didn't use the word 'super.'"

"Speaking it into existence. Go ahead."

"I watched this YouTube video on the power of confession."

"Maybe I really do need to see about getting a priest to go out there with us."

"No—well, it wouldn't hurt. But this video wasn't even coming at it from a religious view. It was one of those crunchy granola girl channels."

"That sounds very reliable, Cory."

"She's a certified life coach."

I raise my eyebrows. "Not helping yourself."

"Just hear me out."

"I'm listening."

"Okay, so, the power of confession. I think it might have to do with why we flopped so hard with the forgiveness thing. How can we offer Regret forgiveness for something she hasn't even taken responsibility for? Like yeah, that could have benefit to the person offering it, but to the receiver? It'd only piss them off. Which is exactly what happened."

"I thought we were on the same page in believing Regret's side of things, though. Wasn't Violet the one who needed to confess? Isn't that our whole issue right now? Because, you know, she's dead."

"No, you're missing the point. There is power in the unburdening." He leans forward, closer to me. "I'm talking power of the mystical variety. *We* need power to release Regret. So *we*, as in you and me, need to confess."

The room grows warm, and I take a long sip of my Sprite. "Confess what?" I ask, even though I already know. The night everything went down, Regret herself asked me to do it. To tell her my biggest regret. She's the only one who I've spoken to about what happened with Rich, and she saw through that faster than I did. She knows that's not my biggest regret.

"We both have things weighing on us."

"Trenton?"

"Shh, shh." Cory brings a finger to his mouth. "I don't think we should talk about it together first. Don't want to waste the power of confession in Ozzy's," he adds with a hesitant laugh.

"Just think about it. It's something we can try next time we go out."

"Next time is my last chance. She said not to go back until Saturday."

"Which is why we are going to go in armed with a few ideas. Did you find anything besides the holy water and sage?"

"When I was reading about the sage, I found a lot about burning items in general. The symbol of it. I was thinking we could gather up some of the dolls and toys in the woods and burn them on the beach. Violet's diary too."

Cory searches his bag for his notebook. "I like that."

The pizza arrives as he finishes writing, and we eat for a few silent minutes. My mind spins the way it does every time Trenton passes through it.

"I need to go to the restroom." I get up from my seat and go to the ladies' room. Straight to my stall. I close and lock the door. Turn my back and lean against the cool metal. The hinge digs into my shoulder blade, but I welcome it. Something to distract me from the flickers of painful memories trying to overtake my mind once again. I inhale deeply. Press my fingertips against the Sharpie writing on the wall. The writing I can find without looking.

I hear echoes of Mom's voice in my head, but for the first time since she went away, it isn't enough. I need to see her. I need to talk to her. There are so many questions I want answered. Questions I need answered. I can't even articulate them, but I feel the weight of them on my shoulders. But there's another feeling just as strong. A sensation that implores me not to go there. Not to open that can of worms. To accept her decision to go no contact instead of continuing to prod the corner of my mind where most of my memories of her are held. They are trapped behind the thinnest veil. One that has already popped a few seams. Is that something I'm ready to unleash? Hard no. Not with everything else going on. And that thought puts an abrupt end to the whirling inside my head. I have this place, haunted by her living ghost, to thank for that.

Someone else enters the restroom. I exit the stall and approach the sink to wash my hands. A woman stands next to me, reapplying her lipstick.

"The pizza here is great," she says before rolling her lips together and releasing them with a smack. "I ate like six slices."

"Yeah," I say with a polite laugh, fixating on the word *six*, half expecting her to mash her lipstick into the mirror and write the number over and over. Six days left.

She throws her hair behind her shoulders and adjusts her necklace. Seeing it makes me remember something from last night. On the dock. The glint of metal. I pat my pockets frantically as if I'm wearing the same pants. As if I'd just tucked the necklace into them. I'm terrified that I lost it. Maybe because it seems like a lifeline to Kira. A reason to see her. An olive branch, of sorts. Like returning a piece of Rich to her may repair some of the cracks that have formed between us. There is a whisper in the back of my mind. One that tells me not to go to her. Not to take that risk. It battles with another voice that says I found that necklace for a reason and should do something about it. I leave the bathroom, not completely sure which voice will win until I reach the table again.

"Thanks for lunch, but I need to go home."

"Wait," Cory says, slipping from his seat. "Let me drive you."

"It's just a couple of blocks, and I could use the alone time."

"You're sure?"

"Yeah." I don't want to explain what has me so frazzled. I don't want him to talk me out of taking the necklace to Kira. I don't want to hear reason. It'll be quick. One small show of good faith and then back to my place. Five minutes tops.

At home, I march straight to my overflowing dirty clothes hamper. I find the sweats I wore to the lake yesterday at the top of the pile and reach into one of the pockets. There's something in it, but it's not the necklace. It's the LX vial. I'd forgotten about that, too. I hide it behind a book on my shelf to deal with later and search the other pocket for the necklace, and there it is. I let the sweatpants fall to the floor but keep the gold chain tight in my grasp. The voices saying I shouldn't go return, this time upgraded from a whisper. None of my visits with Kira have gone well since the party, but this feels like it could be different. She'd probably expect me to throw the necklace in the trash, especially by the way I reacted to it at first. I think about it for only a few more seconds before checking Kira's location on my phone and heading to Layla's.

I hear people talking in the backyard when I get there, so I let myself through the gate. John's leaning against their grill, looking down at his phone. Kira and Layla sit at their wrought iron bistro table. Layla spots me first. Her expression makes Kira turn around.

"What are you doing here, Simone?" Kira asks in a tone that reveals our limited communication has done nothing to soften her.

"Hey, come on." John pockets his phone. "Don't be like that, Kir."

Kira cuts her eyes at him. "Don't tell me how to be." Her words sound personal and aggressive.

John throws his hands in the air, offers me a *yikes* face, and ducks into the house. Kira watches him go, mouth twisted into a hard frown.

Layla scoots her chair back, the legs scratching against the concrete slab. "On that note . . ." She grabs her drink and follows her husband inside.

Part of me wishes she would stay, like it might keep the dark thoughts that have been bubbling up whenever I'm around Kira from reaching the surface.

"I'm not ready to talk to you, Simone."

That sentence alone ignites something red deep within me. If she could just keep quiet, there'd be nothing to worry about. . . . Again I visualize reaching across the table and covering her mouth . . . her nose . . . making it impossible for her to talk . . . to br—

"Simone?"

I shake my head, afraid of my own thoughts. Is it possible I could follow through with the consequences of failing to hold up my end of the deal before the deadline even comes? Surely not. Either way, I need to get this over with quickly.

"Sorry. I'm not here to talk, not really." As I say it, I realize she said she's not *ready* to talk to me. That's a good sign. It implies that one day she will be. There's another side to all of this.

"If you aren't here to talk, then why are you here?" She picks up her phone. "I guess I need to go ahead and stop sharing my location."

"I found something," I say, suddenly aware I don't have a good explanation for how I found it. "I-It was wrapped up in my things. I only just got around to unpacking my bag from the party."

"What is it?"

"The necklace Rich gave you." I reach into my pocket and pull it out.

She doesn't make a move for it, so I place it in the middle of the table in front of her. She barely gives it a second glance. I expected her to be more sentimental. More grateful. The fact that she isn't bothers me. And I'm aware that it's upsetting me far more than is reasonable. "I thought it'd mean a lot to you to have it back."

The tip of her nose reddens, followed by her eyes. It does mean something to her. Finally she reaches for it, eyes watery, hands trembling. "I didn't even know I'd lost it." She fumbles with the clasp, and without thinking, I gently take it from her hands and stand behind her. It takes a couple of seconds before she lifts her ponytail out of the way so I can put it on her.

I reach around her, noticing how tiny her neck is, how thin and delicate the skin over her carotid artery is, how easy it'd be to— One side of the chain drops from my right hand. It sticks to the warm skin of her back. That floral, smoky fragrance I've come to associate with Regret and the lake filters through the air. I close the clasp and quickly back away.

"There," I say. "That's all I wanted." I rush out of the yard, disgusted with myself. I hear her chair slide back. I feel her watching me, and I know she wants to call out. She doesn't, but knowing that she wants to means everything.

CHAPTER 27

"Simma, that you?" Dad calls when I enter through the front door.

It takes me a second to force down the string of sarcastic responses that my overstimulated mind coughs up. "Yes, Dad. It's me."

He trots down the stairs and stops on the last step. "Got a call from Officer Long."

I do my best to keep my expression neutral. "My friends said he started calling people in for a second round of questioning."

"Oh, you knew? Why didn't you say anything?"

I shrug out of Cory's jacket and hang it on the rack. "I didn't think it was a big deal. It's not, right?"

"No. No. There was no urgency about it. They are just doing their due diligence."

I wonder how much he knows. If he's heard about the drugs. "When do I have to go in?"

"Tuesday. After school. I'll pick you up."

I nod and study his face. He looks a little run-down. "You okay, Dad?"

"Oh, I'm fine. Just about to go tidy some things up. Kitchen needs cleaning."

"You've been talking about hiring cleaners for ages. You can afford it. Why not just bite the bullet? You look like you could use some rest."

He scrunches his nose. "Hard to find good service these days. Best to do it yourself."

"Try Delia's Home Cleaning." I pull out my phone to look up their number and text it to him. "John had them come out to clean the cabin before the party. They did a good job. Saw it with my own eyes." And throwing some extra business their way is the least I can do after the help their employee gave me at Ms. Elmira's.

Dad huffs, unsure. "I'll give them a call."

"Great. Go claim your spot on the couch and relax. I need to catch up on some homework."

"Yeah, you do. I was going to give you another week before I said anything."

"On it."

He steps aside.

In my room, I send Cory a quick update, then shoot Kira a message asking if Officer Long set up an appointment with her too. Cory replies right away, but he's not the one I want to hear from. I close out all the open apps on my phone, waiting for Kira to respond, but she doesn't. I did run out of there pretty abruptly. She's probably sick of the hot and cold with me. The logical part of my brain tries its best to make this thought the dominant one. But the emotional side, the unreliable side, whispers other things. And like fog creeping over me, those whispers manage to overtake everything else.

She's angry at you. She's going to say something to the police.

She's going to make them suspicious of you. She hates you. She knows. She knows what you did. She'll ruin you. You shouldn't have made that deal. You have to stop her.

My phone dings, breaking the spiral. I snatch it up, hoping it's her, but it's Cory again.

Cory
Let me drive you to school tomorrow. Talk then?

Me
sure.

The next morning there's a knock on the front door. I walk downstairs to open it, expecting to see Cory, but there's no one. I look up and down the street. Nothing—except for a box of things left on the doormat. Instantly I recognize them as Kira's things, but not just any of Kira's things. Things *I* gave her. Things that mean something significant to our friendship. I'm fuming before I can even bend down and investigate the box further. I find the necklace balled up and tangled in the left corner and whip out my phone.

Me
What's this box about? And the necklace is in it. What makes you think I'd want that?

She responds right away.

Kira
That necklace is not mine. I don't know where you got it or what game you're trying to play, but it's not cute.

I examine the circular golden pendant with the *K* engraved on it. I can see it so clearly. The glint of the gold around her neck in the moonlight on the dock.

Me

I saw you drop it.

That's not exactly true, but explaining how I know would involve telling her that the "dream" she had was real, and I don't think she's ready to receive that. I don't want her to receive it. In the end, I don't have to explain because she blocks me. And with the blocking, the fears that she'll say something to betray me to the police return. I don't know if they are founded or if this is just Regret playing with my mind. Setting up for what she thinks will be my failure. I throw my phone in my purse and get ready for school, taking some aggression out on everything I touch. I move quickly, determined to be out of the house before Gabby Greta announces that I have only five days left. I don't need the reminder.

I grab my things and go wait for Cory outside.

"Good morning," I say through the window when he pulls into the driveway.

I get inside, and he flinches when I slam the door shut.

"Sorry."

"It's okay," he chuckles. "Good morning."

I pull down the sun visor and slide open the mirror. Car mirrors are the most brutally honest things on this planet. I swipe at some stubborn eyebrow hairs.

"You good?" he asks.

"Cory, I'll go ahead and let you know the answer to that question is going to be a hard no unless we, and Kira, make it to Halloween in one piece."

"I meant it relatively speaking, but okay."

I lay my head against the headrest. "Kira blocked me. I'm not looking forward to dodging her at school all week."

"You're going to have to."

"I know that, Cory. I know. Jeez."

It's rare that a silence is awkward between us, but an uncomfortable quiet descends over the car.

"I'm sorry for snapping," I say after a minute or two. "We're supposed to be using this drive productively."

"Right. So let's recap then. We are going to try confession and burning the dolls and diary. Did you really want to look into the priest thing? I can do that today. I'm ahead on my schoolwork."

"I want to throw everything at her that we possibly can."

"How are you feeling about your meeting with Officer Long tomorrow?"

I shrug. "Just want to get it over with."

Cory and I discuss everything we've discovered so far and start outlining a detailed day-of plan for the remainder of the drive to my school. He drops me off out front, and I go straight to my first-period class, hoping to avoid catching even so much as a glimpse of Kira out of the corner of my eye.

At lunchtime, I check my email and there is a new message from Mama Dee's Conjure Shop.

> Thank you for booking your appointment with Mama Dee. Please read the instructions below carefully and follow the link to complete the pre-consultation questionnaire prior to arriving for your session. Failure to do so may result in delays.
>
> Please arrive twenty minutes before your scheduled time.

Would a real psychic need a pre-visit questionnaire? Seems like a scheme to get enough information to social-media stalk clients before a visit so she can randomly drop the name of their great-aunt, calling out from the beyond. I browse the conjure shop's Google reviews, trying to see if anyone else found the questionnaire odd. A few customers noted that it did raise their scam red flags, but the appointment itself turned them into believers. But I guess it doesn't matter either way for me since a reading isn't the purpose of my visit. I just have to hope Mama Dee is willing to open up about her past. That she can even recall memories from seventy-plus years ago. I'm about to click back to my email when a name in the reviews catches my eye. Abigail Dawson. The grandmother of Natalie Dawson—the college student who disappeared this past summer.

Abigail Dawson
6 Reviews 1 Photo

★★★★★ a month ago

Deidra used to teach my Sunday School classes when I was a girl. I'm ashamed to admit that I, along with so many other members of the congregation, shunned her when it came out she was doing these psychic readings on the side. I pray every day, and after the disappearance of my dear granddaughter, Natalie, I've kicked it up to every hour. Some may say I'm rushing the Lord, seeking guidance from a medium, but I prefer to view it as trusting the gifts he bestowed upon others! And my, my, did he bless sweet Ms. Deidra Hightower. All I will say is this . . . I love you and I miss you, Natalie, baby. Justice will be served in this realm and the next!

 Like

I screenshot the review and send it to Cory.

Cory
Whoa. I mean there were rumors about
Mama Dee seeing Natalie's ghost but this
makes it seem like she believes there's been
some sort of foul play

Me
I thought that was obvious

Cory
People assume, but the police haven't
mentioned anyone else being involved

Me
Justice will be served . . . what do you think
she means by that?

Cory
Hard to say. Half sounds like she hired
Mama Dee as a hit man

I send a few laughing emojis, picturing a hundred-year-old woman rolling up, guns blazing.

Me
Maybe you can ask her a few questions for
your blog series on Natalie

Cory
Some other time for sure. But it's not the
priority right now.

My heart swells because he gave the response I didn't know I wanted—the response that proves he is truly all in when it comes to helping me resolve this. I click on the link at the bottom of the email, and it takes me to a purple Google form.

Mama Dee's Conjure Shop
Pre-Consultation Questionnaire

General Information

a. Name:
_____

b. Date of Birth:
_____

Select a Consultation Tier from the list below:

a. Diamond—1 hour, $350
b. Gold—30 minutes, $200
c. Silver—10 minutes, $90
d. Bronze—5 minutes, $50

Personal Background

a. What is your primary reason for seeking this consultation?
_____

b. Do you have any specific questions you would like to focus on during the session?
_____

c. Are there any recent life events you feel are relevant for the consultation?
_____

I select the gold tier, then spend the entire lunch block debating how to answer the personal background questions. On the first, I explain that I'm not actually interested in a reading at all and pray it won't lead to a cancellation. But I want to be clear before I step foot in there. If Mama Dee has the gifts she claims to, I don't want anything to do with it. I don't want any more previews of the future. I don't need anything distracting me or depressing me even more. Not when I have so little time left to figure things out. Memories of Trenton interrupt every other thought as I type my responses, explaining, vaguely, the real reason for our visit. In a different world, I might consider talking to her about him. But in this world, if I get things right, all my painful memories will be obliterated, hopefully only leaving the bright spots behind.

CHAPTER 28

Dad picks me up Tuesday after school to go to the police station. Officer Long lets us know he'll be with us in just a few minutes, so we take a seat in the waiting area. A young boy wanders over, plops into the seat next to me, and stares at me, smiling. Dad waves at him and nudges my shoulder.

"Hey," I say with something close to a smile.

"Hi!" he responds cheerfully.

A woman across the room looks up from a book. "Gabe?"

The little boy pays her no mind. "Today's my birthday."

"Happy birthday," I say. "How old are you?"

The woman spots him then. "I am so sorry," she says, rushing over and taking his hand.

"No worries," Dad says. "Happy birthday, little man."

She brushes some fuzz from his head. "It's not his birthday yet." She gives an exhausted smile. "Four more days!"

The little boy begins to chant as they walk away. "Four days! Four days! Four days!" Slowly, in my mind, his voice transitions into Regret's.

"You all right, Simma?"

"Uh, yeah. A little anxious is all." And you would be too if a ghost witch was using cute little kids to send you ominous messages right before you get interviewed by the police about a death you definitely had something to do with.

"It's okay, baby girl. This is nothing to—"

"No, it's fine, Dad. I'm fine. I think I just need to stand. Walk around."

"Yeah, of course. Do what you need to do."

I go to the front entrance and study a big bulletin board filled with missing person signs. There's no consistency in format, so I assume they were all made by the people's families. I wonder if the board is a way to placate them. A free place to advertise their loss that feels more significant than a utility pole or grocery store. I wonder if it makes them feel better knowing their loved one's picture is hanging in a police station. I wonder if they consider that the officers couldn't even be bothered to post the signs themselves. I spot a fresh one of Natalie Dawson on the far-left side and move for a closer look.

Officer Long approaches then. "Not gonna lie. That one has us stumped."

"Natalie?"

He nods and directs me and Dad to a conference room.

"How do you deal with that?" I ask.

Officer Long raises his eyebrows in question.

"How do you get over the cases you can't solve?"

He thinks for a moment, allowing us to enter the room before him. We all have a seat at the table. "I don't know that I ever get over the ones we can't solve. I also don't know that I ever give up hope that we will one day. But every case we *can* close eases the ache. I like to think in some way, justice for one is justice for another."

His words strike a chord with me, but I don't have time to ponder them as Officer Long quickly moves on.

"How've you been holding up, Simone?" he asks.

"Okay, I guess."

"I know it's a difficult time, and the last place you want to be is in here talking to me, so let's make it quick. I only have a few additional questions for you."

"Okay."

"Did you take any recreational drugs at your party?"

"What?" Dad interjects.

Officer Long holds up his hands. "Let me do my job, Tony. I have to ask."

"No, sir," I answer. I'm still not entirely sure no one attempted to drug me, but it definitely feels best *not* to bring that up.

"Do you know if any of your friends took anything?"

I shake my head. "They were just drinking, and that's not something any of us does often, either."

"Shouldn't be doing it ever until you're twenty-one," Dad says.

Officer Long agrees with Dad but looks unsurprised by my responses. "Simone, did you attend a rave at a warehouse in Sittersville on Friday, September 10?"

I wonder if that means Kira has already been here. Did she tell them about the rave, or did Rich's parents? "No, sir. I've never been to Sittersville. I don't even have a car."

"September 10 is my sister's birthday," Dad says. "We went out for hibachi, then did a game night at her place."

"Why do you ask?" I can't help myself. "About the rave?"

Officer Long scribbles on his notepad. "As you're already aware, teens tend to get into things they aren't supposed to at parties, and a rave is just a big party. They've started popping up around here more often in the past year or so and we've seen some concerning trends since."

"Like what?"

"This one has a lot of questions, don't she?" Officer Long asks my Dad.

Dad gives me a stern look. "Yes, she does. Sorry. Please continue."

"Simone, since the last time we spoke, has anything else come to mind about that night that you feel might be useful to share?"

"Yes, actually." I glance at Dad, who looks taken aback. "Um. Before everyone else got there, I ran into a groundskeeper. Nate, I think, was his name. I'm not saying he did anything, but he was on the property that day before everything got going."

"Why are you just now bringing this up, Simone?" Dad asks.

"Sorry, I was kind of distracted by Rich being found dead."

Dad jerks his head back. "Watch your tone, now. I know you've been through a lot but don't forget who you're talking to."

"Take it easy, you two," Officer Long says. "We've spoken to the groundskeeper. He came up on the security footage, and John Yearwood told us you'd texted about him. Said he watched the man get in his car and drive off, but couldn't be completely sure that he didn't return later in the night."

"Is he a suspect?"

"We can't disclose all that, darling. But if it will set your heart at ease some, we are still looking into this as an accidental death, okay?"

I want to believe him, but his eyes flash over to Dad's briefly. One of those looks shared between adults that very loudly says there is something they aren't saying.

Officer Long asks me a few more seemingly harmless questions before dismissing us. In the car, I replay everything, worried I said the wrong thing. It doesn't help that Dad's unusually quiet. At a stoplight, I spot another poster of Natalie Dawson, and my thoughts shift back to her. When I get inside the house, I grab my laptop and google her, browsing for anything new. Eventually, I land on YouTube, where I watch a handful of reports from assorted news stations. They are all different variations of the same information. I backtrack to my home page, and there's a new set of recommended videos based on my recent browsing. The first is titled "Exclusive: Parents of Missing College Student Plead for Answers." I recognize the person in the thumbnail as Natalie Dawson's mother, but the still image is not familiar in any other way. I click it and skip over an ad.

The video has been recorded in someone's living room—Natalie's family home, maybe. I definitely haven't seen this before. Excited and anxious, I carefully listen to the interview, but can't help but feel let down as it nears its close. Different setting. Same questions. Same answers. It's only the reporter finally acknowledging the person sitting next to Natalie's mom that makes me watch until the end.

"And you're her sister, right?" they ask, voice gentle.

"Yes, sir. My name is Rosalie."

"Is there anything you'd like to say?"

She looks into the camera, eyes glistening. "Just that we love you, Kay. We miss you and want you to come home."

I drag the scrubber back a few seconds and release it.

"Just that we love you, Kay."

Again.

"Just that we love you, Kay."

Kay? Why would she call her that when her name is Natalie? Natalie *M.* Dawson, I learned from a previous video. I scroll down to the comments. User88271 had the same question as me, and a Rosalieee13 was kind enough to reply.

> **Rosalieee13:** Sorry for the confusion! Me and my sister's names rhyme—thanks mom! Friends and family call us by our middle names to avoid mix-ups. Hers is Mikayla, but I couldn't say it when I was little, so Kay Kay it was.

I grab my phone and go to Instagram. Type "Rosalie Dawson" in the search bar. I click on three incorrect profiles before finding hers. The first post on her grid is a picture of her inside a bookstore with a stack of paperbacks in her arms. The next is a carousel post. The caption reads **Happy birthday, sis. We'll never stop looking.** The first picture is of her and Natalie as little girls dressed as Disney princesses. I tap the tag button and try to go to Natalie's Instagram, but it's private. I go back to the carousel on Rosalie's page and swipe. Photo two is a picture of them with their parents on a cruise ship. In photo three, Natalie and a large fluffy dog are playing outside. And photo four. Photo four is a picture of Natalie seated outside a coffee shop. Sunglasses on. Smile on her face. Gold chain with the letter *K* around her neck—but that's not the only thing. Her laptop is covered in stickers, and right in the middle, right over the Apple logo, is a cartoon astronaut vomiting up a rainbow.

CHAPTER 29

I bound from my chair and dump the box of things Kira dropped off onto my bed, thanking God that I didn't throw it all out. I sift through the items until I find the necklace. Once I do, I race back to my phone and compare the pictures. I go to Kira's page and swipe through everything looking for her necklace. When I don't find it, I reluctantly go to Rich's, and sure enough, it's right there in the second post. His arm is thrown around Kira's shoulders as he kisses her cheek. She grins in a white square-neck top. I use my fingers to zoom in on her necklace. I study it and the one in my hand. There is one key difference. Kira's is sans serif. This one, and the one around Natalie's neck, is serif.

I gently place my phone and the necklace on my desk. I've been drawn to Natalie's case since I first heard about it. This doesn't feel like a coincidence. Does it mean Natalie was at Doll's Head Lake? Could Natalie *still* be at Doll's Head Lake? Did Regret see what happened to her? If so . . . if so . . . What was it Officer Long said earlier? Justice for one is justice for another.

I pick my phone back up and call Cory. It's raining outside, but I have to show him what I found in person. He needs to see it for himself. Connect the dots himself so I know I'm not just losing it. I ask him to meet me at the gazebo in the park in ten. He offers to pick me up, but I can't sit still. I'm out of the house and halfway up the street before he can insist.

By the time I make it to the park, my jeans are wet up to the knees. Cory is already there waiting for me. I hand him the necklace without saying anything.

"I thought you were going to give this back to Kira?"

I tell him to look at it closely while I pull up the picture of Rich and Kira. "What do you notice?"

His eyes dart between the necklace and the picture a few times.

"It's not the same necklace."

"Exactly. It's not the same necklace. Now look at this." My fingers shake with adrenaline as I pull up Rosalie Dawson's page again. "Look. This is Natalie Dawson. Look."

He squints. Zooms in. "There's even a tiny chip. . . ."

I snatch the phone back to see because I hadn't noticed that, and sure enough, it's there. "This is hers, Cory. She was at the lake."

"But why is she wearing a necklace with a *K* on it? The person who gave it to her . . . maybe their name starts with *K*?"

"Possibly. But I think it's something to do with her nickname. We can get into that later but . . ." I trail off, mind buzzing so violently I can barely think straight.

"Do you think something happened to her?" Cory asks.

"Yeah, I think something happened to her! She's missing."

"No, I mean, do you think it was an accident or something else?"

I see myself shoving Kira on the dock. That part wasn't an accident. I wanted her to back up. To give me space. But her falling. Her drowning. That *was* an accident. "I don't know. How could we know?"

"What do we do? Go to the police?"

"I think we need to rule out any connection with Regret first. This could be another thread. Another way out of this for me. Maybe breaking the curse has something to do with whatever happened to Natalie. I had my meeting with Officer Long earlier, and he said something interesting."

"What's that?"

"He said justice for one is justice for another. Dorothy Savoie probably died out at Doll's Head, and Regret couldn't get justice for her—Violet made sure of that by trapping her there. But what if getting justice for someone else could satiate her?" And if I'm the one to help break Natalie's case—if I could help her, if I could help someone—it might ease the guilt I feel over what happened to Trenton. And if it did, if that remorse was gone, what would be left for Regret to feed on? What would there be for me to confess? This could be a win in so many different ways. But is this necklace enough to lead me to answers in just four, now almost three, days? With the sticker to consider, too, I think it could be.

"Simone!" Cory shouts.

His tone startles me, and I look up, half expecting to see Regret emerging from the woods.

He takes my hands in his to calm me. "Sorry. You were zoning out. Talk to me."

I give him a quick rundown about the sticker, which I hadn't yet mentioned. I tell him how I saw it on Natalie's computer, and I pull up the picture I took of it on the card at Rich's burial site. "I also saw a guy at the funeral wearing a pin of it."

"So what are you getting at?"

I haven't even organized the thoughts in my own head yet, but it's time. "Rich and Natalie are both connected to those stickers somehow."

Cory nods encouragingly.

"Rich gave Kira a necklace that's similar to Natalie's."

"Mm-hmm."

"Natalie might have died out at the lake. . . ." I bite my tongue because the words that want to come out feel wrong, even though they make perfect sense. "Rich might have known Natalie, Cory. What if it was him? What if he drugged her? What if he *killed* her? What if what happened to him was some sort of cosmic retribution?"

"You said he was out at the dock before you and Kira that night, right? It's possible it wasn't his first time. And didn't you say the whole reason he was there was because he was luring some girl?"

I hadn't used the word *lure*, but when I think back to the messages I read on Shaina's phone, she didn't want to go to the dock. And of course she wouldn't. It was dark and scary out there. But Rich had insisted. He stopped replying when she questioned him about it. At the time, I thought it was because he was worried about Kira catching them, but now I'm not so sure. I rub my temples. "But what would some college girl want with Rich? Why would she follow him out there?"

"I mean, she was only nineteen. And not to be macabre, but she didn't necessarily go out there on her own free will. You already mentioned the drugs. . . ."

"I don't know. It just seems off."

"Okay, how about this. He got to know Natalie at whatever place throws those stickers out. Started up a whole side-relationship with her. Learned her nickname. Got a two-for-one deal on gold necklaces. Realized juggling two girls was too much. Tried to drop Natalie and something went wrong. But it's possible he charmed her to start with, right? I mean, he had that effect on all girls pretty much, didn't he?" Something strange passes over Cory's face. Something he works to quickly conceal.

My own face heats as that familiar feeling overtakes me. That feeling that Cory can see through me. That he knows things about me without me saying them aloud. But he doesn't have magical powers. He's not Regret. He's not Violet.

"Yes," I say, finding it easier to just admit it. "Yes. He had that effect on people. Lord only knows why."

This would make everything make sense. Regret hates murderers. Maybe she witnessed Rich kill Natalie and saw an opportunity to get some kind of justice. Maybe she *wanted* me to make that deal so she could have Rich. The possibility of her being freed is like icing on the cake. And Rich had plenty of regret for her to feed on, even outside of murder. Of course she'd want him.

CHAPTER 30

I skip school on Wednesday. Cory and I ride out to Sittersville to see if we can learn more about the rave Rich attended. On the way, I browse social media for any mentions of it, but I don't find much. We left Fairville early enough that the school day hasn't yet begun at Crescent Hall, Sitterville's only high school, and as I learned last night, Natalie's alma mater. Cory turns in to the student parking lot and finds a spot at the very back. We people watch for a few, trying to decide who might be able to give us more information.

"What about them?" Cory asks, pointing at a group of guys with skateboards.

I side-eye him. "Why them?"

He shrugs. "They look like they know things."

I rub my forehead and suppress a laugh. "What does that even mean? How about we start with people that Rich would be likely to hang around?"

Cory scans the parking lot. "Okay, how about them?" Now he points at a group of guys in letterman jackets standing around a pickup truck.

"Are you going to walk over and ask?"

"Yeah. I don't have any issues doing that."

"I'm sure you don't, but I think I spotted someone better." I get out of the truck. "Just wait here."

There is a girl leaning against her car, reading a book. She reminds me of myself, clearly familiar with the rowdy group of athletes but also in her own world.

"Hey," I say.

She looks up at me and squints, trying to figure out whether she is supposed to know me or not. She glances over her shoulder like maybe I was talking to someone else. "Hey," she replies hesitantly. "Do I know you?"

"No. I go to Pinegrove in Fairville."

She perks up at this. Of course she does. Fairville's been in the news. She's curious about what brought me here, and I have every intention of playing right into that.

"I'm sure you heard about Rich Pearson. The guy who passed away last week."

"Yes, oh my God. It's so sad. And he was a senior, right?"

"Yeah, he was. Rich was . . . my friend, and I'm still trying to make sense of things. There's been all this talk in the aftermath. Stuff that makes me feel like I didn't even know him."

"I'm sorry. That must be tough."

She doesn't know the half of it. "It is. Anyway, I came here because I know Rich went to a rave somewhere in town last month. I was hoping to find some people who were there and get a vibe for who he was in his final days."

"Yeah, I get that. I haven't been to one myself. It's mostly college kids that go, and you have to have an invite."

Natalie Dawson was a college kid. "How do you get an invite?"

"You just have to know the right people."

"Do you know any of those people?"

"I'm not interested in it, to be honest. Those parties are pretty hardcore. Like, 'drugs laced with fentanyl' hardcore."

I nibble my bottom lip, trying to figure out how to respectfully tell her that's not what I asked. "That's horrible. I wouldn't want to go to something like that, either. And if Rich was wrapped up in it, I really want to know how. I need to know who he spoke to. He has a little brother, you know?"

"I'm sure whoever directly invited him won't speak up, but . . ." She stands on her tiptoes. "Hey, Jackie!"

"What's up?" a redheaded girl in platform Converses shouts.

"Come here for a sec!"

Jackie takes her time walking over to us. She has a denim backpack full of decorative pins, and it doesn't take me long to spot the vomiting astronaut.

"Where did you get that?" I ask. Jackie contorts her body, trying to follow my gaze. "The astronaut pin."

"Ohh. You looking for an invite?" She gives me a careful once-over.

That's all the confirmation I need to connect the astronaut logo to the raves. "No, I was just hoping to find out the location of the one they had back in September."

"Is that all? You swear?"

Her intensity makes me nervous. "Yeah . . . why?"

"Because they aren't anything to play around with. The people who started them just use them to turn rich kids into addicts. Extort them for cash until they drop dead."

Rich was a rich kid. His cold, lifeless face appears in my mind. "I don't have much money," I lie. "And I'm not interested in drugs. I just need to know where that specific one was held."

Jackie looks at her friend for a second, debating. Then, with a sturdy exhale, she finally responds, "They never hold them in the same place twice, but I'm pretty sure it was at one of the abandoned warehouses on Orchid Street."

"Orchid Street. Great, thank you. That's helpful," I say, already backing away, resisting the urge to run.

"Hope you find what you're looking for," the first girl I spoke to says.

CORY and I park up the road from Orchid Street and walk to the warehouses. There are several overflowing trash cans lined up outside. One is tagged with a couple of the astronaut stickers.

"Guess we should go in," Cory says.

"Yeah." It's dark and scary looking in there. Instinctively, I grab his hand.

He quickly but gently closes his fingers around mine, and I tug him along through the open door. A rat or some other small furry animal skitters by our feet and I scream. This sets Cory off laughing.

I drop his hand and elbow him in the ribs. "Get it together."

"Sorry. I didn't expect the queen of fright to be spooked by a cute little—" He walks into a thick spiderweb and bats his arms around chaotically, running in circles to try to free himself from it.

I rest my hand on my hip until he settles. "You were saying?"

"Touché." He holds his arm out. "Can I have your hand back? Since we've established that we're both on edge."

"You can have it back, but I know it has nothing to do with you being scared."

He smirks and runs his thumb across the back of my hand.

We dodge several other critters and hazards before making it to the spot where the party was clearly held. There are streamers, pieces of exploded balloons, and trash all over.

"Yo, look at that." Cory points at a busted speaker. Sitting on top is a large bald baby doll with the number three written in the center of its forehead.

"That's how many days I have left. It keeps happening," I say. "Signs. Reminders. The Gabby Greta doll has been counting down every morning too."

"Sounds like overkill. Not sure how anyone could forget about a situation like this."

"I'll make sure to mention that when I leave a review of my experience."

He laughs lightly and walks deeper into the room. "What are we looking for?"

"A supplier of GHB."

"You think they're just hanging around in here somewhere?"

"No, I don't think they are hanging around in here, Cory, but I bet we can find a phone number."

He looks absolutely baffled, but I pull him along until we find a bathroom—and the graffitied walls inside.

"Ohh," he says.

"You take the left side," I instruct.

We spend several minutes scanning the walls before I find something promising right beneath the soap dispenser: TXT 4 GOODS ;) XXX

There's a phone number written underneath. "Found something!"

Cory walks over for a better look. "Emphasis on the *X*?"

"That's what I was thinking."

He pulls his phone from his pocket and starts typing.

"What are you doing?"

"Calling the number."

"You can't just—"

"It's fine. If they sound shady, I'll just say I have the wrong number."

He puts it on speaker, but no one picks up, and the voicemail box is full.

"I'll text them."

"What are you going to say?"

He takes a picture of the note on the wall and sends it to the number along with a rocket ship emoji and a question mark.

"Wait, what's with the emoji?"

He shrugs and points just below the phone number where a bunch of tiny rocket ships are drawn. "Astronauts ride rocket ships to go *high* in the sky? Oh! Three dots!" Cory shouts, staring at his phone, but my mind is spinning.

Kira said Rich had mistakenly texted her a rocket ship emoji that night. What if he wasn't trying to cheat at all? What if he was just looking for someone to do drugs with? That's what everyone keeps saying. Who does party drugs alone? Maybe Shaina was upset that it wasn't something more. Didn't she say as much last week? That Rich only hit her up to smoke and drink? But if that's true, if that's what was really happening on the night of my party, then . . . then everything that went down after was because of a misunderstanding on my part. Assumptions on my part, and . . . and, no. Nope. That is a possibility I can't even entertain right now.

"Response!" Cory inches closer to me so I can see his phone.

Unknown
$25 per. 869 Orchid, 6pm. In or out?

"Okay, so this confirms that Rich could have gotten the GHB from here. Now what?" Cory asks.

"Now we need something that links him directly to Natalie. If he hurt her, if her body is in that lake, then her family could have justice, and hopefully that would satisfy Regret."

Cory deletes the text messages and blocks the number before pocketing his phone. "Let me do some digging. If the two of them were connected, I'm sure there is evidence online somewhere. But to be honest, I think the necklace, the rave, the drugs, and your intuition will be enough if it comes down to it. We'll focus on our other threads in the meantime."

CHAPTER 31

Thursday afternoon Cory and I set off for our appointment at Mama Dee's. We walk down the cobblestone alley where the shop is located, and every step feels like we are being transported back in time. The shops on this strip have not been renovated for decades. They are a perfect snapshot of mid-fifties Fairville. One in every three or so is abandoned. Boarded up. Falling apart. Ancient CONDEMNED signs stapled to the doors. A few older people sit on their stoops in foldout chairs, drinking golden liquid and smoking hand-rolled cigarettes.

Cory points ahead of us. "I think her shop is up there on the left."

"Yeah, that's it." I recognize the purple sign above the door. MAMA DEE'S CONJURE SHOP is written across it in fancy gold lettering. It's the only well-kept building on the block.

I push open the door, and a bell hanging above it dings. The place is dim. Heavy drapes cover the windows, and the only light comes from shrouded lamps. The air is fragrant. Spicy and herbal, but not overwhelmingly so. A woman walks through a beaded curtain that separates the back of the store from the front. She wears a crop top and an open flannel shirt. Her butt-length locs are decorated with small seashells and golden crosses.

"Afternoon. How can I help y'all?"

I glance at Cory, and he gives me a slight nod. "Um, I think we spoke on the phone the other day. I have an appointment with Mama Dee at four PM."

The woman checks the computer. "Simone Washington?"

"That's right."

"Okay. Mama Dee will be ready in just a moment. Feel free to look around the shop while you wait. Few things on sale." She motions toward the clearance area.

I grab a shopping basket and drift to the spiritual cleansing section, carefully reading the handwritten descriptions posted under each product. I fill my basket with various candles, roots, and herbs, then return to the counter.

"Quite the cocktail," the clerk says as she rings the items up.

I bite my bottom lip. "Yeah. My house is . . . old."

"Fair enough. That'll be forty-two fifty."

As I tap my card, a soft bell dings from the back.

"That'll be Mama Dee. I'll keep your purchase under the counter until you're done." She bags my items, tucks them away, then instructs us to follow her.

We pass through the beaded curtain, and what's beyond is the complete opposite of the front of the shop. There's white wicker furniture with navy cushions, a kitchenette with a big bay window that lets in warm, diffuse light, and a dozen or so healthy houseplants.

Mama Dee tends to a kettle on the stove. "Oooh, chile." She looks over her shoulder at me. "Somebody wants you to know you got two days and she's not messing around. Ain't had a message come through that clear in years."

Cory and I lock eyes, and I know this is two hundred dollars well spent.

"Can offer y'all some tea in just one minute," Mama Dee says. "Go on and have a seat."

We do as she says.

She's tall, and her back is surprisingly straight. It's not wrinkles so much that give away her age, but the way her skin droops in places. Some quite dramatically. A few strands of her white hair spring free from her mauve headwrap.

Mama Dee sets the kettle on a tray on the coffee table, where there are already three tiny teacups and an open package of shortbread cookies. She fills each cup and adds a sugar cube without asking for any preferences, which surely she has earned the right to do at her age.

"Simone and . . ." She looks up at us over her glasses.

"And Cory. Thank you for meeting with us."

"Well, you're paying me to do it." She slaps her knee and lets out a hearty laugh. "Can't tell you the last time I had anyone as young as you two come in for a chat. Folks your age are like aliens to me. I don't look at you and reminisce about my past. I look at you, and I am *fascinated*." She puts a strong emphasis on the last word and smiles wide. It must be some special kind of feat that all her teeth are not only present and accounted for, but pearly white, too.

"I read your questionnaire, so I have a good idea of what's brought you here, but let me hear it from your own mouth."

It feels strange to switch gears back to this after spending all day yesterday focused on Natalie and Rich. "Um, since you already know I'm pressed for time, I guess I'll get right to the point. I was looking at old church records at Fairville First Baptist and saw that you were listed as a coordinator for several adoptions in the mid-fifties."

"Every child deserves a loving home. Never had any of my own, but my, I must have fostered at least a hundred."

"That's amazing," Cory says.

She winks at him. "Nothing but a thing."

"I saw that you were the coordinator for the adoption of a two-year-old boy whose birth mother was listed as Evelyn Young. Do you remember that?"

"I remember." She sips her tea. "The whole thing was a farce."

I blink a few times, shocked by her candidness. "What?"

"Evelyn Young never had a baby. And everybody who believed so was a damn fool."

"If it wasn't Evelyn's baby, whose was it? Violet's?" I ask.

Mama Dee arches an eyebrow. "Violet Savoie was a wicked woman. She was the one who brought the boy down to the church. But he wasn't her baby, no. Kin? Yes, but not hers."

Kin. "He was her cousin Dorothy's baby, wasn't he?"

"How'd you come to know that name?"

"We, uh . . ." I scramble for how to answer her question without admitting to breaking and entering and robbery. "We spoke to Violet's daughter."

"Violet's daughter was still in diapers when her mama passed. What's she know about it?"

"She had some boxes of her mother's old things," Cory offers.

"Ahh. I see." Mama Dee lets out a deep chuckle, like she knows the things we aren't saying.

"Did Violet say why she was giving the baby up?" I ask. "Why was Evelyn listed in the records?"

"Violet didn't say much besides some nonsense about the child belonging to Evelyn, and I won't ever be caught encouraging a liar to tell more lies by asking 'em questions. Ain't no secrets around me anyway."

Her eyes glisten, and I'm suddenly uncomfortable. How much does she know about *my* secrets?

"So what's the truth?" Cory asks. "Why did she give up a baby that didn't belong to her?"

"First off, let me tell you the energy wasn't right when she came in with that child. That's the only reason I gave her the time of day. For the boy's sake. I had a feeling letting her walk back out the door with him would be something I'd regret my whole life and Lord knows my life has been a long one. So I sat there and let her lie through her teeth. And when she was finished and gone and left, I did what I do." She nibbles on the edge of a cookie, then wipes the crumbs from the corner of her mouth. "The baby was covered in sand. She must have brought him straight from the lake. Materials, they hold memories inside." She rubs her thumb and index finger together like she is sprinkling sand across her quilt. "The sand in his pockets told me a story."

I make a couple of mental notes about this. One, to make sure I don't leave anything behind here. And two . . . Natalie likely crossed through that same sand. I don't know if she was dead or alive at the time, but maybe her memories, maybe her story, is embedded in it, too. Maybe Mama Dee could help us reveal it. "Can you share it with us? The story from the boy's pockets?"

She studies us carefully. "Tell me why I should. You two are deep into some dark town history. I want to know how you landed there. I want to know how it ties into this strict deadline you're on."

I decide honesty is the best move here. At least some of it. "Did you hear about the recent passing of Rich Pearson?"

"The young football star, yes. He passed at a party out by Yearwood Lake. I hadn't thought much of the location. It's been so long. . . . But . . ." She waits for me to continue.

"It was my birthday party. I thought it'd be a fun spot for the Halloween season. Do you know about the dolls and stuff out there?"

"I've heard about them. Go on."

"I wandered out to the lake late at night and . . . well, we have reason to believe Regret—I mean, Evelyn's spirit is trapped there. We want to set her free."

"How do you figure she's trapped? I've heard rumors, but Violet is long gone . . . I thought . . . Usually . . ." She trails off.

"I s-saw her." I stutter over my words, deciding how much of my shame I want to reveal to this woman.

She places her hand in mine. I have to actively resist pulling away. I'm afraid she'll see straight to my soul, and if she does that, she'll run me out of this place. But she doesn't. So I have to assume she either didn't see, or she only saw the parts that might earn me sympathy.

"What did the sand in the boy's pockets tell you, Mama Dee?" Cory asks.

"This will be the second time I share this story, and I'm only telling it in case what you say is true. Evelyn Young's soul doesn't deserve to be trapped in that ungodly place."

"Who did you tell the first time?" I ask.

She looks at me like I have two heads. "The police, of course. But it was a different time back then. They didn't care much about a colored woman carrying on about some other colored woman from out of town. And they especially didn't care to hear it from me. Not after word started going around about my . . ." She taps her temple.

"We want to hear it," I say. "We want to hear from you."

She looks at the ceiling for a few moments. I can almost see her mind searching, grasping for long-buried memories, a bit of light returning to her eyes, life returning to her body as she finds them. "It was a Saturday afternoon. Early summer. Beautiful day after some rain. Evelyn had been sharing her cabin with Dorothy and Dorothy's son, Nathaniel. Evelyn, an only child herself, likened him to a little brother.

"All the girls were young. Eighteen. Nineteen. It was rare for such young girls to be on their own that way. And back then, folks didn't appreciate rare. There was a mold you were expected to fit in, and the people who didn't fit it weren't treated kindly. Anyway, Evelyn had taken the boy and his toys to have an adventure in the woods while Dorothy stayed behind to prepare supper." Mama Dee closes her eyes. "The memories clung so tightly to that sand, I could smell it. Wild onion and garlic. Rabbit. Carrots. Potatoes. A fine stew. Dorothy was there humming a tune to herself." Mama Dee pauses and hums a few chords. "A man came out of the trees. Startled her at first. But he told her he meant no harm. That he heard her pretty singing and smelled her delicious meal. Said his belly led him straight to her. That made her laugh, and being the kind soul she was, she offered him some. She turned to the cabin to grab an extra bowl and . . ." Mama Dee takes a long, deep breath, smooths the wrinkles on her skirt. "He just . . . struck her down. No rhyme or reason."

"Who was he?"

She rubs the pad of her ring finger gently across her forehead, knuckles swollen. "I can't bring his face to mind. When I try, I don't see nothing but darkness. Pure evil. It was Violet who showed up next. Fresh in from town. She caught him there trying to hide the body. I reckon only reason he ain't kill her too is because the Savoies were a prominent and respected family. That, and she was willing to negotiate. That demon man offered her money, knowing the Savoies was secretly broke. Violet, accustomed to a certain level of luxury, accepted his offer. She helped that man toss her own cousin in the lake to save her family's bank account."

I nibble at my thumbnail, wondering just how many bodies have been dumped there. And now I know I wasn't the only one to make a slimy deal on the banks of Doll's Head Lake. A part of me sympathizes with Violet. Hopes that her story isn't as black and white as it seems. Kira's life, my life, and my future were at risk. That's why I did what I did. "Is it possible that the man . . . could he have threatened Violet?"

"I wish it were. But the devilish grin that spread across her face before shaking his hand said otherwise. When Evelyn returned with the boy, fresh honeysuckle and tobacco leaves in her apron, she found Violet covered in blood. She set little Nathaniel down and he sat there, playing in the sand, completely unaware of the violent end his mother had met only minutes prior. Violet told Evelyn the truth of it. Most of it. But Evelyn was disgusted. She didn't want a thing to do with that horrible cover-up. Violet couldn't let her tell and didn't have the heart to kill her, either, so she did what she did, and that was that. A curse to keep her ugly secret. Knowing what I know of Evelyn, I imagine her heart broke for the boy. Being taken from his mother like that. She would have been proud to care for him herself, I'm sure of it."

"Whatever happened to him?"

"My only cousin on my daddy's side took him in. They lived up in St. Louis. She and her husband loved him right and raised him up good. He went to college, got married, had a little boy of his own. He's passed on now."

"Mama Dee, is there anything you can think of that might help us free Re— Evelyn?"

She purses her lips and points to the hutch next to the back door. "If you go on over there and look on the top shelf, there's a box. I got a photo of the boy and some clippings about his accomplishments. Maybe seeing he did all right for himself will shake her loose. She may well think Violet tossed him in the lake all those years ago."

My eyes widen. "I think she *does* think that. Or something like it. She said Violet was a murderer."

"We know for sure she, at the very least, was complicit in one. You take that box on home with you. I haven't got any use for it anymore. And take those, too. Tiger's-eye." She points at two necklaces hanging from her aged vanity mirror. "For your protection. If Evelyn has been trapped as long as you say, might be her magic has strengthened. And if she's been angry all this time, chances are it has darkened, too. You babies be careful, you hear? You be careful and let me know how it all ends up."

"Yes, ma'am." I bite my lip, afraid to ask my next question, but the worst she can say is no. "One more question . . . The thing you did with the sand? To reveal the memories trapped in it. Can you still do that?"

"I find"—she inspects her fingernails—"that materials only like to open themselves up to me a single time. Doesn't mean you wouldn't have luck yourself."

"Oh, but I'm not—"

"You cannot enter into an arrangement like the one you find yourself in without some transfer of magic. It is what connects you to her. Surely you've felt it? A foreign presence within? Powerful feelings that do not belong to you?"

"Yes, ma'am." I certainly have. Every time I get near Kira.

"That's her magic. I think you might be surprised by what you are capable of."

She motions at a notepad and pen, and Cory rushes to pass it to her.

We wait a minute as she scrawls across the paper before tearing it from the pad and folding it in half. She extends her arm out to me. "Here."

"What do I—"

"You read, and you believe. That's it. I wish you both the best of luck. I need to rest now."

"Thank you so much, Mama Dee," I say.

Cory and I collect my bags from the front.

"This is it. We got it. I wish we could just go back to the lake right now," he says as an ominous roll of thunder echoes in the distance.

We exit the shop and stand under the awning, watching the absolute downpour in front of us.

"Want to wait for it to let up or run for it?" he asks.

"I'm afraid," I say.

"It's just rain, Simone. You—" He sighs and does his typical neck slap when he realizes I'm not talking about the rain. "Come here." He leads me to the bench on our right. "What are you afraid of?"

"I'm afraid I'm not good. That I don't deserve Kira's friendship or yours."

"Look, I can only speak for myself, but I'm not asking you to be good. I don't need you to be good."

"Yeah, but *I* do. I want it. It feels like no matter how hard I try, something in me just . . . sabotages it."

"Then stop trying."

"I'm scared of what will happen . . . of who I'll be if I don't try."

"Well, I'm not afraid, and I'll be here with you no matter what."

"Even if it turns out I'm right? Even if there is something dark at the center of me?"

"Something dark like what? What's the worst-case scenario you are imagining?"

"I don't know. Like, what if I'm a demon or something? What if I'm like that man from Mama Dee's story?"

He snorts out a laugh.

"Cory, I'm serious."

"Simone, that man was a literal cold-blooded killer."

"Yeah, and I might be one soon too if we don't get this right."

"Good thing we're going to get it right then." He gets up from the bench and squats down in front of me, resting his hands on my knees. Some humor still lingers in his expression, but he holds eye contact in the way that simultaneously calms and frightens me. "If it turns out you're a demon, I'll follow you to hell."

I close my eyes and take a deep breath. "The thought of you suffering eternal damnation on my account is *not* comforting, Cory."

"That's proof right there that you aren't evil. And an evil person wouldn't go to the lengths you did to save their best friend."

"That wasn't a hundred percent selfless. I was covering my own ass, too. And it cost Rich his life."

"Nobody's asking for one hundred percent, Ms. Honor Roll. Life is messy. All you can do is do the best you can, and that's what you always do. You've never intentionally done wrong by anyone."

I could say something about intent versus impact or give Cory a lesson on what the path to hell is lined with, but the rain is letting up now. "Come on." I take his hand and jog for his truck. Before we reach it, I am struck with the explicit thought that I'm meant to finish the rest of this on my own. I stop short, and Cory runs into me. As he rushes out an apology, I throw my arms around him, the bags in my hands clanging unceremoniously against his back. He returns the gesture, pulling me close to him.

"I don't know how this will all play out, but thank you." I peel myself away and run around to the passenger side of the truck.

Cory settles in the driver's side, then puts the key in the ignition. I remove the folded piece of paper from the inside pocket of my rain jacket and scan Mama Dee's tight handwriting.

1. Select a small vessel in which to place your material.
2. Seal and shake thrice.
3. Warm to body temperature.
4. Recite these words: What secrets contained within you, transfer them unto me.
5. Believe.

CHAPTER 32

I go upstairs to my bathroom and strip off my damp clothes as soon as Cory drops me off. My mind replays Mama Dee's story over and over again. I told Cory it was the *man* I was afraid of having something in common with, but it's Violet who I already do. Violet the betrayer. The friend who didn't speak up when she should have. The woman who let the lives of people she supposedly loved be ruined to protect herself. I stand in front of the mirror. I know logically that the face reflected back at me is mine, but all I see is Violet Savoie. Our similarities go so much deeper than our experiences with death at that lake. I fight hopelessly against the memories threatening to resurface, knowing that I will fail. From the moment Mama Dee began speaking, it was just a matter of time. I could feel it in the pit of my stomach. The awakening of ugly things.

I step into a scalding shower and sit down on the floor of the tub. The porcelain presses uncomfortably against my tailbone. I lean forward so the water runs directly on top of my head. My braids stick to my back, and I stare at the faucet until my eyes burn. When I am forced to close them, my mind lets every detail from the night of Trenton's death that I've kept blocked for years—the true biggest regret of my life, the one Regret could smell on me—rush forward.

Kissing Cory is not the only thing I regret about the night of Trenton's death. There is something darker. Something shameful and complex. My memories blend with the visuals my mind created as Mama Dee told the story from the sand. I cling to that disorientation as long as I can, but eventually, the things I never experienced fade. And the things I did come into sharp focus.

I sit in my room in near-total darkness after getting home from Cory's. The house is not quiet. Dad makes back-to-back phone calls, muttering. Sometimes angry. Sometimes frantic. Sometimes sad. No actual words reach me, but his feelings are clear in his tone. I think he is talking to the parents of my friends. Other parents would be shocked and heartbroken about what has happened, too. They would want to lean on each other and make sure they do their best to support their children through it. Mom isn't home yet. She was probably on the other end of most of the calls he made. Maybe all of the ones he received. So I am not surprised when Dad goes tearing out the side door the moment her car pulls into the driveway. I walk over to the window so I can see him. The garage door opens automatically—Mom using the fob in her car. Dad moves as quickly as he did in his NFL days, dipping under the slowly rising door and disappearing into the dark garage. Mom's car comes into view then. A single headlight casts its glow across the yard. It flickers. Temporarily submerging everything into blackness. I had noticed one of her headlights was out two days ago, but I forgot to mention it. I squint into the night because now, I notice, the headlight isn't the only thing amiss about the car. There is a large dent in the hood, and the windshield is cracked. Dad waves her into the garage and she stumbles out of the driver's seat, clearly under the influence. Just like she has always been lately. She and Dad do a good job keeping the severity of her drinking problem hidden. Dad throws a blue tarp over her car. They rush out of the garage, close the door, and enter the house. Their voices, muffled before, are clear now. They are just below my feet. Dad isn't even trying to whisper like he had on the phone.

"Get yourself together, Camille." A cabinet door slams shut. "We are done. I am sick of cleaning up your messes. He was a kid. He was her friend. Did you even know that?" Mom tries to speak, but Dad cuts her off. "You. Killed. Our. Daughter's. Friend."

There is a silence that seems to stretch on forever.

My mother killed Trenton.

My mother drank and drank and drank, and then she got into her car and stole Trenton's life from him. And worse, she left him there. In the street. All alone. Worse still, she never confessed. Worse still, she went to his funeral. Looked his parents in their eyes. Never could bring herself to tell them sorry for their loss. No doubt the words would have caught in her throat. Revealed their hidden meaning. And she would never, ever risk being caught.

My mother is a monster. So what does that make me? Born from a monster. Raised by a monster. Is it any wonder that I knew the truth and said nothing? Two years and I've pretended I didn't see what I saw or hear what I heard. I convinced myself of a lie. Mom's car had disappeared from the garage by morning. It was back the next day, washed and repaired, all evidence of the tragedy it was involved in erased. I watched Trenton's family plead on the news for anyone with information to come forward. I'd hugged them and told them how much their son meant to me. But he couldn't have meant that much, could he? A real friend, a good friend, would fight for the justice he deserved. But I couldn't confront my mother. I tried a dozen different times. On my last attempt, she told me they had a suspect. An elderly man who should have stopped driving a long time ago. Dad backed her up, and that's what gave me permission to accept it as the truth in my mind all this time. I don't know if it was completely made up, if they framed him somehow, or if the police truly had reason to suspect him. I didn't care to know. I just wanted something easier to process, and a stranger being responsible was so, so much easier.

But part of me still knew Mom needed help. She needed an intervention, or there was a chance something awful would happen again. A few weeks later, I tried to make sure she got the help she needed. I sent an anonymous email to her boss so she'd be "randomly" substance tested. So she'd get fired. So she'd realize she was at rock bottom and take the opportunity to rebuild. I should have known it wouldn't work. If what happened to Trenton wasn't a wake-up call for her, nothing would be. All my stupid email did was make her fall deeper into her addiction. Me, always with the best intentions. Always ruining everything. And I know I could say something now. Try to right my wrongs. But why should I trust that any of it would turn out how it should? It never turns out how it should. Why should I risk derailing my life even more? What good would that serve? Especially now with this mess with Rich and Kira.

I spiral, not sure which, if any, of my thoughts are justified or if it's all my strong self-preservation streak talking. My intense, compulsive need to put myself first, protect myself first. Something encoded in the DNA of each of us, but something everyone else has seemed to learn to override. I can't even lie and say it was loyalty to and love for my mother that made me keep my mouth shut. I was worried about what would happen to *me* if everyone found out what my mother did. There is not an altruistic bone in my body.

Violet, the betrayer of Evelyn and Dorothy. Simone, the betrayer of Kira and Trenton. Violet, the protector of an evil man's secrets. Simone, the protector of a sick mother's secrets. Violet, who forever changed the course of Evelyn's and baby Nathaniel's lives. Simone, who stood by and allowed Trenton's and Rich's families to experience the most severe form of heartbreak without the refuge of the truth. Perhaps I'll go the way of Violet soon. Dead young. Karma come to snatch me violently away. Or maybe selflessness is something I can learn, but there are certain questions I need answers to before I'll ever have a shot. Questions with answers that only my mother can provide.

I stay in the shower long after the water runs cold. I stay until I am shivering, and my skin is pruned. Until Dad bangs on the door, demanding to know what's taking me so long. Until he threatens to knock the door down if I don't answer him.

"I'm okay." It comes out as a croak. I reach forward and turn off the water. "Dad, I'm fine!"

I get out and don't bother to dry off before putting on my robe. I unlock and yank open the door, dripping icy water everywhere. Dad startles when he gets a look at me.

"Simone, what the hell is going on?"

"I need to see Mom," I say.

"I'm not sure that's a good idea right now. You've been going through it. She's been struggling with her own stuff, too."

"You're always ready to drop a hint about forgiving her. Why the hesitation when I'm finally ready to talk?" I don't know why I put any value in his opinion anyway. As if his hands are clean in all of this. As if he's not just as complicit, more so even, than me in hiding the truth behind Trenton's death. He was the adult. He made filthy decisions too. This whole family is one large, ugly stain.

He drags his large hand down his face. "I'll take you to see her this weekend."

"I can't wait until the weekend."

"Simone, I don't think it's a—"

"Never mind." I squeeze by him, holding back a wave of tears.

"8908 Lainey Drive," he says, defeated, just before I reach my bedroom door.

CHAPTER 33

"Hi, I'm Gabby Greta, and I love you! I'm Gabby Greta! Can you count to . . . one? One . . ." Her voice drops on the last word, and the speaker box crackles long after she finishes speaking.

Ten seconds. What started as nearly half a minute of her squeaky robotic voice has whittled down to just ten seconds. I counted. Ten seconds to announce that my life could take a drastic turn in just a day and a half. But I feel strangely calm. Meeting with Mom later, talking to her, clearing the toxic air between us, that's the last of my ideas. A last-ditch attempt to enter those woods tomorrow, conscience clear. No regrets. A possible loophole if everything else goes wrong.

I walk through the halls at school like a zombie, counting down each hour until I see Mom. Each hour until my final showdown with Regret. I haven't told Cory about my plans this afternoon. I don't want him involved in it. I don't need his penetrating eyes analyzing me when I'm done. So I told him I wanted to be alone today. And he understood, because of course he did.

"Hey, Jere?" I call when I see him in the parking lot after school.

"Hey." He stops walking and waits for me to catch up. "What's up? Need a ride?"

"Yes," I answer hesitantly, feeling bad that he jumped straight to that, but that's pretty much all I've used him for lately. "Sorry. I don't mean to treat you like a chauffeur."

"Nah. I know it's not like that, Simone."

"Good because, um . . . I was wondering if you could drive me someplace that's not my house."

He twirls his keys in his hands. "Where to?"

"To visit my mom. She lives about fifteen minutes away."

He raises his eyebrows. "Mom, huh? That's big."

"Yeah. It's just with everything that happened to Rich, I was thinking it might be time to hash things out with her."

"That's real. Come on. I don't mind."

We get into his Jeep and set off, comfortably making small talk most of the way. He slows when we turn onto her street, double-checking the GPS. "Is this it?" He pulls to a stop outside a beige stucco building that isn't bad looking, but definitely not where someone might expect the ex-wife of a retired NFL player to live.

"This is it." I hop out.

"I'm going to wait here for you. Just text me if you need something," he says through the rolled-down passenger window.

I nod, walk up to the door, and press the buzzer next to Mom's name.

A crackle of static comes from the speaker that makes me think of Gabby Greta. "Simone? Is that you?"

I guess Dad gave her a heads-up. "Yes. It's me."

The door remotely unlocks, and I enter the stuffy lobby, a row of mailboxes on one side and a desk with no attendant on the other. The door locks behind me with a loud *clink*.

I walk up the stairs to her apartment and tap on the door.

"Come in," she calls.

I turn the knob and push the door wide, but I don't go inside.

Seeing my mother for the first time in two years feels nothing like I thought it would. There is zero fanfare. It's as if this is my tenth time crossing her path today. Uneventful. Normal. Nothing to fuss over. I don't know if it's a sign of our closeness—one of those pick-up-like-we-never-parted things—or if it's an indication of the ocean between us. She stands at the kitchen island, wiping down the faux-marble countertop. The place is pristine and furnished with expensive-looking things. The opposite of what you'd envision based on the outside. Mom is the reverse, pristine on the outside. Hair perfectly styled. Makeup just right. Clothes steamed, ironed, and expertly tailored to her body. All the ugly things hidden inside behind the distractingly beautiful exterior. I was on track to be a replica of her. But cracks have begun to show. Dark things have begun to ooze, carrying an odor that screams untrustworthy. Bad. Irredeemable.

She lets the rag rest on the counter and takes me in. "You look so grown-up."

I say nothing, still observing the space from the door.

"Come in." She takes a few quick steps toward me, arms outstretched like she might go in for a hug, but then she stops and crosses them over her chest.

I enter the apartment and close the door behind me.

"Have a seat wherever you want. Can I get you something to drink?" She heads for the cupboard without waiting for an answer.

I take a seat in an armchair in the living room, and a few seconds later, she places a glass of cold water on a coaster on the coffee table in front of me.

"Happy belated birthday." She sits on the couch.

"It wasn't a happy birthday at all."

"I—I know. I'm sorry. I heard about Rich. About your party. I wanted to come to you so badly."

"So why didn't you?"

She looks down, fiddles with the hem of her shirt. "I asked your father to send you to me whenever you were ready."

My eyes water. "You're the mom. Why did I have to make the first move? Are you *that* angry with me?"

Her eyebrows knit together. "Angry with you about what, Simone?"

"Your job! The email I sent. Isn't that part of the reason you left?"

She lets out a huff of air and shakes her head. "So that *was* you? I hadn't been positive."

"Yes, it was me. I wanted you to see how badly your life was falling apart. I wanted you to get help. To go to rehab. To get a fresh start at things." I look around the apartment. "And I guess you eventually did the last one. Just without your family."

"That's not why I left, Simone. Like I said, I wasn't even sure it was you who sent that email. And I didn't care. That was so minor in the grand scheme of things."

"Oh, I know," I say looking her directly in the eyes. "That's the real reason I'm here."

She licks her lips and rubs them together, gaze cast to the side. "What is it you think you know, Simone?"

"I know what you did. And as much as I want forgiveness for the things *I've* done, I didn't come here to offer you any."

Her eyes slowly shift to meet mine.

"I know it was you," I say. "I saw the car. The dent. The broken windshield. I heard you and Dad arguing."

Her eyes redden. "I don't know what you want me to say."

"I want you to take accountability for ruining *everything*!" I cry. "I need you to tell me it's okay that I didn't tell the police what I knew. That it was okay that I wanted to protect my mom, even though it meant my friend wouldn't get the justice he deserved. That it was okay that I didn't want to be the girl at school with a mom in prison. I need you to say it because I can't go back out there to her with all of these regrets hanging on me, Mom. I can't. I'm scared."

She slowly stands. "Go back out where and to who?"

I sniff and look up at her, confused by her intensity. "I—Home. Kira—I just meant—"

She holds up her hand. "Don't lie to me, Simone. You just threw the darkest part of my soul into the light. You just said you don't want any regrets."

"I know, but you wouldn't understand. I can't—"

"Let me ask you something." She sits back down, right on the edge of the couch cushion. "That cabin where you had your birthday. Where Rich passed. It's out behind the CPRC?"

I give a slight nod, and my heart rate picks up.

"Did you go into the woods? With all the dolls?"

Again, I nod.

"Did you go to the lake?"

I can't move or speak.

"You did," Mom breathes. "You did, and you saw her."

I burst into tears. "How do you know?"

Mom drops to her knees from the couch, scoots the foot or two to my chair, and throws her arms around me. "Because I saw her, too," she says, rubbing her hand over my head. "And I wish with everything in me that I'd taken the deal she offered."

CHAPTER 34

I try to get Mom to go first, but she refuses to say anything more before I explain what happened when I saw Regret. Jere texts to check in on me, and I tell him he can go. That this is going to take a while. Then I start talking. Mom covers her mouth, and her face contorts as she tries to hold back tears when I tell her what happened to Kira.

She grips my hand when I finish. "I'm so sorry you had to make that choice, Simone. And I don't blame you for choosing the way you did. For taking the deal. I don't blame you one bit, knowing what I know now."

"What do you know?"

She drops my hand and readjusts herself on the couch. Takes a minute or two to collect her thoughts. "I did my best to keep my drinking a secret. It was easy at first—home after work with a bottle of wine. But your father started to get concerned, so I worked harder to hide it. I started slipping alcohol into discreet bottles so he wouldn't know what I was drinking. And that made everything worse. Those bottles started traveling with me. I wouldn't dare be caught drinking alone at a bar or anything, so I found some private spots around town."

"And one of them was Doll's Head Lake?"

"Mm-hmm. It's beautiful out there. I got accustomed to watching the sunset. Time would get away from me, and I'd tell your father I was working late, but he always could see straight through my lies. One evening, I drank a little too much and passed out on the dock. When I woke up, Regret was there. She showed me my future. The hit-and-run. Losing my job. The divorce." She chokes up for a second. "Me and you getting into a horrible, horrible fight that ended in you delaying college, in you turning to alcohol just the way I did. *That's* why I haven't come around. In the future she showed me, I came to you. That's what set you off down a bad path."

"What happened after she showed you your future?"

"Same as you. She offered me a deal. I figure out how to free her and she'd free me from my addiction."

"And if you failed?"

"If I failed, my problems would be exposed to the whole community. Camille Washington, the town drunk."

"That's all? Your stakes were so low compared to mine! Mom, why didn't you take the deal!?"

She shakes her head and gives a small, sad smile. "My prefrontal cortex is more developed than yours."

"What does that mean?"

"It means I didn't believe in witches or ghosts, or premonitions. It meant there was no way in hell I'd make a deal with someone called Regret who was surely just a figment of my drunken imagination. I didn't think it was real until a few months later when everything she showed me would happen actually started to happen. First it was trouble with your dad. Slipups at work. The night I hit Trenton, I went back out to the lake. Begged for another chance. But she didn't even bother to show herself." She stands. "When is your deadline?" She counts on her fingers. "It's got to be close."

"Tomorrow," I say.

"Tomorrow! Do you have a plan? What have you figured out?"

I share with her everything that Cory and I have learned so far.

"That's good," she says, nodding when I finish. "I think that's good. I think one of those will work."

"You do?"

"I do. But tell me this, when Regret says she wants to be freed, what exactly does that mean to you?"

I lift my shoulders up toward my ears. "That she's ready to move on to the afterlife? What else could she mean?"

"She never got the chance to live. Not if she got trapped there as young as you say she did."

"She said she's called Regret because she feeds on it, not because she has any. I don't think there's any unfinished business for her here."

Mom walks to her coat closet and pulls out a box. She sets it on the coffee table. "You have to be careful, Sim. I've done a lot of research over the past couple of years, and I've read many stories about trapped spirits and how to release them and everything that can go wrong in the process."

She pulls some books out of the box and spreads them across the table.

"These spirits can be sneaky, to get what they want. And I use the word 'spirit' loosely, because are we even sure Regret is dead?"

"She told me she was stuck somewhere in between."

"Exactly. She has been there for decades. Her body isn't a human body anymore." She flips through her notes. "I read about something similar where this couple 'freed' a being that was haunting their house. Her physical form disappeared, but her spirit was still stuck there, undead and angrier than ever. I'm not trying to scare you. I just want you to be prepared for anything. If something goes wrong, if you aren't successful, call me. Come to me. I'll drive you far out of town before anything bad can happen with Kira. We'll get on a plane. Start a whole new life somewhere far away together if we have to."

I nod. Lip trembling.

Mom's eyes soften, thinking I've grown emotional because of this out she's offered. But she has it wrong. I'm disappointed. Disappointed that her plans always involve running away. Avoiding. This backup plan is as much about her as it is me. A chance for her to reclaim the life she wants instead of living out the one she deserves. She hasn't learned much at all since I saw her last. I'd be foolish to take her advice. I'm going to face whatever I have to face tomorrow, but the urge to make my mother happy still runs strong. So I slip on my grateful daughter mask and pretend to be thankful for her lifeline. Relieved by it. I reach for her and she hugs me, shushing my tears.

"Listen to me, love." She pulls away and looks me in the eye. "From what you've figured out, Evelyn wasn't a bad person. Regret is just Evelyn stuck between her own rock and a hard place. Try not to bring fear with you into the woods."

"I'll try."

"And one more thing," she adds. "About Trenton. If carrying my secret ever gets too heavy, know that I will never fault you for doing whatever you need to do to release the burden."

Again, I can see she's proud of herself for saying it, oblivious to the cowardice in it. Because she could release me from the burden herself at any time. I don't want my mom to confess and go to prison. But at the same time, I want a mom who'd be selfless enough to do it.

AFTER assuring me a dozen times that she hasn't had a drink in six months, Mom drives me back to Fairville. I have her drop me off around the corner from Cory's house. I walk to his front door, and he opens it before I can knock.

"Hey. I thought you wanted to take some time to yourself today?"

"I changed my mind. Can I come in?"

He scans my face, trying to get a feel for my mood. "Of course."

I slide past him and walk to his bedroom, sit on the edge of his bed. "I went to see my mom today."

His expression goes blank, and it takes him a couple of seconds to speak. "How'd that go?"

"It was . . . eye-opening?"

"Yeah? What'd you talk about?"

I shake my head, not wanting to rehash it. There's nothing I can tell him that'll have any impact on tomorrow. The past two weeks have been so tense. So stressful. I just want to claim a couple of hours of calm.

Cory sits next to me and takes my hand.

I look around his room. "It feels good to be here."

He tucks his Venom pillow behind him and laughs lightly. "Could use a little updating."

I bite back a grin, slipping out of my sneakers and turning to sit on his bed cross-legged. "I don't mean the décor, Cory. It feels good to be here with you." I scoot closer to him.

He looks down at my knee pressed against the side of his thigh, then back at my face, very obviously sizing up the vibe here. I maintain eye contact and reclaim his hand to try to make myself clearer. He swallows hard, Adam's apple bobbing.

"Tomorrow's a big day."

I appreciate him saying that. Doing what Rich didn't do under those bleachers. Acknowledging how other things going on in my life could be influencing my behavior in this moment. Giving me a moment's pause to ask myself if I'm okay with that.

"Yeah. Tomorrow's a big day. But in the meantime, I'd like to be a normal eighteen-year-old girl."

He turns to face me, the gentle curve of his mouth faintly exposing his dimples. He inches closer, testing the waters. When I don't falter, he pushes my braids behind my shoulder and runs his thumb across my cheek. "Proceed or left turn?"

"Proceed."

Cory closes the gap left between us and kisses me, and I let all my secrets dissolve on his lips.

Me, the girl with all the masks, and I can't seem to find a single one.

CHAPTER 35

Gabby Greta doesn't make an announcement on Saturday morning. I wake up early and stare at my phone until the time she usually speaks comes and goes. I wonder if she might announce that today is the day. If she will tell me precisely how many hours I have left. But there is only silence, so I get dressed and spend a few hours reviewing my notes and preparing for what's to come.

Around one, I grab my laptop and go to Cory's website. He said he would post the last entry of the series today *before* going back out to the lake. He wanted to speak some positivity into existence, and I could certainly use a taste of that right now.

BLOG ENTRY 078 / OCTOBER 30

**CATEGORY: FAIRVILLE URBAN LEGENDS
EPISODE 3, PART 3**

Welcome back, fright fiends. We've reached the end of this series on the witch of Doll's Head Lake. My partner and I had a productive visit with a well-known Fairville resident who cleared up many of our remaining questions about Regret's story. That resident is none other than our beloved Mama Dee. As the only town centenarian, she's seen a thing or two, and we knew we had to speak to her—plus, there's the whole psychic thing. Very useful.

But let's back things up a bit. In the last entry, I revealed Regret's birth name (Evelyn Young) and had just started piecing together some notable relationships in her life. In particular, her friendship with a now-deceased woman named Violet Savoie. We were able to visit Violet's daughter this week, which . . . conveniently . . . afforded us the opportunity to read some of Violet's handwritten diary entries. Violet painted a murderously dark picture of her friend Evelyn, but our consultation with Mama Dee proved it all to be a farce. Violet was the one who cast the curse that eventually created the witch called Regret. Why'd she do it? To cover up a murder that would free her family from crippling debt.

Yes, that's right, friends. This was all about money.

So how do all the creepy dolls play in, you ask? Well, that murder Violet was so intent on covering up just happened to be the murder of her very own cousin. And her cousin had a son who Evelyn adored. Cursed to live out the rest of eternity on the banks of the lake, poor Evelyn "Regret" Young never would have learned what became of the boy. But I'm pleased to tell you, he lived a good long life. It's hard to say who began the tradition of leaving toys at the lake, but it's one I hope continues. If you take a visit out, leave something kind behind. Whisper to the trees that the boy lived and loved. Maybe our Evelyn will get the message soon and have a shot at the same in the great beyond.

Keep it creepy, friends.
C.

She'll be getting the message soon, all right. Cory is planning to pick me up at five so we can get to the lake at dusk like Regret said, but I have no intention of waiting for him. I don't want him to come with me. I don't know how things will turn out, but at the very least, I want to be sure he is safe.

It's raining, but my weather app says it's scheduled to let up by four. That's when I'll go. The first thing I want to try is Mama Dee's spell. I think it'd be best to do it when I know Regret won't come creeping out of her cabin, and I've yet to see her make an appearance during daylight. I sit down to review Mama Dee's notes, but a loud banging on the front door prevents me from even getting started. I go to the top of the stairs. Dad's already almost to the door.

"Who's that?" I ask.

"Kira," he says as he unlocks the dead bolt.

"Stop!" I shout.

Dad drops his hand like the lock suddenly turned molten. "Simone, what's wrong with you?"

"Don't let her in." I can't see her today. I don't even want to give it a chance. "Tell her to go home—but keep the door closed!"

"Simma, don't be ridiculous."

Dad and I both look to the door as Kira's muffled voice carries through.

I walk halfway down the stairs so I can hear better.

"Simone! Simone, are you in there? I need to talk to you!"

I desperately want to know what she wants, but for all I know, it's Regret that placed her on my doorstep this morning. A trap. Her coming to claim her prize before my final hours run out.

"Why didn't she call you?" Dad whispers. "What's going on?"

"Because I blocked her last night." I am determined. I can't be influenced by an emotional text or phone call, and I know I would. She has that effect on me and everyone else, too, including my dad.

"Mr. Washington!" Kira shouts. "Are you there? I need to talk to Simone!"

"Oh, come on, Simone. Don't make me leave her hanging out there."

I make a pleading face and prayer hands. Kira has a persuasive effect on everyone, but my persuasive effect on my dad is stronger.

She feebly knocks once more, waits a moment, and then we hear the sound of her shoes as she jogs down the three front steps of the house, the sound of her car door opening and closing, the sound of her driving away.

"What was that about?" Dad asks in his normal speaking voice.

"Nothing, Dad. Girl stuff. We're in a fight."

"Why? You two should be supporting each other right now. Not fighting."

"We'll work it out. I just need some space."

He looks like he wants to push the issue, so I get ahead of it. "Can you make us something to eat? You haven't made your meatballs in a while."

"Been thinking of that secret recipe, huh?" He walks toward the kitchen.

I follow behind him, not wanting to engage in his banter. There are things he and I need to discuss, but hopefully, after today, I won't even remember.

"Whoo-ee, this place is a mess." He pulls a skillet from a pile of dishes in the sink and bangs around the cabinets in search of a fresh sponge. "We're doing some deep cleaning after we eat."

"Did you ever call that cleaning company I told you about? Delia's?"

"Oh yeah, I did," he says, voice muffled by the pantry.

"They all booked up or something?"

Dad turns to face me, arms filled with ingredients. He sets them on the island. "No. I reached out, but are you sure it's called Delia's?"

"Yes. Delia's Home Cleaning."

"Hmm. When I called they said they didn't clean any cabin."

"The place looks more like a vacation home than a cabin. They were probably confused. Did you mention John by name?"

He pulls some eggs out of the fridge. "No. I thought that cabin belonged to his aunt."

"It does, but he hired them to clean it. Delia is his best friend's mom or something. I'll call them for you in a few." Because there is no way I will spend the hours I have left before meeting Regret sweeping and mopping.

Once we finish our meal, I go back upstairs to my room. I put my phone on speaker and let the line ring while I organize some items on my desk, preparing to return to Mama Dee's notes once I handle this.

"Good afternoon. This is Delia's Home Cleaning. How can I help you today?"

I'd hoped I'd get the guy we met at Ms. Elmira's, but it's not him. "Hi, I'd like to make an appointment. You guys were recommended to me by John Yearwood. Y'all did a clean for him about two weeks ago." Saying "two weeks ago" feels strange in my mouth. It feels like an eternity and like no time at all has passed.

"We actually haven't had an opportunity to do a cleaning for the Yearwoods yet, but I'm so grateful to John for promoting my business. Such a kind young man."

"Wait, so you didn't do a clean at that house in the woods behind the CPRC? It's where Rich Pearson—"

"I know what happened there, sweetheart. And I also know none of my staff did a clean there. Someone else called asking about it too. I think John had every intention of scheduling something but didn't get around to it."

I try to recall John's exact words. He never did explicitly say they came; I assumed they did. I only asked him to remind me of the company's name. But why wouldn't he clarify and say he didn't use them? Maybe he wanted me to believe he'd hired out? The Yearwoods never want to be seen as cheap or cutting corners.

"Would you still like to make an appointment?" The person on the phone sounds deflated now, like she believes this confusion has cost her my business.

"Yes, ma'am. I'm interested in your full-home deep-clean service."

I schedule an appointment for Wednesday and hang up, then sit there gnawing on the inside of my cheek. Antsy. Anxious. I review my notes and Mama Dee's directions for an hour before yanking aside my curtains to see if the rain has let up at all. When I confirm that it hasn't, I go back to straightening up my room. A habit I inherited from my mother. The last thing I choose to deal with is the box Kira left at my doorstep. Sifting through, I can see she packed it in a hurry. There are a few things in it that don't belong to me and have nothing to do with our friendship. A Mickey Mouse key chain. A stapler. A small cardboard box addressed to Johnathon Yearwood. I squint at it before lifting it out. It's light. Something inside clinks. For a moment I wonder why Kira would have something addressed to John, but he and Layla stayed at the Davises' for a few months while their home was being renovated. I carefully open the box. The cardboard rubs against itself, making a noise that sends an uncomfortable sensation up my spine.

When I glimpse what's inside, I drop the box onto the rug and jump to my feet. I dash to my bookshelf. Shift things around until I find what I hid there a few days ago. The empty dropper vial labeled LX. Slowly I approach the box on the floor and pry it the rest of the way open so I can compare what's in my hands to what's in the box. The tiny glass bottles are a perfect match, but they're generic. Someone could buy these anywhere. Amazon. Walmart.

The dollar store. I try to convince myself of this until I find the sheet of sticker labels tucked behind the vials. Each printed with LX in the exact font of the bottle that likely held the GHB that ended up in Rich's system. I flip the labels over and on the other side are four stickers. Astronauts. Vomiting up rainbows.

My head spins. What does this mean? Did John supply the GHB that everyone had at the rave? Is that how Rich got it? Is it possible that John met Natalie? Could he have . . . ?

I pace. Pieces of every interaction I've had with John Yearwood flicker through my mind. He didn't want us to have the party at the cabin. Now I believe there is a good chance he lied about getting it professionally cleaned. And yet the place was spotless. It's his aunt's cabin, but for some reason he has access to all the security cameras. We lost power the night of the storm, but the CPRC, less than a mile away, didn't. Could it have been him? Could he have tampered with it? Regret hates murderers. But it wasn't just me, Kira, and Rich in those woods that night. Someone else was there. Their phone went off. An Android. John has an iPhone, but he wouldn't use his main phone to sell party drugs. What if Regret wanted me to name John instead of Rich? But if she didn't want me to name Rich, then why show me the future where he throws me under the bus?

I sit on the edge of my bed. Shove my fingers into my braids and rest my elbows on my knees. Contemplating. I can hear the TV from downstairs. Mama Dee's commercial. *I'm Deidra Hightower, but y'all can call me Mama Dee! Come to Mama Dee's to get what you need. Come to Mama Dee's, set ya mind at ease!*

Something about the way she says her last name stands out. It floats around my brain, trying to find the memory that's the matching puzzle piece. The groundskeeper's face is the first thing to surface. Without giving myself time to overthink, I grab my phone and text John. I write casually like I haven't just spent the last several minutes wondering if he could be a killer.

> **Me**
> Hey. What was that groundskeeper's name? Nate...

Typing bubbles appear.

John
Hightower. Why?

Everything's coming together now. Right on time. I don't know exactly how it all connects, but the cards are on the table. Mama Dee said Dorothy's son, Nathaniel, was adopted by her cousin on her father's side. That means his name was Nathaniel Hightower. Mama Dee also said he grew up and had a son of his own, and my gut tells me he named his son Nate. Nathaniel Hightower Junior. Nate is right around the perfect age. And if he's done any digging into his family history, it's no surprise he found himself interested in working near Doll's Head Lake.

I get out of bed and pull my curtains aside. It's still pouring rain. It'd be dangerous to go out into the woods right now, but what difference does that make? *I* am the danger today. I am a threat to Kira until this ends, and I can't wait any longer. I need to know what happened. I need to arrange all these clues in some way that makes sense. I need Mama Dee's incantation to work.

I snatch up the bag I packed last night with Violet's diary and all the supplies I'll need and toss in the LX vial, too. Without bothering to grab a raincoat, I sneak past Dad, who's knocked out on the couch, and grab the keys to his SUV. Being in the driver's seat again feels so unnatural, yet familiar all the same. Like riding a bike. I crank it up and pull out.

CHAPTER 36

I use the ten-minute drive plus an extra five minutes parked outside the cabin to amp myself up. The rain has calmed to a drizzle now, but it's just chilly enough to be uncomfortably aware of the temperature. I go to the back of the SUV and grab one of Dad's old jackets. I don't want my choice to not bring my own to be something else for Regret to nibble on. I'm about to close the back when I spot a toolbox in the corner. I pull it to me and sift through, looking for something I might be able to protect myself with. I find a utility knife. Not like I could stab a ghost, but sliding it into my pocket gives me a tiny bit more confidence, and I need every piece of that I can get.

With no other reason to delay, I enter the woods and power forward until I can smell the lake water. It's then that fear finally overtakes my adrenaline. I have to close my eyes to make the transition from the woods to the beach. I'm afraid Regret will be in front of me when I open them, but dusk is still half an hour off. I take a deep breath and open my eyes. The sand is dark and compact, and the water is high from all the rain, but everything else looks the same. Calm. Peaceful. Beautiful, even. I try to imagine what it was like when Evelyn, Violet, Dorothy, and her son were here, coexisting happily. I guess everything changed for them as suddenly as it did for me. Only their story involved a violent stranger, while mine was truly a tragic accident. I instinctively look over my shoulder, making sure I'm alone before walking to the edge of the water by the dock.

I take out my materials and Mama Dee's instructions, then kneel. My knees sink into the thick sand. I place the tiger's-eye necklaces Mama Dee gave me around my neck and am relieved to find no feelings of embarrassment or ridiculousness creeping up. Those are the feelings that surface when there's doubt. I don't have space for doubt today. Mama Dee said the magic is already in me. All I need to do is believe. I wouldn't be in this situation I'm in if magic weren't real, so that part isn't difficult. Putting that belief in *myself* is harder. Imagining myself as the conjurer of the magic that is clearly so strong in this place is harder. But hard doesn't mean impossible.

I set everything up according to Mama Dee's instructions. I chose one of John's vials to be my vessel in hopes that any connection he or the vials themselves may have with this place will help the right memories resurface. For even more assurance, I wrap Natalie's chain around the outside of it. I take a pinch of sand from the ground and rub the wet granules between my fingers so they will loosen, and then I sprinkle them into the vial. I put the top on, shake it three times, then clench it in my fist. I bring my fist to my mouth and blow on it to add some heat, then I lower it to my chest. Press it against my heart.

"What secrets contained within you, transfer them unto me."

Thunder cracks and a torrential downpour erupts from the sky. The wind is knocked out of me, and the scene around me changes in an instant, like someone kicked me over and I sat back up in a different time. It looks almost exactly like my last two visits here, only this time, instead of my head being submerged in the lake, it's rain that drenches me. It takes a few moments for the new scenery around me to sharpen. The downpour fades to a soft drizzle like the roar of a full audience's applause wound down to a few lonely claps. The decaying wood of the dock comes into focus first. Plank by plank. My eyes trail up it, and at the end, there is a dark figure. Regret? No. A male. Rich. It's Rich, dammit. I've brought back the wrong memory. Kira and I will emerge from the trees any second. I'll see her fall again. I'll see myself push her. See her die again.

The figure shifts, startling me, and I realize I have it all wrong. The rain that's falling on me is not the cool rain of fall. It's warm now. The trees are full and green. It's summertime. And the dark-haired man at the end of the dock is not Rich. No. Now that I can see his profile, I can tell without a doubt that it's John Yearwood. And there is something in front of him. Someone. A woman with long blond hair caked with dirt and sand and something else sticky and dark. She is as still as the stones tied to her body. Natalie Dawson. A chill runs up my spine, and slowly, I turn to look behind me. Regret. As she existed in this memory. But she only hovers by her cabin door. Why doesn't she go to John? Why doesn't she offer him the same deal she offered me? Is it because she knows his intention and mine were different? Or maybe it's because it is garishly clear in the color of her skin, the cloudiness of her open eyes, that Natalie has been gone more than the few minutes Regret claims she has to make a difference. Natalie didn't die here. She is being dumped here.

As soon as I draw this conclusion, John pushes her body into the water, and I see it. The glint of her gold chain as it catches between the planks. He watches her sink to the bottom, then walks back down the dock. I can't help the panic that spreads through my veins as he gets closer, even though this version of him and this version of me exist in different timelines. There is something off about his face. The friendly, golden retriever mask is gone.

What's beneath it is cold and void of empathy. He lifts his foot to step off the dock, and then it's over. As quickly as it began, it's over. I grab at more sand. Shove it in the vial. Try to start the scene up again. Find out something more. Mama Dee said the secrets only reveal themselves once. But what did I learn, really? John dumped Natalie's body. I assumed it was him or Rich. But I don't know how he killed her or why or, technically, if it was even him at all. I don't know whether he was involved with the death of Rich or not or how any of it ties back to Regret and my own perilous situation. What good was—

"Simone?"

Every muscle in my body freezes at the sound of John's voice from behind me. He had to shout so he's not close. Still by the tree line.

"Simone, is that you? What the heck are you doing out here?"

No, John. What are YOU doing out here? I force myself to stand. To face him.

"Are you okay?" he asks. My eyes drift to the gold watch on his wrist. I'd forgotten his aunt owns a jewelry store. He probably helped Rich get the necklace for Kira and bought one for Natalie at the same time.

"You never replied to my text after you asked about Nate Hightower. I was up at the cabin doing some maintenance, and then I saw you walking off into the woods." He takes several steps closer to me. "It's not safe to be out here alone. It'll be dark any minute."

"I didn't see your truck."

He huffs out a nervous laugh. "Layla dropped me off. You should come inside, though." He looks beyond me at the items scattered on the ground. "What do you have there?" he asks, gaze shifting to my clenched hands.

I brace myself. He's only seconds away from connecting the

dots. I see it on his face when his eyes make out the vial, when they move from the vial to the necklace grasped in my other hand.

John drops his head and curses under his breath.

I hope Regret is listening because it's time for a confession. "Did you kill Natalie Dawson?"

He takes another step toward me. "What do you intend to do if I did, Simone?" The question drips with annoyance.

I hadn't gotten that far. Him showing up here wasn't a part of the plan. But it could work in my favor. Maybe Regret will take him. He might not regret whatever he did to Natalie, but I'm sure he regrets not fighting harder to not have my birthday party here. I'm sure he regrets the thing that led to him getting caught.

"Did you kill her or not?" I push.

He puts his hands on his hips and looks off to the right. "I had to make a choice, and I chose me. She put me in an impossible situation."

A metallic taste fills my mouth as I bite the inside of my cheek. Once again I find common ground between me and some vile person. How many times can I shrug it off as a coincidence before I have to accept myself as the common denominator?

When John turns his face back to me, his eyes are ablaze with rage. "You've put me in an impossible situation, too."

He lunges forward, and I hesitate for just a moment, debating which way to run—a horrible mistake. It's the half-second difference between making it to the trees and him being able to wrap his fingers around the collar of Dad's jacket and yank me to the ground. I struggle against him, screaming for help while he shouts at me, angry at me for making him have to do this.

"You don't have to do anything!" I get in a good swing. Feel something give in my hand and his face as I do, but it only enrages him more. He pins me down and raises his fist, but before he can strike, a shout comes from behind him. Someone jumps on his back and the weight of them both crushes me. I see a flash of golden-brown curls. Kira.

John puts his attention fully on her, rolling over and freeing me in the process. I lie on my back, gasping for air as she fights him mercilessly. Hitting, kicking, scratching. But he doesn't fight back. Instead, he does his best to defend himself, to push her off. There is something new trapped behind his eyes. A touch of fear, like a cornered animal. He knows he can't get away with hurting Kira. He finally squeezes in one firm shove that lands her flat on her ass.

"What the fuck, Kira?" John spits out a mouthful of blood-tinged saliva. "It's real noble for you to try to protect your friend and all, but there is so much you don't know."

She laughs sarcastically. "Oh yeah?"

"Yeah. She—" He points at me, arm covered in long angry welts, and I take the opportunity to interject.

"He killed Natalie Dawson."

"I know," Kira answers, rising to her feet, looking all too eager to continue her assault on John. She glares at him. "I know you were cheating on Layla with Natalie. I didn't want to believe it. I didn't want to hurt my sister by even suggesting it." She looks to me. "And it's part of the reason it was so hard for me to hear you out about Rich. I was a coward. It was easy to deny, deny, deny. But if I hadn't been so afraid, I could have cut Rich loose sooner. He would have had no reason to be sneaking around. He might still have his life." Her eyes bored into John. "If I'd told Layla that I saw you and Natalie standing a little too close in the alley behind Ozzy's, maybe things wouldn't have escalated the way they did. Maybe Natalie would still be here."

"You're giving him way too much credit," I say, but Kira holds out a hand to silence me, eyes steady on John.

"Layla told me you guys are broke. So what are you doing for money, huh, John? Selling drugs to kids?"

"Yes," I say. "That's exactly what he's doing." Neither he nor Violet have any qualms about dirty money.

"What I can't figure out," Kira starts, "is why you killed Rich. He had plenty more money to spend."

I want to ask how she knows that for certain, but John Yearwood is a killer regardless. And there's something about the way he looks standing there with the trees behind him. I can picture it so perfectly. Dorothy cooking. A man coming from the woods. Could it have been a man whose family would purchase the land she stood on only months later? A stiff breeze kicks up, dislodging dry leaves and raindrops, and I run with the image in my mind. I can feel it in my bones. It's the missing puzzle piece. The thing that links all of this together.

"How many?" My words come out soft as I still try to organize my thoughts. "How many women have Yearwood men dumped in that lake?"

John narrows his eyes at me.

"Which one killed Dorothy Savoie? Was it your grandfather? Do y'all have some kind of sick family tradition?"

He cocks his head to the side. "Oh, you've been digging deep, I see."

"So it's true then? You admit it?"

"I can't tell you exactly how many. But I can tell you there will be two more today." He charges me, but again Kira leaps on him, this time before he can actually reach me.

My vision suddenly goes cloudy. It's disorienting, making me squint and stumble. A dull ringing kicks up in my ear and then . . .

Let me in.

I hear Regret's voice in my head as John and Kira struggle, but I don't see her.

I will not harm you. Let me in.

My gut says to trust her and before I even consciously agree, it's like my body is overtaken by a massive wave. Everything goes black and I can feel Regret's full presence inside me. It's powerful. It's just. It's hungry. When my vision returns, I focus on John Yearwood like a laser. My muscles move against my will, and I run at him. My hand moves to my pocket, fingers searching for the knife that's hidden there. I know what's coming. I know exactly what's coming, and I don't want to see it.

A wish granted, my vision goes black once again, and the world goes silent. But I can still feel. I feel my arm jerk forward. I feel the give of flesh. I feel the sudden flow of warm, viscous liquid. When all of my senses are restored, I see John's motionless body on the sand, surrounded by a pool of blood.

I can feel Regret's satisfaction, her sadness, her heart—until another wavelike sensation knocks the wind out of me.

"Oh my God," Kira says, her eyes slowly moving from John's body over to the knife still clutched in my hand and then finally to my face.

Her expression, the fear in it, stirs up something dark inside me. I crack my neck, trying to make it go away. "You need to leave, Kira."

"Simone, it's okay. No one saw. We can—"

"You don't understand." I back away from her. Throw the knife as far away from me as I can. Why do I still have these feelings? These urges. I turn to put distance between us when I spot movement in the trees. Cory bursts onto the beach a second later, carrying a can of gasoline and dragging a bulging linen bag behind him.

"Why the hell did you come without me?" He dumps the bag filled with dirty toys collected from the woods into a pile.

Kira asks what's going on, and the sound of her voice sets my teeth on edge.

"Simone, I—" Cory stops speaking mid-sentence. He's spotted John.

"Both of you need to leave. Now," I say.

Cory shakes his head free of shock. Of course he'll have no issue believing there is a good reason for the sight in front of him. "Have you seen Regret yet?" he asks, now drizzling the pile of toys with gasoline.

"No," I say. "Not exactly."

"Well, maybe this will get her attention." He strikes a match and sprints away as it all goes up in a plume of toxic fumes. As the dark smoke billows into the sky, I realize it's only a matter of time before firefighters show up. This has to end now.

"Regret!" I scream, running to my bag and tossing the diary into the flames. "Where are you? Show yourself!" I gesture at the fire, at John's lifeless body. "Was this not enough?"

The remaining light of day seems to dissipate on fast-forward. A dark cloud forms between me and Kira. She backs away as it materializes into a woman. Regret.

"Baby Nathaniel is okay," I blurt. "He's passed on now, but he lived a good life. Violet didn't hurt him." I scramble to pull the evidence from my bag then hold it out to her with trembling hands. It's the last thing I have to throw at her. "Is this enough? Please say it's enough."

She looks at the fire and Cory, and then, with a snap of her fingers, the flames cease. She approaches me slowly and takes the newspaper clipping from my hand. Her fingers gently graze the young boy's face in the photo, then she looks up at me. I feel a new sense of deep familiarity when her light gray eyes meet mine and all my thoughts of harming Kira fade away. I can literally feel the dark energy release from my pores.

Regret focuses on John. She takes a few hesitant steps toward his body and looks down at him in disgust. "Drag his body to the lake," she demands. "When their bellies are full, when they are free, I will be too."

"They?" I ask. "Who?"

"Look," Kira and Cory say simultaneously.

I turn to face the lake like the rest of them. Grayish orbs of light—a dozen or so—hover across the water. A layer of thick fog encroaches, and they move with it. As they get closer, I see that they are women. Angry, hungry-looking women. The closest one's eyes are glued on John. She is young and blond and bears a striking resemblance to Natalie Dawson.

"Take him to the lake!" Regret insists.

"We—we can't just dump him," Kira says. "What if—"

"Do you want your friend arrested for murder?"

"I didn't even kill him!" I shout.

Kira looks at me and the blood on my hands with deep concern.

I point at Regret. "She—"

"Is that the story you will tell the police?" Regret asks. "Do as I say and all of this will go away!"

No one makes a move toward John.

"Do as I say!" Regret's voice booms like thunder.

I run to John's side, lifting his left arm from the ground and pulling to little effect. "Help me!"

Kira stands there, jaw slack, eyes flitting between the ghostly figures on the lake and Regret's eerie form.

"Cory!"

He springs into action at the sound of his name, running across the sand to help. Together we drag John just a couple of feet before Regret's voice locks us in place.

"Wait," she says. "You must first lay yourselves bare. There must be no ounce of remorse lingering, or else at the end, I will be drawn to it like a magnet."

"What does she mean?" Kira asks, voice shrill. "What's she talking about?"

Cory thinks for a moment before dropping John's arm. "Like we talked about," he mumbles to me. "Confess," he says louder. "Your biggest regret. Say it out loud. Do it, and we can get out of here, and then we'll explain everything."

Kira stutters, confusion and fear tripping her up.

"Just do it!" Cory shouts. It's aggressive, but it's the push Kira needs.

"Layla." She looks at me. "If I had said something about the cheating. If I'd been more like you, Simone, Natalie might still be alive. That's what I was coming to talk to you about this morning. I've felt so guilty ever since she went missing. I suspected him the whole time. And I knew he and Rich connected at a rave in the spring. I knew Rich was getting roped into some messed-up stuff, but I didn't speak up. Now he's dead, too."

"And it's that one who can stake the final claim there." Regret points at John's body.

"So John really did kill Rich? I thought maybe, but we . . ." I trail off because Kira doesn't know yet. She doesn't know about the deal I made.

"John saw the boy called Rich running away from the lake in a panic, muttering about needing to call 911. He thought he'd spotted the blond girl's body. Even with my manipulation of time, I could not erase that memory from John's head. I know now it is because our futures were intertwined." Her eyes find the bloody knife, then shift back to his body. "John killed the boy and made it look like an accident."

"Manipulation of time? What do you mean? Why was Rich in the woods?" Kira asks. "Why was he in a panic?"

Regret stares me down. "Do tell."

I can't say that regret is what I feel about everything that went down here with Kira and Rich, but it *is* something that needs to be put out there. Taken off my chest. Confessed. "Kir, do you remember telling me about that dream you had? About falling into the lake?"

She nods.

"It was real. Only I pushed you. But it was an accident," I add quickly. "Y-you . . . died. You were dead. And she"—I glance at Regret—"she offered me a deal." I explain the details of it. "It was you or Rich. I had to choose. And then I had to figure out how to free Regret, or you'd be gone again. I would have hurt you."

Kira's lip trembles. She doesn't seem to be able to form words, but she doesn't look angry.

"That's not all." I pause just one moment before unleashing the shame within me from the night of Trenton's death. The part about being late. About kissing Cory. But I hold my other cards close. The one about what happened between me and Rich at the football stadium. The one about what Mom did. I hold those close to me because Regret has already removed my homicidal urges toward Kira. And she's already admitted to mishandling our deal. A hiccup. A run in a stocking. *She* did not trade Kira's life for Rich's. If some being above her was owed a soul, I just offered John Yearwood's. Driven by Regret or not, it's my fingerprints on that knife. I did the hard thing. I owe her nothing. Most certainly not my deepest regrets. Finally, a little taste of control over my own life. And maybe I like that more than constantly fighting, and failing, to be honest and good.

"My turn," Cory says. "Simone, it's been weighing on me every time you bring him up. You know how I feel about you now, and it's the same as it was two years ago. Only back then, Trenton . . . I think he had a crush on you, too. And if I'm honest, I wanted to shoot my shot before he got the chance." His eyes fill with tears. "I lied to him about what time the movie started so me and you could have a few minutes alone. And it worked. While I was telling you how I felt, while we were kissing, my phone was buzzing in my pocket. It was him. I knew it was. Texting, wondering where we were. But I didn't care. I thought I could just explain it all to him later but—"

"Enough! Do it now," Regret says. "Drag his body to them now!"

"What if he washes up? Will we be caught?" Kira asks. Her use of *we* is not lost on me, even though I was the one who drove the knife into him.

"They will devour him and all evidence of his presence here."

Cory, Kira, and I share a couple of seconds of eye contact, each agreeing that this is what we are going to do. A choice that will link the three of us together for the rest of our lives.

Cory snatches up the knife and moves to John's feet. Kira, silently crying, takes one of his arms. I grab the other, and we carry him to the end of the dock.

"On three," Cory says as we swing John's lifeless body to get momentum.

I hear Gabby Greta in my head as he counts.

"One. Two. Three."

The moment we release him, the gray orbs swarm. With eerie moans and screams, they envelop his corpse just as it breaks the surface of the water. I take the knife from Cory and toss it in, too. The water grows turbulent, violent, as the three of us run back to shore, where Regret stands at the water's edge, arms spread wide, face angled up toward the sky.

We slow down and circle around to see what will happen. Behind Regret, one by one, the orbs burst free from the water and float upward until they blend in with the stars. Regret releases a deep exhale after the last one. I expect her to gently fade into translucence and beam up into the sky like all the others. I wait for all my awful memories to go with her.

But it doesn't happen.

Her pale gray eyes flick open like she is surprised by this too. Her form pulsates like it wants to go but cannot. Her mouth curves downward. Her stomach growls like thunder. And she screams with rage. She screams so loud that cracks form in her skin, like dry desert sand, and her eyes widen, as if she's just made a realization. Then she smiles sadly.

"Oh, darling girl," she says directly to me. "You have so much left to learn." Regret's form begins to disintegrate. She crumbles from the bottom up like a sandcastle. With a few mumbled words, and a look of resignation laced with hope, she dissolves into dust.

I take a deep breath in, and the heavy scent of honeysuckle and tobacco curls around me.

CHAPTER 37

TWO MONTHS LATER
CORY GOODING

Simone Washington is a liar. By omission, at least. People debate whether or not that counts, but in my book, it definitely does. I don't have a problem with it, though. Not when it comes to her. Not when I know the truth about something she can't bring herself to speak aloud. Something she couldn't bring herself to mention the night we attempted to free Regret.

Kira is still alive, and Simone isn't in jail, so we were all spared the consequences of what Regret promised would happen if Simone didn't hold up her end of the deal, but Simone also didn't get the benefits they agreed upon, either. The two of us have dissected that night a dozen times since, and we both agree that the loophole was the fact that John killed Rich, not Regret—that and Simone's bold choice to lie about her biggest regret. It took me a while to call her on it. To tell her that I knew the truth. But after everything we went through, it seemed dumb as hell to keep walking on eggshells and keeping secrets. Something had to give after all that, and I'm glad it gave in favor of our friendship. A friendship that will be tightly bound forever, not just because we illegally disposed of a body together, but because I know Simone's mother killed Trenton.

I've known since the night he died.

I guess that makes me a liar, too.

A couple of hours after me and Simone found out about the accident, I started to worry about her. I walked to her house and up to the side door, like I had so many times that summer, but I heard her dad shouting and lost my nerve. I could see that the light was on in her room, and as I pulled out my phone to text her to come to the window, a car pulled into the driveway. I wasn't doing anything wrong, so I don't know why I ducked behind the hedges. But I'm glad I did. Because I saw, and I'm not sure what would have happened if anyone knew that I did. I saw the damage to Mrs. Washington's car. Every crack and dent. The dark stains trapped in the crevices of the spiderwebbed windshield. I saw Simone see. The flash of her curtains. The shock on her face.

I ran home the second I got the chance. Simone thought it was all her. The two years we went without talking. But she's not the only one who didn't speak up. She was never the only one bogged down by regret. I'm still working through it all, and I probably won't ever fully get over lying to Trenton about the movies, but I'll be okay. And Simone . . . well, Simone carries regret differently these days, but it seems to be working out just fine for her.

I pop some ziti from Ozzy's into the oven to reheat for Grandma. She sits on the couch watching the news. I'm drawn to her side when I see John Yearwood's photo on the TV screen.

"The search is still on for Fairville resident Johnathon Yearwood, a key suspect in the murder of nineteen-year-old Natalie Dawson, whose remains were recovered from Yearwood Lake just last month. Information provided by Mr. Yearwood's wife and sister-in-law proved that he was involved in a volatile romantic affair with Ms. Dawson prior to her disappearance. Upon a full search of the lake, the remains of at least four other women were found, one of whom was confirmed to be the grandmother of a groundskeeper hired to maintain a nearby property owned by the Yearwood family. It is unclear if Johnathon Yearwood, or any other members of the Yearwood family, have knowledge of or are associated with the deaths of these other women, but we are following this case closely and will report back as any new developments arise."

"That poor young lady." Grandma shakes her head. "All those women. Shows you really got to watch who you associate with."

At least Simone made it so they can all rest in peace. So their families can get closure one day. She made an anonymous tip about Natalie and the lake. It took guts to do that, knowing what she did to John. She had to go out on faith that what Regret said was true. That there'd be no trace of what happened to him and no trace of who did it. I think by now she's in the clear.

My phone dings, and I smile when I see it's Simone.

Simone
Sure you're still up for going to the party tonight?

Jeremiah Hutchinson is hosting a New Year's Eve costume party, but it was Simone and Kira who did most of the planning. Simone never got to throw her big Halloween party, and Kira wanted something to keep herself busy in the aftermath of everything with John. I used to think Simone's Pinegrove friends were kind of shallow, but she's invited me to hang out with them a few times now, and they're actually cool people.

Me
Wouldn't miss it. Need to see this costume you've been keeping a secret.

Simone
♥ pick me up at 9?

Me
see you then

I drive to Simone's house, jog to the front door, and ring the doorbell. Her dad greets me a few seconds later.

"Cory. Good to see ya. How's it going?"

"Good—" I start, but the sight of Simone coming down the stairs makes it difficult to find words.

Her father looks over his shoulder. "Hey! Look at that. Straight outta the 1950s. Where'd you get that outfit?" he asks.

Simone doesn't just look straight out of the 1950s, she looks exactly like the photo we saw of Evelyn Young. From that hat tilted just enough to shade her right eye, to the dark lipstick, to the cream-and-brown shoes.

"Ms. Tandy helped me find everything at the thrift store," Simone answers, looking at me. "Where'd you get *your* outfit? Walmart?"

I adjust the scratchy black cape around my neck. "Don't hate. My mask is in the car."

Simone rolls her eyes and grabs a coat from the rack. "See you, Dad. I'll be home just after midnight."

"Mm-hmm, you sure will be. I'll be up waiting." Mr. Washington throws a stern look my way before turning back to Simone. "Don't forget to call or text your mom. Tell her happy New Year."

"I won't," Simone says, walking out the door and toward my truck.

I cringe, imagining Simone giving her mother New Year wishes knowing she has every intention of finally going to the police about what she did. She's deep into mission "set things straight."

I crank the engine and turn up the heat, giving her another once-over. "Does that even count as a costume . . . considering?"

"Don't start, Cory," she says playfully.

It's a quick drive to Jeremiah's. I park at the end of a long line of cars, then slip on my gold phantom mask. "What do you think?"

"Perfect."

We walk toward the driveway, and there's a girl sitting on the curb next to a friend, bawling her eyes out, mumbling about drinking too much. Simone's stomach rumbles, and she inhales deeply as we pass them. "Smells good out here."

"Yeah, I don't think I'm ever going to get used to that. You at least gotta be more slick with it, Sim. You're gonna scare somebody."

She looks at me, a shadow passing across her eyes, then shrugs. "Sounds fun."

That's a classic Simone thing to say, but I study her for a moment. The costume is blurring lines that are usually distinct to me.

"Come on, Cory." She holds out her hand and nods toward the house.

Inside, we split off in different directions. She dances with Kira and her other friends while I hit the snack table and game room with some guys from work. Simone finds me ten minutes to midnight so we can count down the New Year together.

"Where's Gabby Greta when you need her?" She laughs.

"Sitting on your bookshelf being creepy as f—"

"Did you see that?" she interrupts.

"See what?"

"That guy over there. Dressed like an astronaut. He was at Rich's funeral. Look at the patch on his arm."

It's an astronaut vomiting a rainbow.

My stomach sinks as I feel her energy shift.

"Do you think he's selling drugs? Do you think he knew John?"

"I don't know, Sim. Maybe it's time to ease off the vigilante-redemption thing."

"I don't have a choice," she says softly.

Before she leaves my side, I notice that her usually dark eyes are pale gray. It changes her appearance entirely. Like a mask. She always did say she had a lot of those. But this one is different. This one has a mind of its own. One day I'll figure out how to help her shake it loose. But they've been happy this way. A symbiotic relationship. Second chances for both.

I move a little closer so I can hear the conversation between her and the astronaut.

"And who are you supposed to be?" He gives her a long look up and down.

She glances my way, still with those light gray eyes.

"Come on," he pushes. "What's your name?"

Her lips curve into a sly smile. "They call me Regret."

ACKNOWLEDGMENTS

I am so incredibly blessed and grateful to be here writing the acknowledgments for my second published book—but man, finishing this one was a ride! Other authors gave me a heads-up about the infamous book two struggles, and *They Call Her Regret* delivered. I thoroughly enjoyed writing this book, but it certainly tested me both creatively and personally. The challenges were real, but I'm thankful for all I learned along the way. I truly couldn't have made it through without my amazing support system.

To my mom and dad, who have never, ever stopped believing in me—I love you so much and appreciate every word of encouragement, every hug, and every thoughtful piece of advice. You two are absolute rock stars, and I am so honored to be your daughter.

To Marion, Stacey, and the rest of my beautiful family, y'all showed up for me in such a big way through the publication of my first book. That carried me through writing this one more than you know. Really, that groundwork was laid my whole life just by having you all around. Thank you.

Endless thanks to my wonderful agent, Molly Ker Hawn. Your

guidance and wisdom are invaluable. I am so happy to have you in my corner.

Thank you to my incredible editor, Tiffany Shelton, who saw my vision for this book and helped me sharpen it every step of the way. All my gratitude to Anto Marr for the perfect, deliciously spooky jacket design. Thank you also to Ashley Quintana, Alyssa Gammello, Daisy Glasgow, Cassie Gutman, and the entire team at Wednesday Books who helped get this book polished and in the hands of readers. You are all amazing.

To Alex Antscherl, Isabelle Tucker, Tim Hardy, and the rest of the Bloomsbury UK team: Thank you so very much for your hard work and enthusiasm. Huge thanks to Michelle Brackenborough for designing *another* gorgeous cover. And a special thank-you to Sara Jafari. Your early insights were priceless.

All love and appreciation to my beautiful writer friends: Megan Davidhizar, Emily Charlotte, Christine L. Arnold, Valo Wing, Lally Hi, S. Hati, K. A. Cobell, P. H. Low, Sana Z. Ahmed, Laurie, Veronica Bane. You all are the best part. Thank you for the brainstorming sessions, early reads, feedback, advice, and fun.

Thank you to Wes. You were there when the idea for this book was born. You were there when the idea for *Needy Little Things* was born. Those early stages of the process are so delicate. Thank you for helping me nurture vague little pitches into intricately plotted books. And thank you for reminding me to drink water and rest. You're so cool. I love you.

To my girls! Chris, Tonika, Hannah. Thank you for decades of friendship. Thanks for loving me through every season. For dreaming with me. For so perfectly understanding my humor and providing countless laughs. Thank you for showing me how beautiful and comforting and safe true friendship can be. And thank you for not reading too much into the complicated, sometimes toxic friendships I tend to work into every book. Y'all are my ride-or-dies. Love you always.

Massive shout-out to my coworkers and students! I am honestly tearing up just thinking about the support you gave me when *Needy Little Things* came out. From attending my events, to stopping by my classroom with copies of my book for me to sign, to frequently checking in about what was coming next. Your excitement for me, your belief in me, got me through some really tough rounds of edits!

To the booksellers, librarians, and school media specialists who put stories into the hands of readers: Thank you. Your work is so important and it is an honor that you embraced mine.

And finally, to you, reader—whether *They Call Her Regret* is your first book of mine or if you've been here since *Needy Little Things*—thank you for picking up my work. You inspire me to keep showing up to the page. I am forever grateful.

HAVE YOU READ

'Memorable, fascinating and full of emotional complexity, this is an original, layered YA thriller'
Guardian

'An unexpected twist on an important story, *Needy Little Things* weaves a skilfully crafted tale that grips readers from start to finish. A gem of a novel!'
Angie Thomas, author of *The Hate U Give*

ABOUT THE AUTHOR

Channelle Desamours is a high school science teacher from Atlanta, Georgia, who loves writing tales about magical Black girls. When she's not napping to recover from her five-AM writing sessions, she can be found building tiny homes on *The Sims 4* or tending to her houseplants. She is also the author of *Needy Little Things*.